The Marine
by Mau

'This would be a big mistake,' Travis said, his gaze shifting from her eyes to her mouth and back again.

'It doesn't feel that way,' Lisa told him.

'It will tomorrow.' And if he had one active brain cell, he'd break this off and walk away now. While he could.

She turned her face into his palm, then looked at him again. 'All my life I've worried about and planned for tomorrow. For once I'd just like to claim today and let tomorrow take care of itself.'

An invitation? It was one he couldn't refuse, even if he wanted to.

Pulling her closer, Travis bent his head. His gaze locked with hers, he moved in slowly, deliberately, giving her time to change her mind. Praying she wouldn't...

Wild About a Texan
by Jan Hudson

'I would appreciate it if you would forget that night ever happened.'

A slow grin lifted one corner of his sensual mouth, a mouth that had haunted her for months after their encounter. She still remembered the taste of it, the feel of it on—

'Not likely, darlin',' he said in a slow drawl as he ran a knuckle along her jawline.

Her spine started to soften, then Olivia caught herself and stiffened her resolve. She wasn't going to fall into his trap again. There wasn't room for a man in her plans. Certainly not a man like Jackson.

'Forget it,' she snapped. 'There will never be a repeat performance. Now, if you'll excuse me…' She tried to push past him, but he blocked her way.

'Not so fast,' he said, pinning her between his arms and the wall. 'Now that I've found you, I'm not about to let you get away…'

Dear Reader,

Welcome to the truly sensual world of Desire.

In our first two-in-one volume Anne Marie Winston brings us *Billionaire Bachelors: Garrett*—the final story in her BILLIONAIRE BACHELORS series; and Barbara McCauley rounds off her SECRETS! series, for the moment, with *In Blackhawk's Bed*. But watch out for more from both of these very popular authors later in the year.

Maureen Child finds us another of her trademark military hunks in *The Marine & the Debutante*, one of her BACHELOR BATTALION novels; and Jan Hudson produces an honest-to-goodness, gorgeous, millionaire rancher in *Wild About a Texan*.

In our final volume, Katherine Garbera brings us a billionaire businessman who meets his match in *The Tycoon's Temptation*; and in *Dr Destiny* by Kristi Gold a handsome doctor and his best friend, Cassie, share a night of passion and discover they're going to be parents—to twins!

Enjoy!

The Editors

The Marine & the Debutante
MAUREEN CHILD

Wild About a Texan
JAN HUDSON

SILHOUETTE®
DESIRE™

*Silhouette, Silhouette Desire and Colophon
are registered trademarks of Harlequin Books S.A.,
used under licence.*

*First published in Great Britain 2003
Silhouette Books, Eton House, 18-24 Paradise Road,
Richmond, Surrey TW9 1SR*

The publisher acknowledges the copyright holders of the
individual works as follows:

The Marine & the Debutante © Maureen Child 2002
Wild About a Texan © Janece O. Hudson 2002

ISBN 0 373 04859 9

51-0303

*Printed and bound in Spain
by Litografía Rosés S.A., Barcelona*

THE MARINE & THE DEBUTANTE

by
Maureen Child

MAUREEN CHILD

is a California native who loves to travel. Every chance they get, she and her husband are taking off on another research trip. The author of more than sixty books, Maureen loves a happy ending and still swears that she has the best job in the world. She lives in Southern California with her husband, two children and a golden retriever who has delusions of grandeur.

Visit her website at www.maureenchild.com

Books by Maureen Child in the BACHELOR BATTALION series

Silhouette Desire

The Littlest Marine
The Non-Commissioned Baby
The Oldest Living Married Virgin
Colonel Daddy
Mum in Waiting
Marine Under the Mistletoe
The Daddy Salute
The Last Santini Virgin
The Next Santini Bride
Marooned with a Marine
Prince Charming in Dress Blues
His Baby!
Last Virgin in California
The Marine & the Debutante

This book is dedicated to the men and women
of the United States Marine Corps. Their courage
and devotion to duty allow the rest of us to enjoy
the freedom of living in the best country in the world.
Thank you all from the bottom of my heart.
Semper Fi

One

"**I**f I get shot saving some spoiled little rich girl," Travis Hawks muttered, "finish the job and kill me."

"Deal," J.T. whispered.

Travis sent the other man a quick look. In the darkness, all he could see of his friend's face were the whites of his eyes—and his grin. Camouflage paint disguised his features, just like the other two men on the recon team.

"You agreed to that mighty damn fast," Travis said with a wry smile as he checked the load in his rifle for the third time.

"What're friends for?" he asked. "You'd do the same for me, wouldn't you?"

A slight rustle from the bushes had them both spinning around, alert and ready. Deke poked his head through, whispered, "Travis, go get the girl and let's get the hell outa here."

"Right."

"Your charges set?"

"You need to ask?" he asked, already dropping to his belly for the crawl to the squat, stone house just fifty feet from them. Hell, Travis was the best damn explosives man in the Corps and everybody here knew it. Most days, he was even better than Jeff Hunter, the Gunnery Sergeant who led their team, though Travis wasn't stupid enough to say that out loud. And when it came right down to it, his expertise was probably what had gotten them roped into this mission.

Which just went to show that pride in your work could get you into all kinds of trouble. But it wasn't time to think of things like that now. Instead he focused his concentration on the job. Flattening out on the dirt, rifle cradled in his arms, he used his elbows to drag his body across the open ground between the team and their target.

Voices drifted to him on the still night air. And though he didn't exactly speak the language, the tone told him the men guarding the woman were relaxed. Good. He hoped they stayed that way.

Sweat pooled at the base of his neck despite the near-freezing temperature. It got damn cold in the desert at night. His knees and elbows propelled him quickly to the stone house, and as he slowly came to his feet alongside the blacked-out window, he quietly released the breath he'd been holding. So far, so good.

Just as he'd expected, there were no guards posted on the perimeter. Apparently, these guys felt pretty secure. Bad for them, Travis thought, good for us.

He lifted the window sash and prayed that the intel they'd received before starting this mission had been completely accurate. If there were guards in the room with her, then all hell was about to break loose. Travis paused for a heartbeat or two, to listen. When he was convinced that it was still safe, he slipped into the darkened room, moving as quietly as combat boots allowed.

His vision already adjusted to the blackness, Travis had no problem locating the woman. She was lying on her back upon the only piece of furniture in the room—a narrow cot. Her deep, even breathing told him she was asleep. In a few steps he was beside her. Clamping one hand over her mouth to keep her quiet, he waited for her to wake up.

Instantly she did just that.

And he almost wished she hadn't.

She fought against his hold on her like a tiger coming out of her cage looking for dinner. Arms, legs, teeth joined the fight, and Travis was hard-pressed to contain her. Keeping his hand over her mouth, despite the teeth digging into his palm, he pinned her to the cot beneath his own body and muttered, "U.S. Marines. Knock it off, lady. I'm here to get you out."

She stopped fighting just as quickly as she'd started.

He stared down at the whites of her eyes and watched them narrow dangerously. Then very deliberately she reached for his wrist and yanked his hand from her mouth.

Finally, he thought. A little gratitude.

"It's about time," she snapped, and shattered his little hero fantasy.

A flash of anger shot through him, followed by a blast of sheer fear. He threw a glance at the door across the room, then looked back at the woman who was about to blow this whole damn thing.

Keeping his voice no more than a whispered threat, he ordered, "Lady, shut up and get moving."

"Fine," she said softly, already swinging her legs off the cot and standing up. "But for heaven's sake, you people took your own sweet time about getting here."

"Oh, for the love of—" He didn't even finish the oath. Didn't have time. Had to get moving before her captors took it into their heads to check on their little pot of gold. "Follow me," he said, and headed for the window and escape.

"I need my purse."

"Forget it," he muttered, peering out into the darkness before turning to help her across the sill. Stunned, he saw she hadn't followed him at all. Instead she was flat on her belly, reaching under the damn cot for her damn purse.

He stalked back across the room and grabbed her elbow. "There's no mall here. You don't need daddy's credit cards. And there's no time for this, princess," he muttered.

She yanked free of his grip, then, meeting hostility with pure venom, she said, "I've waited two weeks for you. You can wait another minute for me."

Short of hitting her over the head and dragging her ass out of there, he didn't have much choice. Through his headset, he heard a whispered question come through loud and clear. "Where the hell are you?"

Scowling, Travis touched the black band at the base of his neck, pressed the sensitive throat mike to his larynx and muttered, "Waitin' on princess. Comin' right out." He kept one eye on the closed door and mentally ticked off the seconds as they passed. There were too many of them. They were asking for trouble, he told himself. This couldn't be good. "Move it, lady."

"Got it," she said, and stood up, holding a white leather saddle bag dangling from what was probably a real gold chain. She slipped it over her head so that the chain lay across her chest and the purse settled at her hip. Then she nodded at him, and Travis grabbed her and propelled her toward the window—and freedom.

"Come on, now," he prodded. "Climb out and let's get gone."

She sat on the window ledge, gathered up her skirt and started to swing her legs through. Then she stopped. "You know," she said softly, "you could be a little nicer, here. I *am* the victim, remember?"

Travis sucked in a gulp of air. He was seriously beginning to doubt that. In fact, another few minutes of this and he was going to start feeling some real sympathy for her abductors.

He bent down, put his face just a breath away from hers and whispered, "Listen up, princess. We got about a minute and a half to get clear of this place and still have time to make the chopper pickup. Now, you want to move that pretty ass of yours before I kick it into gear?"

Her eyes widened and for a second, there, it

looked as though she might argue. Then apparently she changed her mind. Swinging her legs over the window ledge, she dropped onto the desert floor and waited for him to follow.

There was just no time to throw her to the ground and try to slink out the way he'd come in, Travis told himself. Instead he took a tight grip on her upper arm and dragged her along behind him as he made a run for cover.

Stumbling and muttering under her breath, she managed to keep up. Barely. And as soon as he hit the low clump of bushes where the others were waiting, he dropped into a crouch, pulling her down beside him, then released her.

Deke glanced at her before fastening his gaze on Travis. "Jeff's at the rendezvous point. Let's move."

"Move where?" the woman asked.

"Right behind ya," Travis muttered, ignoring her and her question.

In seconds Deke and J.T. had melted into the low-lying bushes, and Travis pushed the woman after them. "Get going," he said, then added, "and keep low."

Thankfully, she kept quiet and did as she was told. Travis threw one last look at the stone hut behind them, then moved silently off after her, guarding their escape. His mind blanked out as it always did at times like this. He did *what* he had to, *when* he had to. He didn't think. Didn't question. Just moved on instinct.

His gaze swept the landscape, back and forth, but kept drifting back to the woman in front of him. Her stupid full skirt snagged on every bush she passed. He shook his head and clenched his teeth together to keep from shouting at her to hurry up. Already the others were too far ahead of them. She was slowing everything down.

"Damn it," he muttered under his breath. "Can't you move any faster?"

Lisa Chambers stopped dead and glared at him over her shoulder. She'd had just about enough. Two weeks of sitting in that cramped little hot box, surrounded by men who wore bandoliers of ammunition with the aplomb her father's friends wore cummerbunds; and now this. She was hot, tired, hungry, cranky and she'd gone *way* too long without a bath. She for darn sure wasn't going to stand for some Southern-fried Marine cursing her for walking too slowly.

Cold night air crawled over her skin, sending bone-deep shivers to every inch of her body. The gold chain across her chest chafed her neck and the solid slap of her purse against her hip was beginning to throb.

Hard to believe that in the span of a few minutes a person could experience so many different sorts of emotions. When she'd first awakened to the feel of a man's hand across her mouth, her first reaction had been sheer terror—followed, naturally, by the instinct to defend herself. For one brief, horrifying moment, she'd thought her captors had finally decided to do more than keep her isolated and afraid.

Then the very next instant, relief had crashed down on her as she'd heard that purely American voice drawl the words, "U.S. Marines." The "cavalry" had been so long in coming, she'd about given up hope.

Tears she didn't have time to shed stung her eyes, and she blinked them back with practiced ease. She hadn't shown her captors any weaknesses, and she wouldn't let her rescuer see any, either.

"You know," she said, sarcasm dripping from her words, "a little sensitivity wouldn't be out of line here."

He didn't even look at her. Well, she was pretty sure he didn't. In the moonless dark, he was almost indistinguishable from the night, so it was hard to be sure. Unlike her. In her sunny-yellow dress, she probably stood out like a spotlight on an empty stage. And that thought gave her a cold chill deep enough to have Lisa give the surrounding darkness a quick, wary look. When she turned back toward

him, she saw the whites of his eyes narrow dangerously at her.

"Lady," he said and his slow, menacing Southern
drawl drifted in the air, "you want sensitivity, call
the Navy. You want help, call the Marines." Then
he dropped to one knee and pulled something from
under the closest bush. Flicking her another quick
glance, he ordered, "Get a move on, darlin'."

"Darlin'?" she repeated, but her voice was lost
in the blast of a nearby explosive.

Lisa gasped and staggered back a step or two. Her
gaze locked on a fireball that roared up as if thrown
from the bowels of hell by a demon bent on destruc-
tion. Light showered down on them and the area,
but before she could do much more than notice that
the Marine was running at her, he had hold of her
arm and she was moving, too.

His hand made one warm spot on her body, but
his grip was anything but tender. The fabric of her
skirt caught, then ripped free as he half dragged, half
pushed her along the path. Her high heels sank into
the sand as if the desert itself was trying to hold her
back. The delicate pumps were perfect for a day of
shopping or even a night of dancing. But they
weren't exactly prime jogging equipment. Her feet
ached, her head was pounding, and she wondered
absently if she would survive her rescue. Her
"hero" stayed just a step behind her, obviously

guarding her back, but she almost wished he was in front of her so she'd know where to go. She had no idea. Only knew that she wanted out of this place. Now.

She wanted to be back in the States. Back at her father's house. In that glorious, sky-blue bathtub that dominated the bathroom in her suite of rooms. She wanted freshly fluffed towels, lit candles sputtering on the sea-foam colored tiles and a chilled glass of wine at her elbow. She wanted running water, hair dryers and *toilet paper*. Oh, God, please help her to get out of this mess, she prayed frantically.

"Damn it," he muttered, and she heard that curse with a sinking sigh.

"What now?" she demanded, still moving, due to his hand shoving at the small of her back. "What is it? What's wrong?"

"What isn't?" he grumbled, and stopped dead.

Lisa stopped, too, waiting for him. He might be irritating, but as far as she was concerned, he was the rescuer and she was going to stick to him like glue.

"Keep going," he shouted, the need for silence apparently lost with the first blast.

"Where?" she demanded, not moving another step.

"Son of a—" His voice broke off and he pulled another something out from yet another bush, and this time she was close enough to watch him. His fingers moved surely, efficiently. He flipped up a small, clear-plastic dome, flicked a silver switch and then moved his thumb to a bright-green glowing button. He punched it, and another blast rocked the desert night.

This one was closer and Lisa stared at it, awe-struck by the fierce beauty of it. But beneath the roar of the explosion, she heard shouts. Angry shouts.

And she knew her captors were chasing them.

"This can't be good."

"Darlin', none of this is good," he muttered, jumping to his feet and grabbing her hand. "Let's get the lead out, huh?"

They ran.

And ran.

And when she thought she'd drop, when she was wishing she could take her aching legs off and throw them away, they ran some more.

"Runnin' late. Not gonna make it," he said, more to himself than to her.

She swallowed hard, fought for breath and still managed to ask, "You mean the helicopter?"

"Damn straight."

"We have to make it."

He threw her a worried look. "The extraction point's up ahead."

Extraction? Sounded like a dental visit, which would have been more fun than this.

From far off she heard the dull slap of a helicopter's blades whipping the air. Her heartbeat thundered in her chest. Close, she thought. So close. They'd make it. They had to make it.

Every step was a trial.

Every breath a victory.

Behind them she heard voices. Shouts. And the occasional gunshot. Lisa winced and instinctively ducked her head as they ran forward. The wash from the chopper blades pushed at them. In the indistinct light she saw other men—two, then three—sprinting for the helicopter. A Marine stood in the open door, an automatic weapon in his hand, spitting gunfire, covering their escape.

Then that Marine crumpled as if he'd been a puppet and someone had cut his strings. A moment later she heard a rifle shot, followed by several more in quick succession.

"Get down, damn it!" the man behind her said, crouching and pulling her down with him.

"Why are we waiting?" she demanded, looking up at him, trying to read his expression through the camouflage war paint he wore.

"We won't make it," he said tightly. "Too much open ground. They'll pick us off."

"We—we *have* to make it," she said, shifting her

gaze back to the helicopter where another Marine had taken the place of the first one. He fired quick, staccato bursts from his weapon, and flashes of fire erupted from the barrel of his gun.

"Can't."

"No." She couldn't go back to that place. To being a prisoner. She wouldn't. Lisa half stood, determined to make a run for the only way out.

But she didn't get a step.

He yanked her back down with such force, her butt slammed into the ground. His grip on her upper arm tightened and he pulled her around to face him.

"We can't make it. And if they sit here much longer waitin' on us, they won't get out, either."

Panic reared its ugly head. He couldn't mean what she thought he meant. "What are you saying?"

He didn't bother to explain. Instead he stood up briefly, hitched his rifle high over his head and waved it in some sort of silent signal.

"No," she said, hoping he hadn't done what she thought he had. "Don't do that!"

"Come on," he said tightly, dragging her off to the right, deeper into the shadows.

Lisa looked back as the helicopter lifted off, taking her only means of escape with it.

Two

Travis kept a tight hold on the woman's hand and ran for it. He could only hope that their pursuers were still far enough away that some fast running and clever hiding would do the trick. If they could get gone quick enough, the men still firing rifles at a now-disappearing chopper, would assume that their prey had escaped in that helicopter. *If* he could get the woman stumbling along behind him to shut up and move. As he'd already learned, that was no easy task.

"Are you out of your mind?" she demanded.

He had to give her credit. Even in her fury, she

kept her voice low enough that it wouldn't carry across the desert.

"It's been said," he agreed, darting a quick look back over his shoulder. No pursuit yet. Good. Keep moving, he told himself.

"You waved them off," she continued, stunned disbelief coloring her voice. "I *saw* you. The helicopter was there. They were waiting for us. Our only escape and you waved them off!"

He shot her a glare that would have terrified a lesser woman. Naturally, it didn't have the slightest effect on the one woman he wanted it to.

"You're insane," she muttered.

"I'm startin' to agree with you," he snapped. Who else but a crazy man would volunteer for such a mission? He could have been on leave back home. Of course, then his sisters would have been ragging on him. But at least *they* were family. "Now shut the hell up and follow me."

"Like I have a choice," she managed to say breathlessly.

They kept going, and one part of Travis's mind gave quiet thanks for the terrain. This wasn't the kind of desert that you found out in the middle of the Mojave. The *real* desert was farther out. This area was more like the landscape that he grew up with back in Texas. Sand, sure, but more rocky. With clumps of bushes and a few sparse but hardy trees. A ring of low-lying hills, which probably passed for mountains around here, surrounded them, and he was hoping to find refuge there.

The darkness was their friend.

They could lose themselves in the night and hopefully, before dawn, they'd be huddled in a cave somewhere and he'd have a chance to think of alternate escape plans. While he ran, making sure the princess was keeping up with him, his mind worked the problem. He had water. And rations. And a radio and weapons. He could do this. *They* could do this.

It was just going to take some creativity. Adapting and overcoming. Hell, he'd been trained for just this sort of thing. And damned if he wasn't going to pull it off.

"Come on," he urged quietly. "Just keep moving and everything'll work out."

"Like it has so far?" she wondered aloud.

He threw one look at the star-studded sky and silently asked, Why me? And more important, Why her? This would have been a helluva lot easier if he'd just been asked to rescue a reasonable person. But this woman had been trouble from the get-go, and he suspected that it wasn't going to get much better.

They walked for hours, until Lisa was ready to throw dignity to the wind and beg the guy in charge of this little forced march for a rest. But she doubted he would even hear her. Long accustomed to the darkness, she had no trouble seeing him clearly. Tall and rangy, he moved effortlessly across the rocky ground. He never seemed to get tired. He never let go of her hand, and his gaze continually scanned their surroundings, constantly on alert. His profile was sharp, dangerous looking, without an ounce of softness in it. The camouflage paint only made him look scarier—more remote. His jaw was hard and square and his nose had obviously been broken at least once…. Her sympathies were entirely with the break*er* not the break*ee.* She hadn't had a good look at his eyes yet, but she had the distinct feeling they'd be all business, no matter the color.

Well, if she had to be stranded in the middle of nothing, she told herself, it was better to be with a man so clearly equipped to handle it. A stray notion shot through her mind and she laughed shortly at the thought of her last fiancé trying to survive out here. James hadn't been able to hail a cab in Manhattan successfully.

"Was that a laugh?" he asked, slowing his steps.

Grateful, Lisa slowed down, too, and instantly felt her calf muscles cramp. She winced, nodded and admitted, "Yes, I laughed. Maybe I'm hysterical."

"Swell."

She looked up at him. Darn him, anyway, he

wasn't even winded. "I'm kidding," she said, then added, "I think."

Releasing her hand, he gave her a long, thoughtful look, swung his pack to the ground and said, "Sit for a few minutes. Take a breather."

"Oh, thank heaven," she muttered, and dropped like a stone. Then she had to shift slightly to inch *off* the stone she'd landed on. Perfect. Well, why shouldn't her behind ache as much as every other spot on her body?

"Here," he said, handing her a beige, flask-shaped canteen. "Have a drink. Not much, though. I've only got two and they've got to last us."

Lisa nodded, too tired to argue, which was saying something, she supposed. Unscrewing the cap, she lifted the canteen and took one big mouthful of warm, wet, wonderful water. Then she swallowed, letting the liquid slide down her throat like a blessing, before handing the canteen back. She hadn't even realized just how thirsty she was. And right now, the metallic-flavored water tasted better than the finest bottle of wine.

Now that they'd stopped running, the cold night air had caught up with her. She shivered and clapped her hands to her upper arms, rubbing them up and down, trying to create some warmth. Funny how running and being terrified will keep you all toasty.

"Cold?"

She nodded.

He shrugged the small pack off his back and swung it to the ground. Then, setting his gun to one side, he quickly undid the buttons on his sand-colored uniform shirt and pulled it off, revealing a Marine-green T-shirt that looked as though it had been molded to his brawny chest.

"You don't have to do that," she said, both grateful and embarrassed to be taking the shirt off his back.

"Just put it on, princess."

Well, so much for gratitude. She snatched the shirt out of his hands and shoved her arms into the long sleeves. The cuffs hung well past her wrists, to flop over the edge of her fingertips. But it was warm—the fabric still held a touch of his body heat along with his scent.

He stood up again, grabbed his rifle and gave another quick look around.

She looked down to see the mammoth shirt hanging to nearly the hem of her dress. Oh, if her friends could see her now. Lisa Chambers, girl fashion plate, dressed as a miniature soldier. But she was warm and that was saying a lot.

"I, uh…" Gratitude came hard, considering that he wasn't one of her favorite people at the moment.

"Forget it." He cut her off, clearly not interested

in thanks. "Now, you stay put," he said. "I'll be right back."

"What?" Panic reared up inside her, and she shot a wild look around her at the surrounding darkness. *Anything* or *anyone* could be hiding out there. "You're leaving me here? Alone?"

He shot her a grin. "Gonna miss me?"

Her stomach flip-flopped. Amazing what an effect that smile could have on an exhausted, thirsty, hungry, obviously delusional woman.

"Don't worry about it," he said, before she could come up with a witty reply. "I'm just goin' back to make sure I've covered our tracks well enough."

"I didn't realize you *had* been covering our tracks," she said, looking back over her shoulder as if she could actually see into the darkness and the trail he'd been working to erase.

"That's my job," he said, already moving off into the shadows.

"Who are you, anyway?" she demanded. "Daniel Boone?"

He glanced back at her and gave her another one of those grins. "Nah, the name's Travis Hawks, ma'am. But I appreciate the compliment."

"Well, my name's Lisa Chambers," she retorted as he disappeared into the darkness. Her voice dropped to a whisper as she added, "It's *not* 'ma'am.'"

What felt like hours but what was probably only a few minutes, passed, and she heard him approaching. At least, she *hoped* it was Travis Hawks.

It was.

She released a breath she hadn't realized she'd been holding as he moved to her side. Then she noted he wasn't even breathing heavily.

Tipping her head back, she looked up at him. "Aren't you even tired?" she asked, disgusted that he showed no signs of the fatigue swamping her.

He spared her a quick glance, then lifted his gaze back to the wild, arid landscape. "I'll be tired when we get where we're goin'."

"Well," she said, "I had no idea I was in the company of a superhero." Muffling a groan, Lisa pulled her right foot onto her left knee and massaged the tight knot in her calf. "And where *is* 'where we're goin',' exactly?" she asked, mocking his drawl.

"There," he said, ignoring her gibe as he pointed to a low range of mountains.

She squinted into the distance and felt her heart drop to the pit of her stomach. "You're kidding," she said, "right?"

"No, ma'am."

"Lisa," she reminded him, "not 'ma'am.' And that's probably another five miles," she protested, already thinking about the extra aches and pains headed her way.

He reached into the inside pocket of his shirt and pulled out a fabric-covered map. He studied it for a few minutes, then shifted his gaze back to her. "More like three."

"Well, heck," she said, sarcasm dripping from her words. "That's different, then. What're we waiting for?"

Folding the map and tucking it away again, he dropped to one knee beside her and reached for her leg.

"Hey!" She stiffened and tried to pull away, but let's face it, she was so tired a snail could have overtaken her. Let alone Mr. I'll-Get-Tired-Later.

"Relax, princess," he said, his fingers kneading the tight flesh. "I'm just tryin' to help."

She muffled a yelp and told herself to stop him. She shouldn't be letting him do this. She hated him. She hated what he was forcing her to do. Heck, she'd walked more today than she usually did in a month of treadmill exercising. And it was all *his* fault. If he hadn't waved off that helicopter, she'd be winging her way toward an American Embassy somewhere, already anticipating a hot bath and a good meal and some fresh clothes. So, yeah. She hated him and she should be telling him all this while at the same time making him stop massaging her legs. And yet…it felt so *good*. Pain shimmered inside her, blossomed, then disappeared under the wash of warmth drawn from his fingertips.

He moved from one calf to the other, his strong fingers easing away the tightness in her muscles until she almost wanted to weep with the pleasure of it all. Okay, she thought. Maybe he's not so bad. Maybe he's doing the best he can. Maybe he's sorry that he's working her so hard. Maybe…

"Okay, that's it," he announced. "Let's get movin'." He dropped her leg as if it were a seashell; picked up, examined, then discarded as useless.

And just like that she hated him again.

"That's your idea of a 'rest'?" she asked. "Three whole minutes?"

Standing up, he held one hand out to her and pulled her to her feet. "Sun'll be up in a few hours," he said sagely, his gaze drifting across the far horizon. "I want to be tucked away nice and quiet before that happens."

She shifted her gaze to the same horizon and realized that the sky did look just a bit brighter. They'd been walking all night. No wonder she was tired, for pity's sake.

"And you think I'm going to be able to walk three more miles in under three hours?" If the way she was feeling at the moment was any indication, she'd be lying in a crumpled heap inside of a half hour. Her own fallen image rose up in her brain, and Lisa imagined the headlines—Billionaire's Daughter Found Dead in Desert. And, of course, there'd be pictures. Of her mummified body wearing her once fashionable, now pitiful, designer dress.

Now there's an epitaph.

"You'll make it," he said, his words shattering the thoughts in her mind with the steely ring of determination in his tone.

She looked up at him. Funny, she hadn't noticed until just this minute how tall he was. At least six-three. At five-nine, Lisa was no munchkin, but he made her feel tiny in comparison. Maybe she could make it. With his help. He didn't seem the kind of man to give up easily. If he had, they would have been captured hours ago.

"Okay, general," she said, bravely swallowing the knot of fear lodged in her throat. "You lead, I'll follow."

"Ooh-rah," he said, and gave her a smile that nearly knocked her over.

"Ya-hoo," she answered, hoping she'd see that smile again really soon.

Travis wouldn't have admitted it under torture, but he was beat, down to the ground. The cold was keeping him awake for now, but if he didn't get some sleep soon, neither one of them was going to get out of here. Which was why he nearly shouted in joy when he spotted the cave.

If he hadn't been looking specifically for just this, he never would have noticed it. A slight overhang of rock jutted out from the side of the mountain, looking like nothing more than an extrawide crevice. Yet, on closer inspection, he found a narrow but deep cave that would be a perfect place to hide.

Every bone in his body cried out for rest, but before he could, he had to make sure the place was safe. Leaving the princess at the mouth of the cave, he took his rifle and snatched a chem light out of his equipment belt. Cracking the hard plastic case, he then shook it until the crystals inside glowed a soft green. An ordinary flashlight or a flare would be too bright in this all-encompassing blackness. Too easy to spot from a distance. This thing would give off enough light to see by and still be hard to spot by their enemies. Carefully he inspected the shelter. The eerie green light glowed and cast soft, indistinct shadows on the rock walls. His right hand gripping the rifle, he held the light up high in his left as he squinted into the darkness.

"What do you see?"

He winced as her voice seemed to echo in the stony enclosure, and he hoped to hell the place was as empty as it seemed.

"Quiet." His voice was hardly more than a raspy

hush of sound. And still it traveled back to her with no problem.

"And what does quiet look like?" she muttered.

Travis grinned reluctantly and shook his head. This damn woman was as stubborn as he was. A moment later, though, the smile on his face faded as he concentrated on the task at hand. The walls were solid, no holes where critters could crawl or slither through from somewhere else. There was no sign of human habitation in here, but there was always the threat of snakes. Growing up in Texas had given him a healthy respect for the reptiles, and he sure as hell didn't want any surprises while they slept.

Damn, his eyes felt heavy. Gritty. As though he hadn't slept in a year. He blinked, shook his head again and focused. As he did, a slight movement caught the corner of his eye, and he turned his head to follow the snake's movement. Just one, it was moving fast across the sandy ground.

"Damn it," he whispered, knowing he couldn't risk a gunshot to kill it. He'd been prepared to fire on a hostile human, but he'd rather not risk a rifle shot being heard for miles for the sake of killing a snake. Gritting his teeth, Travis set his rifle down, grabbed his knife and killed it, neatly slicing its head from its body.

Then he stood and gave a last look around. Everything else was secure. If the snake had had friends, they were long gone. The cave wasn't much, but it looked damn good to him at the moment. They were safe—for now. They could get some rest and hide until he figured out the best route to get out of this country.

"What's going on back there?" she called, and he heard the fear in her voice.

That woman could drive a saint right out of heaven, he thought. But then, a part of him couldn't really blame her for being scared. She'd already been through more than most folks would face in a lifetime, and to give her her due, she hadn't folded. And Travis admired grit in a person, male or female.

Of course, that didn't mean he didn't wish she was anywhere but there. But wishes wouldn't do a damn bit of good. They were stuck together. And the fact that she was too blasted good-looking for comfort shouldn't come into it. She was his responsibility—nothing else. He'd best remember that. "It's okay," he said. "You can come in now."

"Good," she said, and her voice told him how quickly she was making her way down the length of the cave. "I was getting worried back there by myself. You know you could have left me one of your little Halloween pumpkin light thingies."

"It's a chem light. Not the kind used in pumpkins."

"Whatever," she said, and he watched her walk into the circle of soft-green light. "The point is, it's really dark in here and I—"

Her voice broke off as her gaze fastened on the dead snake. She took several deep breaths, slapped one hand to her chest and said, "Oh, God."

"It's dead."

"That's supposed to make me feel better?" Eyes wide, she backed up and looked around frantically as if expecting to see a pack of snakes sneaking up on her flank.

He bent down, picked up the carcass and held it up admiringly. At least a three-footer. "You'll think better of it once it's cooked."

"Cooked?"

Travis could have sworn he heard her gag.

"Waste not, want not," he told her.

"Look before you leap," she countered.

"He who hesitates is lost," he said, figuring this could go on awhile.

"He who eats snake will get sick," she told him.

"That's not an old saying."

"It's one of my favorites," she said. "As of right now."

Travis laughed shortly and set his pack down, then laid the snake alongside it. Jamming the end of the light into the sand at his feet, he said, "Have a seat. I'm going out to gather some brush. We can make a small fire.''

''You're leaving me here?'' she asked, lifting one hand to point at the snake. ''With *that?*''

''Trust me,'' he said tightly, ''*you're* more dangerous than he is.''

She swung her hair back from her eyes, and in the green glow those blue eyes gleamed like sapphires. Her face pale, her features drawn with fatigue and fear, she was still pretty enough to take a man's breath away.

And he realized he'd been right.

She *was* dangerous.

Three

——

An hour later they were crouched beside a fire so tiny it hardly qualified as flames. But still, the hiss and snap of the burning brush was…comforting, somehow. Except of course, for the snake meat sizzling on a stick.

Lisa cringed just a little and shifted her gaze from the fire to the man opposite her. She watched as he used a rag from his pack to wipe the camouflage paint off his face. With steady, long strokes, he slowly revealed more of his features. Jet-black eyebrows. And his eyes. Darned if they didn't look like melted chocolate—rich and dark—and they had almost precisely the same effect on her. A twinge of hunger, mixed with expectation. In the weird green light, his features looked sharp. Resolute. His nose had character, she decided, and combined with that strong, square jaw, he probably could have made a fortune as a model. Instead, he made his living by dragging women across dark deserts while crazy people shot at them.

"We'll stay here until dark," Travis was saying. "Then I figure we'll head for El Bahar. It's not far and the king there is friendly to the U.S."

"Uh-huh," she said, and though she heard the snap in her tone, she couldn't seem to stop it. "And how far away is this place?"

He pulled out his map, checked it for what had to be the tenth time in the past hour, then glanced at her briefly. "Not far."

"How far?"

"A day or so," he said, deliberately ignoring the sarcasm in her voice. "But once we're in their territory, you'll be safe."

"Day *or so?*" She tried to keep the groan out of her voice but she was pretty sure she hadn't succeeded. Then, rather than concentrate on the march ahead, she focused on the last word he'd said.

Safe.

For the past two weeks of captivity, that was a word she'd concentrated on often. Before being snatched from her spur-of-the-moment shopping trip, Lisa'd never realized just how much she took her own safety for granted. It wasn't something you normally thought about. It just...*was.*

She doubted she'd ever be that complacent again. In fact, she'd probably be looking over her shoulder for years.

But she hadn't let her captors know she was scared, and she refused to give in to fear now.

"Once we're in El Bahar," he was saying, "we'll go directly to the American Embassy and call for a ride home."

"My father can send his jet."

One black eyebrow lifted, and he shook his head, chuckling wryly under his breath.

She had the distinct feeling he wasn't laughing *with* her. Stiffly she asked, "What's so funny?"

"You," he said, reaching to rotate his stick of snake meat in the fire. "A regular plane ride's just not good enough, huh? Have to call for a private jet."

All right, maybe that *had* sounded a little snooty. "I only meant—"

"Relax, princess," he said, interrupting her neatly. "I know just what you meant."

"Really."

Shifting position, Lisa folded her legs in the most ladylike manner she could manage. Wincing slightly at the movement, she tucked her torn, dirty dress down over them and shrugged out of his shirt. With the rock walls cutting off the wind, and the tiny fire, she'd finally warmed up again.

"Yes, really," Travis said, shaking his head again and leaning back against the cool rock wall. He had her number. Had had it from the moment she'd opened her eyes and looked up at him back there at the shack. And he didn't mind telling her so. "I've known women like you most of my life," he said. "The rich girls, counting out daddy's money and buying what they could never earn."

"Now just a darn minute." Her eyes flashed, outrage obvious in her tone.

"Struck a nerve, huh?" he asked, and without waiting for an answer, he went on. "Let's just look at your story so far. You decide to visit an area rife with civil unrest to do some *shopping* and promptly get snatched."

"The papers at home didn't say anything about the dangers of—"

"And then," he said, his voice easily overriding hers, "when you're in trouble up to your pretty neck, you just expect Daddy to pay the demanded ransom."

"Why wouldn't he?" she asked. "I'm his only child."

"For which he's probably grateful," Travis commented and took real pleasure in the murder he saw glinting in her eyes. "My point is, even if he'd paid the ransom, there was no guarantee you'd be released."

"Of course they'd have released me. Why wouldn't they?"

"Darlin'," he said, "after spending most of the day with you, I'm only surprised they didn't offer to pay your dad to take you off their hands."

"You have no right to say such—"

He waved off her indignation. "But back to our story. See, this is where me and my friends came in. The government convinced your daddy to hold off on paying up and to send us in instead."

"It's your job, isn't it?"

"My *job* is to help people who need it. Even spoiled little rich girls whose only job is to look gorgeous and spend cash that isn't theirs."

And she was gorgeous, he admitted silently, his gaze moving over her quickly, thoroughly. Even after all she'd been through, she looked damn good. Blond hair that just dusted across her shoulders was tucked behind her ears now, and a soft fringe of bangs stopped just above her finely arched eyebrows. In the firelight her eyes looked as blue as the sea at dusk, and her mouth looked delicious. Her teeth continually tugged at her bottom lip until it was all Travis could do to keep from offering to help with that little chore. Damn, this was not the time or the place or hell...*the woman* to be having these thoughts about.

He'd do well to remember that she was nothing more than a mission gone wrong. If she hadn't held him up. If she hadn't wasted so much time looking for her damn purse. If those expensive but worthless high heels had made better time in the sand...if any of those things had been different, he would already be rid of her. They'd have parted ways and he never would have had the time or opportunity to notice that her right breast was just a little fuller than her left.

Oh, man. Travis got a grip on the suddenly rampaging hormones charging through his bloodstream and reminded himself that she was no different from the girls back home. Those girls, backed by their daddies' oil money, had run roughshod over anybody in their way. And when it came to guys like him—they were happy enough to snuggle up in the dark, but they never brought his kind home to daddy.

Travis Hawks didn't come from money and as far as he could tell, having it hadn't done those girls— or this one, for that matter—any good.

"I resent that."

He blinked and drew himself back to the conversation at hand. Hell, fighting with her was one sure way to keep his mind on the job rather than on fantasies that didn't stand a snowball's chance in hell of coming true. "I bet you do," he said. "But you're not denying it."

"I do deny it," she said hotly, and leaned toward him. Firelight mirrored in her eyes until it looked as though her gaze was shooting sparks at him. "I am *not* spoiled. And for your information, I'm on the boards of some very worthwhile charities. I *do* work."

He nodded sagely, but there was amusement in his eyes. "Oh, I'm sure your telephone dialing finger gets a real workout."

That blond eyebrow lifted again and disappeared behind her bangs.

"So you work," he said. "Do you have to live off what you make? I don't think so."

"I see. Because I don't have to worry about income, what I do is worth nothing?"

"I didn't say that."

"You most certainly did."

All right, maybe he shouldn't have started any of this. It was none of his business how she lived. His job was simply to return her to the lap of luxury and get the hell out of Dodge. They had another few days together, and there was no sense in being outright enemies, for Pete's sake.

"You know what you are?" she asked, tilting her

head to one side and studying him as if he were smeared on a glass slide beneath a microscope.

"I'll bet you're about to tell me."

"I'd be happy to," she said, a soft smile curving that luscious mouth of hers.

She looked like a woman with a point to make, and Travis, like any other sane man, battened down the hatches and waited for the blow.

"You're a snob."

A short, sharp laugh shot from his throat, ricocheting off the rock walls to echo mockingly.

"A *snob?*" he repeated.

"That's right."

"Honey," he said, "I don't make enough money to be a snob."

"That's just it," she countered, folding her arms beneath her breasts and nodding at him. "You're a reverse snob."

"Oh, this should be good," he said, intrigued in spite of himself. He watched her with interest and couldn't help noticing again just how damn fine she looked, sitting there all smug in her dirty designer dress.

"Because you don't have money, you're prejudiced against those who do."

"Darlin'," he reminded her, "*you* don't have money. Your daddy does."

Her eyes narrowed, and he had the distinct feeling

that if she could have reached him, she just might have slapped his face. But since she couldn't, she kept talking. Which was, he thought wryly, worse than the slap would have been.

"You're a snob, and changing the subject won't alter that one fact."

"Yeah, right."

"Why else would you make assumptions about me?" she asked, drumming her fingertips against her upper arms. "You don't know me at all."

"Sure I do, princess," he drawled, letting the words slide out slowly on purpose. "I've known you most of my life."

She sniffed. "Trust me, if we'd ever met, I would remember."

"Okay, not you specifically," he continued. "But your kind."

"My *kind?*"

"Yep." His mother would be shamed to know it, but he was beginning to enjoy himself here. Nothing quite like a good argument to get your mind off your worries. And he pretty much figured that, by now, the "princess" was so mad at him, she wasn't thinking about her captors or about how small their chances of getting out of here were—or anything else for that matter except maybe taking his head off.

Oh, not that he'd started all of this because of the

kindness of his heart. No, she irritated him beyond measure. With her stylish clothes and her whining about having to run for her own life. But now that she was giving as good as she got...now that he saw that fire of temper in her eyes...damned if he wasn't having a good time.

"Oh yes," she said nodding, "that's a very cogent argument."

"Ah," he replied with a chuckle, "fifty-cent words. Trying to confuse the 'help'?"

"You're really a pain in the—"

"Now, that's not very ladylike, is it?" he asked, cutting her off just in time.

Inhaling sharply, she drew a long, deep breath into her lungs and held it. That did amazing things for her bustline, though Travis knew that if she realized he was noticing, she'd cut it out.

"I refuse to argue with you anymore."

"Can't think of a good comeback, eh?"

She shot him a glare that probably turned the rich boys she was used to into a pillar of ice. Travis wasn't impressed...or intimidated.

After a long minute or two she unfolded her arms and reached for her purse. Ignoring him completely, she flipped it open and began to rummage inside.

"You're a very annoying man," she muttered beneath her breath.

"Yeah and you're a walk in the park."

Her head snapped up and she gave him another one of those "mistress to half-wit servant" looks.

"I'm so happy I can amuse you," she said wryly. "You know, you may be used to this sort of thing, but I'm not."

"I can see that."

"And," she continued, keeping her hands fisted inside her purse while she looked up at him, "I don't appreciate being harassed by the man who was sent here to save me."

"And I don't appreciate listening to you complain, when it was your fault we missed the ride."

"You waved the helicopter off."

He leaned in close, locking his gaze with hers. "One man had already gone down. I waved 'em off so everyone else wouldn't die while they waited on us."

"That's not fair."

"But accurate."

She inhaled sharply, let it out again, then asked, "That man. Do you think he's…"

Travis closed his mind to that thought. He didn't know who'd been standing in the open doorway of the chopper. But whoever he was, he was a fellow Marine, and Travis sure as hell didn't want to think the man had been killed because Travis hadn't been able to move the princess along any faster.

"I don't know." He narrowed his gaze at her. "But one man hurt was enough, don't you think?"

Her lips flattened into a thin line, and her eyes glimmered with what he thought might be tears. But he couldn't be sure, and in an instant that softness was gone again.

"Fine," she conceded. "It was my fault. Forgive me for not wearing my sneakers and jeans. But I didn't expect to be kidnapped and held for ransom. If I'd known I was going to have to make a desert trek…"

"You wouldn't have done a damn thing different."

She straightened her shoulders and lifted her chin. Swinging her hair back out of her face, she asked, "You really don't like me very much, do you?"

A spurt of irritation shot through him. And that irritation was aimed at both her and himself. She'd been right about one thing, anyway. He *didn't* have the right to judge her. She was his mission, pure and simple. And beyond that, there was nothing. With that thought in mind, he said, "I'll tell you what, princess. Four of us, my friends and I, came into this little hellhole to pull your pretty butt out of trouble." He leaned in toward her again, mindful of the fire. "We raced across the desert, laid down cover fire, risked a chopper pilot and his crew—got one man wounded, maybe worse—and not once…not once, since the moment you opened your eyes to look into mine, have you even said, *Thank you.*"

Even in the firelight, he saw the flush that stained her pale, smooth skin, and Travis knew he'd hit his mark. For all the good it did him.

Then, even more irritated that he'd said too much, he picked up the stick, pulled it away from the fire and gingerly tested the snake meat with two fingers. Glancing at her, he said, "It's done."

"Uh-huh." She wasn't convinced.

"You'll like it."

"Let me guess," she said. "Tastes just like chicken."

"Pretty much," he agreed.

"I'll never know for sure," Lisa said, watching the skewered meat as if half expecting it to still be able to strike. "No way am I going to eat a snake."

"We both need to eat," he said, his tone deliberately patient. "And believe me when I say that this snake tastes better than a tuna-casserole MRE."

Confusion shone in her eyes before she warily asked, "Okay, I admit it. I have to know. What exactly is an MRE?"

"Meals ready to eat," he said shortly, and pulled a thick, green plastic, rectangular package from his pack. Stabbing the end of the shish kebab stick into the dirt, he ripped open the plastic and pulled out a flat, brown-cardboard box. He held it out to her. Stamped on one end, were the words Tuna Casserole.

"Good Lord," she said, looking from the box to his dark brown eyes. "They expect you to eat something that comes packaged like that?"

"Yep," he said with a shrug, then added, "and it's not half-bad, either. But the snake'll be better."

"No thanks."

His features tightened briefly. "Up to you, but you'll be almighty hungry before too long."

Lisa smiled and pulled her hands free of her purse. Travis's gaze dropped to what she held. Two big chunks of bread.

"You have food in there?" he asked, surprised.

"Why else would I need my purse?" she retorted. "Like you said, there aren't many malls out here."

Travis winced slightly as he felt his own words coming back to bite him in the ass. "Where'd you get it?" he asked softly.

She shrugged and began to pull more food out of that saddlebag of hers. Pieces of dried meat, parts of oranges, a handful of dates. "Every time they fed me, I hid half of whatever it was. Then, when they forgot to feed me, I'd at least have something." She shrugged as if it didn't matter, and that shrug hit him hard.

"You hid part of your food," he repeated, look-

ing at her with a new admiration. And damn it, respect filled him, too. She'd survived. It probably
hadn't been easy, either. He would have figured that
a woman like her would collapse under the conditions she'd been living in. But she'd not only stood
up to them, she'd come out on top. She'd done what
she had to do to survive. She'd used her head, protecting herself, looking out for the future. Not many
people would have been smart—or strong enough to
keep back extra food just in case.

The princess had just gone up several notches in
his estimation.

"It only made sense," she said, obviously trying
to make light of what she'd done. "After all, who
knew if they'd get tired of feeding a spoiled little
rich girl. I thought it would be smart to store some
food…just in case."

Travis nodded thoughtfully and met her gaze. "It
was smart. Damn smart. Most people would have
eaten when they were hungry, not thinking about
tomorrow."

She smiled then, and something inside Travis's
chest lurched hard against his rib cage. Much to his
own surprise, he realized it was his heart.

"Would you like some bread to go along with
your snake?" she asked, holding out a chunk of flat
bread toward him.

"Yeah, princess—*Lisa*," he corrected. "I believe I would. Thanks."

Her fingers brushed across his skin and Travis tried not to think about the warmth blasting its way through his veins at her slightest touch. Then her gaze locked with his, and she very clearly said, "No, Travis. Thank *you*."

And staring into those sea-blue eyes of hers, he knew a bridge had sprung up between them.

It might be a little shaky...but it was there.

Four

With the words she should have said hours ago, something indefinable changed between them. Lisa felt it. And she knew he did, too. She pulled her hand back and tried not to notice the tingling in her fingertips. But it was as if she'd touched a live electrical wire rather than the callused palm of a man's hand. Her skin hummed with an energy she'd never felt before, and she wasn't at all sure what to do about it.

This possibility had never occurred to her.

She'd never counted on such an instant, overpowering attraction.

Especially to a man who was so completely the opposite of what she'd always thought of as "her type."

Lisa would be the first to admit that she hadn't shown great judgment in the past. After all, you couldn't make and break five engagements and not start doubting your ability to choose wisely.

Her string of fiancés proved that much. A doctor, a lawyer, an investment banker, a college professor and a stock broker. The closest she'd ever come to the "wild side" was her professor. He taught parapsychology and though it was weird, he *was* a professor. And though none of them had worked out, they had at least made sense.

This thrumming, pulse pounding, dry mouth response to a man she hardly knew did not.

But knowing that didn't change a thing.

The men in her past had been professionals. They were a part of her world. She understood them in a way she would never be able to understand this man with the serious Daniel Boone fixation.

And it didn't seem to matter.

Something flashed in Travis's chocolate eyes, and Lisa sucked in a quiet breath. Something hot and liquid settled low in the pit of her stomach and sent out tentacles of awareness that reached every corner of her body. Wow. If just touching his hand could do that to her, she wondered what a kiss would be like.

Her gaze locked on his mouth and her insides trembled. Oh, this probably wasn't a good idea. She had who-knew-how-many days left to be in his company and he'd already made it pretty clear what he thought of her. So there was no way this was going anywhere. Still, she thought as her gaze lifted to meet his, a private little fantasy or two couldn't do any harm, could it?

"What's running around inside that head of yours?" he asked suddenly.

Lisa flinched guiltily, as if he could read her mind and see for himself the direction her thoughts had been taking. And the idea of that was simply too embarrassing to contemplate. So she had to think quickly to come up with something to tell him.

"Uh…" she stalled for a moment, then blurted, "I was just wondering what smells so bad…the cave, the snake or the fire." Brilliant, Lisa, she thought on a silent groan. Just brilliant.

But he accepted her statement at face value, for which she was grateful. "It's the fire," he said. "Actually, it's the brush we're usin' for fuel. Now, if we were back in Texas…" he paused and a soft smile creased his harsh features. "I'd toss some mesquite onto those flames and you'd think you'd died and gone to heaven, on the smell alone."

''Texas, huh?'' she asked. A Marine *and* a Texan. Heck, no wonder he'd been so sure of their ability to traverse the desert before sunrise. He was probably convinced he could walk on water.

And a part of her wouldn't have been surprised to see him do it.

Oh, dear. She could be in big trouble, here.

''Yep,'' he said, and that proud smile on his face widened, deepened.

Again that lightning-fast sizzle of awareness splintered through her bloodstream, and Lisa wondered frantically how to stop her reaction to him. This wasn't the time or the place or the *man* for these kinds of feelings.

She was sitting in a *cave* for pity's sake. In the middle of a desert. *Get a grip, Lisa,* she chanted silently, but the way her heart was thudding in her chest, she had a feeling it wasn't going to do any good.

He started talking about home, and she watched pure pleasure light his eyes as he described his family's ranch, the horses, the sunsets and so much more. He talked about his family, about the small town where he'd grown up, and with every word, he painted a picture. A faraway look softened his gaze as if he was staring at a memory so good, so cherished, it was enough to wipe away thoughts of their current situation. Lines of tension in his features eased away, and his lips curved into a smile that made her wish she could see what he obviously saw so clearly.

Lisa suddenly felt very alone, and a slender thread of envy wound through her. Plainly, he loved the home he carried in his heart. She wondered what it must be like to have a *real* home—a home where people and places were so familiar they were like a part of yourself.

Raised by her father after her mother's death when she was three, Lisa had grown up in boarding schools. And when vacation time rolled around, there was no family homestead to head for. It was Spain or Paris or Switzerland. Not that she was complaining or anything. After all, most people would have loved to see all those places.

But she'd never had the comfort of her own room. Her own private space to dream or sulk in. She'd gone from hotels to rented villas, with never a place to belong. And even thinking it made her feel guilty. So many people had real problems that hers looked trifling in comparison.

Still, a twinge of regret for things she'd never known struck a familiar chord deep within her and brought to life an old ache. But she pushed that pain down into a dark hole inside and covered it over, as she'd done all her life, with a bright smile.

''My brother'll tell you that sage makes the best

fire," Travis was saying, "but for me, it's mesquite, every time."

"Your brother?"

"One of 'em," he said with a half shrug.

Another thing to be envious of, she thought briefly. How many nights had she lain awake, hungering for a sibling to argue with, share secrets with?

"I'm an only child," she said.

His mouth quirked in a half smile. "When I was a kid, there were a lot of times I wished I could say that."

"Trust me," she said, smoothing the hem of her torn, dirty dress over her knees, "it's not all it's cracked up to be."

"Yeah, well, now that we're grown," he said, "I guess I'm glad to have 'em."

"How many brothers do you have?"

"Three," he said. "And two sisters."

"Six kids?"

"We do things in a big way in Texas."

"Apparently."

"And we all know how to cook," he said, holding the still-steaming snake meat out toward her.

She eyed it with distaste, then looked up at him. "I thought we'd settled that already."

Both black eyebrows lifted and his mouth quirked into a taunting smile. "Scared?"

"Not scared," she said with a sniff. "Discerning."

"Chicken, you mean."

Lisa shook her head. "You really think you're going to get me to try that stuff by pulling a third-grade dare?"

"Bwaack, bwaack," he said, and she had to admit he did a pretty decent imitation of a chicken.

"Oh, for heaven's sake," she muttered, reaching out to snatch a piece of the meat. Before she could change her mind or get too sick to swallow, Lisa popped it into her mouth and chewed.

After a long minute she swallowed and looked into his waiting eyes.

"Well?" he asked.

"It wasn't terrible," she admitted, unwilling to give him more than that. But blast it, the stupid snake *did* taste good. As long as she didn't remind herself exactly what she was eating.

"Want some more?" he asked, a knowing smile on his face.

She sighed and said, "You're really loving this, aren't you?"

"Yeah," he said in that slow drawl of his. "I think I am."

"Gracious in victory, I see," she said wryly.

"Princess," he said, clearly enjoying himself

now, ''the only good loser is a guy who's used to losin'.''

Firelight flickering on his harsh features, a steely look in those dark eyes of his, he looked to Lisa like a man who was definitely not used to losing.

At the American Embassy in El Bahar, Gunnery Sergeant Jeff Hunter snapped into the telephone. ''Yes, sir. We'll wait for further instructions.''

He shot an irritated look at the two other men standing nearby. J.T. and Deke both looked as itchy footed as he felt. None of them were comfortable staying here at the embassy while Travis and the Chambers woman were somewhere out in the desert. Nothing worse than standing around waiting.

And with that thought uppermost in his mind, he interrupted the Colonel on the other end of the line. ''Sir, if you give us the word, my team can be back in the field inside an hour. We'll find Hawks and the woman, then call for an evac.''

''Under no circumstances are you to take your team back out,'' Colonel Sullivan ordered. ''This was supposed to be a covert mission. We can't risk sending you back in. At least, not yet.''

Disgusted at the fact that politics were now running what should have remained a military operation, Jeff shook his head at the two men watching him. J.T. cursed under his breath and Deke's scowl got fierce enough to boil blood.

"Understood, sir," Jeff said, not liking this one damn bit. Another minute of "yes sirring" and he hung up, dropping the receiver into the cradle with a loud crack.

"They're not letting us go in, then?"

"No," Jeff said, glancing at Deke. "They don't want to take the chance of having this whole thing on CNN by nightfall."

"So instead," J.T. muttered, "they're hanging Travis out to dry."

"Basically." Jeff shoved one hand across the top of his head and tried to figure out where this had all gone wrong.

"What about the woman?" Deke asked. "Isn't her father rattling enough cages to get some action?"

"Mr. Chambers," Jeff told him with a narrow-eyed stare, "doesn't know what happened. Yet."

"Travis'll get her out," J.T. said. "There's not a better man for this job."

"True," Jeff said, walking to the wide window of the Ambassador's office. He stared out at the busy street below, then lifted his gaze to the desert far out in the distance. It was a hard, dangerous land out there. Good thing Travis was every bit as hard and dangerous himself.

* * *

An hour later Travis stood at the mouth of the cave, letting his gaze slide slowly across the scorched landscape. The sun shone down from a sky that looked white-hot. In the distance, waves of heat shimmered, bending the land and tricking the eye. He narrowed his gaze on the wavering lines that resembled a large pool of water. But he was no stranger to mirages. He'd seen his share of them back in Texas on blistering summer days. He knew damn well that a desperate man could be fooled into chasing water that didn't exist until it was too late and the last of his strength gave out.

Taking a tighter grip on his rifle, he shifted his gaze from the mirage to slowly scan the area. No sign of anyone out there—but that didn't necessarily mean anything. He couldn't take anything for granted. It was up to him and him alone to see that Lisa Chambers made it out.

Which meant that he was going to have to stay focused. And not on her. Travis reminded himself that hormones had no business here. Hell, he'd been doing this job for years and never once had he found himself *talking* with the mission like they were on a date or something. Disgusted with himself, he knew that one slipup here could mean recapture or worse. He didn't need to have his concentration divided. He couldn't afford to see her as anything but what she was.

His responsibility.

Oh, they didn't need to be enemies. Hell, this whole rescue thing would work a lot better if they weren't. But they didn't need to be friendly, either.

What was needed here was a cool, detached professionalism. And if that meant pulling back, being a hard-ass, then that's just what he'd have to do. Better she not like him than start giving him the kind of smile he'd just seen. How was a man supposed to keep his mind on the dangers at hand when a woman like her turned on the charm?

Nope. This'd be a damn sight easier if she went back to snarling at him. Which shouldn't be at all hard to accomplish.

Turning, he slipped back down the narrow passage until he reached the end of the cave where he'd left Lisa, waiting.

"Did you see anything?" she asked, and he heard the fear underlying the calm of her words.

"No," he said shortly. "But that doesn't mean much. Still, we should be safe enough here. We'll hole up until nightfall and then leave. It'll be cooler walking at night and easier to lose ourselves in the shadows."

She nodded, but clearly wasn't looking forward to it. He didn't blame her. Hell, no way was she used to this kind of life. Probably hadn't walked farther than the curb to hail a taxi in years. But, he thought, steeling himself against a swell of sympathy, the harder he pushed her, the sooner they'd be out of here and back where they both belonged.

Which was nowhere near each other.

"Get some sleep," he said, and kicked out the last of their tiny fire. He used the toe of his boot to stomp out the dying embers until there was nothing left of them. Motioning her back against the wall of the cave, he stretched out in front of her, placing himself between her and whatever danger might approach.

"Sleep?" she repeated. "Here?"

He turned his head to look at her and told himself not to notice the fear in her eyes. "Well now, I called the Hilton, but they were full up."

"Very funny."

"I try."

"Try harder," she told him, squirming around on the rock floor, looking for a comfortable spot—and obviously not finding one.

"Pretend you're camping." He didn't even look at her when he spoke. At the moment he didn't have the energy.

"I've never been camping."

"There's a surprise."

She muttered something he didn't quite catch, but he heard the rustle of her dress across the dirt as she settled down.

"Look, princess," he said, feeling fatigue ease up from his very bones, "we're stuck here. We can't leave now. It's too damn hot out there. We wouldn't make a mile with our water supply so low."

"Yes, but—"

"We've got a chance for some sleep, and we're gonna take it."

She glanced at the dark passage leading toward the outside world, then shifted her gaze back to him. "And what if someone comes in while you're napping? What then, fearless leader?"

Well apparently she, too, had decided to back off the whole friendship thing. Which was just as well, he told himself. It was much safer for both of them that way.

Closing his eyes, he muttered, "Trust me. The guys who kidnapped you are probably throwing a party to celebrate you being gone. If they've got any sense at all, they're not lookin' for you."

And if they were, he thought, he'd hear them long before they got close enough to snatch her again. He'd learned long ago how to sleep with one eye open. As long as she was with him, she was safe.

He'd see to it.

Five

She moaned in her sleep, and Travis went on full alert.

First things first, he glanced at the entrance to the cave and saw that no one had discovered them. They were still alone. But Lisa's pain shimmered in the air around him. Going up on one elbow, he stared down at her and scowled to himself. In the dim light, he saw her features tighten, her brow furrowing as she twisted her head from side to side. Almost frantically she whispered words he couldn't quite understand.

But he heard the fear clearly.

A cold, hard hand fisted around his heart as he watched her battling demons in her sleep. Back teeth grinding together, Travis fought with his own instinct to protect. She wouldn't welcome his comfort, he knew. Hell, they'd been at each other's throats for hours. But at the same time he couldn't just sit here and watch her torturing herself with nightmares.

"Lisa," he whispered and reached out one hand toward her. He stopped short, though, and curled his fingers into a tight fist to keep from touching her. Keep it impersonal, he told himself sternly, trying to ignore the single tear rolling down her cheek.

But seeing a strong woman cry was enough to curdle his blood. What the hell was she dreaming about? Her captors? What had they done to her? During their forced march across the desert, he'd pushed her to the edge of her limits and then beyond. But she'd stood up to it. She hadn't broken. And damned if it didn't bother him to see her in the grips of something she couldn't fight.

"Princess," he said, his voice a little louder now as he tried to reach her through whatever torments she was experiencing.

"Don't." The single word came loud and clear and for some weird reason, it made him feel better. She was strong. Probably stronger than she knew.

Even in her dreams she was fighting back. Holding on.

He opened his fisted hand and touched her upper arm gently, trying not to be distracted by the cool softness of her flesh. But that was hard to do since the moment his skin came into contact with hers, heat swelled up and boiled his blood. Damn. It was like the shock of static electricity.

He swallowed hard and muttered quietly, "It's okay, princess. You're safe."

Whether it was the sound of his voice or the touch of his hand, she instantly quieted, turning her head toward him and moving closer on the rocky ground. He stretched out again and held perfectly still as she cuddled in, dropping one arm across his chest and burrowing her head into the hollow of his shoulder.

One corner of his mind knew that she didn't have the slightest idea of what she was doing. She was simply looking for comfort, the way a child in the dark might grab at a teddy bear. But the feel of her body curled into his sparked a reaction down low in his gut and threatened to swamp all of his high-and-mighty notions of keeping his distance.

He lay awake, staring into the darkness for a long time, while she slept deeply, trustingly, in his arms.

Lisa woke with a start.

Her eyes flew open. Her heartbeat thundered in

her ears. She swallowed hard, focused on the soft pillow beneath her head and for a long, frantic moment couldn't remember where she was.

Then, as the new aches and pains began to register, it all came flooding back to her. Oh, yeah. The cave. With supermarine.

How could she have forgotten any of it? Even for a minute? Heck, every inch of her body hurt. That wild race across the desert had just about wiped her out. *And,* she'd eaten *snake,* for pity's sake, then spent hours arguing with a man whose head gave new meaning to the phrase *solid rock.*

She grimaced as she shifted position carefully, and it wasn't until that moment that she realized her "pillow" was actually Travis Hawks's shoulder.

Oh, for heaven's sake. How embarrassing was this? All she'd done was fight and argue with the man, and then the minute she falls asleep, she snuggles up close? Well, the only discreet way out of this was to slip away from him before he woke up.

And she would do just that, she told herself. In a minute. The problem was, he just felt so darn good. Strong. Solid. She listened to the steady beat of his heart and felt...*safe.* Silly, she knew, considering the fact that they were hardly out of danger.

But there it was.

Ever since appearing in that horrible little room

to rescue her, he'd put her safety first. Even now, he lay alongside her, his body between hers and the mouth of the cave. His body between her and danger.

Okay, she told herself, uncomfortable with that particular line of thought, no need to start giving him more brownie points than he'd already collected. Besides, she was already in his debt. She didn't want to have to be forced to actually *like* him, too.

But whether she wanted to or not, Lisa's mind kept spinning on the subject of Travis Hawks.

Had he slept? Or had he stayed awake and on guard?

And why, she wondered, did she care?

He'd insulted her, exhausted her and infuriated her. So why should she care? The easy answer of course was, she shouldn't. This was his job. He did this all the time. She was just the latest in his no-doubt-impressive line of rescues.

Nothing special.

Lisa frowned at that bitter pill and some of the soft glow she'd been feeling faded away. Naturally she was nothing special to him. She'd never been special to anyone. Why would he be any different?

"I can hear you thinkin'," he said, his deep voice rumbling through the cave and dancing along her spine.

"Geezz!" She jumped, slapped one hand to her chest to keep her heart from flying out of her chest and pushed away from him to sit up straight. She felt a flush of heat rush to her cheeks and was grateful for the darkness. Served her right, she thought. Indulge in a little self-pity party—think some warm, fuzzy thoughts, and get caught at it. That would teach her.

Thank heaven he couldn't read minds. She cringed and, to cover her own discomfort, she retreated into arguing with him again.

"So since you couldn't run me to death, you've decided to *scare* the life out of me?"

His gaze shot straight to hers. Even in the shadowy darkness, she felt the power of that gaze, and something inside her did a slow flip.

Oh, boy.

"Not till we get where we're goin'," he said.

Figures that Captain America would come out of a deep sleep ready to march. "I take it we're leaving?"

"If it's dark enough," he told her, and got to his feet quickly. Looking down at her, he said, "Have another drink of water. I'm going to check things out."

She watched him walk away and marveled at how quietly such a big man could move. In seconds he was back. "Sun's gone down. Time to head out."

Lisa smothered a groan as he packed up the few things he'd carried with him. He gave her another drink of water, took one himself, then helped her to her feet.

"Better put my shirt back on," he said, snatching it up off the ground to hand to her. "Gonna be cold again in no time."

She slipped it on, then paused for a long look at the man standing within an arm's reach of her. His chest looked impossibly broad. His square jaw screamed defiance. The weapon he held was deadly. But the look in his eyes as he stared at her told Lisa that nothing and no one would hurt her.

And her bruised heart felt warm and full.

"Come on, princess, you're doin' fine."

She huffed out a breath that ruffled the bangs drooping over her forehead, but the glare she shot him let Travis know exactly what she was thinking. And he figured if she was carrying a gun, he'd have been a dead man a couple hours ago.

"How...far...have...we...come?" she asked, every breath interrupted with a gasp or a moan.

He took the hint and stopped. "A couple of miles."

"It feels like more," she said, and dropped to the ground. Staring up at him, she continued, "I hate to sound like a three-year-old in the back of a station wagon, but—how much longer?''

A brief smile crossed his face as he reached into his breast pocket for the map he'd already consulted several times. Going down on one knee beside her, he unfolded the thing, angled it to catch the moonlight and did some fast figuring. ''The city's still a ways, but we're almost in El Baharian territory.''

''That's good, right?''

''Right. Once we're safely on their side of the border, we can relax.''

''Relax. God, what a wonderful word.'' She sighed, pushed her hair back from her face, then rubbed at her calf.

Travis frowned and found himself wishing there were some other way. If he could contact his team, they'd be able to call in another chopper. But the throat mikes they wore on the mission were too short range to be of any use. Nope. They were on their own and that meant walking out. Whether it beat the princess into the ground or not.

''You're doin' great,'' he said, knowing she probably wouldn't care what he thought, but he had to at least give her this. He had to tell her that she'd done a better job of keeping up than a lot of boot Marines might have.

She slowly lifted her head and looked at him. ''Was that a compliment?''

He cleared his throat, scraped one hand across his face and when he'd stalled as long as possible, he muttered, "Yeah. I guess it was."

She stared up into his eyes and in the moonlight she looked too damn good. That pale-yellow dress of hers looked like spun gold in the silvery light. Her blond hair was messy and tumbled around her face in the kind of waves that made a man want to comb his fingers through them.

His mouth dried up, and it had nothing to do with the lack of water. Travis's insides were twisted into knots, and a hard ball of need settled down low in his gut. He wanted to pretend nothing was happening, but he was a man unused to lying. Even to himself.

And the truth of the matter was the princess was getting to him. Oh, she complained and argued, but hell, that only made the trip interesting. Beneath that spoiled-rich-girl exterior, there was a thread of steel. And that thread kept her moving despite her fear, her exhaustion. Hell, despite *him*.

"Thank you, Travis," she said and her voice came soft and quiet. "Strangely enough, coming from you, that actually means a lot to me."

He could see she meant that, and it pleased him. "You earned it."

"I know," she said, and gave him a smile that slammed into him with the force of mortar fire. But he shook the feeling off to listen to her. "I'm dirty and tired and sore, but I'm doing it. And I'm going to make it the rest of the way, too."

"Yeah," he agreed, nodding. "You will."

He handed her the canteen and offered her a drink. She took it gratefully, and after she'd handed it back, he took a swallow himself, letting the water soak into his dry mouth before allowing it to slide down his throat. It took care of his thirst, now all he could hope was it would cool the fire building inside him.

But the way he was feeling, he suspected that would take a lot more water. Say, a lakeful.

"Those shoes working better for you now?" He shifted the conversation, hoping to get his mind off his hormones as he carefully stowed the canteen.

"Yes." She drew one foot up and examined what was left of her expensive but useless footwear. "Although Ferragamo would have been highly insulted to see you using that knife of yours to whack at his creation."

Not as insulted as she had been, he was willing to wager. He could still see the look on her face when he'd sat her down and broken off the spindly heels. Personally, he was a fan of high heels. They did amazing things for women's legs—especially, he admitted silently, hers. But they weren't exactly made for trooping through the desert.

Along the horizon a sliver of pale blue edged the night. Sunrise was coming. Already the stars looked a bit less bright. Squinting, he narrowed his gaze and took in the surrounding area. For miles in every direction, there was simply nothing. They'd long ago left the rocky terrain behind and had entered the real desert. Sand dunes stretched out forever, and Travis knew they'd need to find some kind of shelter before morning. To be trapped on the sand during the day would be asking for trouble.

Not only would they be out in the open, they'd also be at the mercy of the sun. No caves around here, he thought, but there was something she'd probably like a hell of a lot better. Plus, it was in El Baharian territory. They'd be safe. And with any luck, they could make it there in just under a couple of hours.

Standing up again, he held out a hand toward her. "Time to go."

Obviously tired, she didn't even argue. She slapped her hand into his and moaned quietly when he pulled her to her feet. For one long moment she stood there, her hand in his. His thumb scraped across the tops of her knuckles, and he watched her shiver. Damn. He didn't know if it was good or bad that she was just as affected by a simple touch as he was.

Finally, though, she pulled her hand free, and Travis didn't even want to admit to himself just how empty his felt without hers in it.

Then she swayed unsteadily and fell into him. His arms came around her in an instinctive move and he heard her breath catch as her breasts pressed against his chest. Heat—pure, undiluted, hot-as-the-halls-of-hell heat—swamped him and he was pretty sure she felt it, too.

Their gazes locked for one long minute before she slowly…reluctantly, stepped back and away.

Damn.

"Okay," she said, her voice over-bright in a futile attempt to cover up the awkwardness of the moment. "Let's get this over with."

Travis nodded. Good idea, he thought, but knew he wouldn't forget the feel of her in his arms. "Right. If we set out at a good clip, we'll be able to make our next stop in about two hours."

"'Good clip,' eh?" she repeated with a smile. "Is that Marine-speak?"

"Close enough."

She put her hands at the small of her back and stretched, leaning her head back, staring up at the sky.

Travis, though, couldn't take his gaze off her. Even with his too-big shirt hanging off her slim body, she looked feminine enough to stoke the hunger riding him. Strange, he'd started out on this mission resenting her and now…hell, he didn't know what he thought anymore.

"Beautiful, isn't it?"

"What?"

She turned her head to look at him and waved one hand at the star-studded sky above them. "This. I mean, granted we're not here under the best of circumstances. And I'd probably enjoy this a lot more if I were standing on a balcony of a great hotel, but it really is beautiful here."

Travis tilted his head back to look at the wide expanse of glittering sky, taking a moment to enjoy the view, something he'd never done before while on a mission.

"The air's so clear here," she was saying, her voice a soft hush of sound in the night, "the stars look close enough for you to be able to reach out and grab a handful of them."

Amazing, he thought, watching her as she turned in a slow circle, taking in the spectacular night sky. Even in these conditions, she took the time to admire the night sky. He wouldn't have thought her the type to notice anything outside a department store. But then, she was surprising him a lot, wasn't she?

"Don't you think it's beautiful?" she asked again.

Travis looked at the woman beside him for a long moment before saying, "Yeah. Beautiful."

And he knew for damn sure he wasn't talking about the sky.

Six

"**W**ater," Lisa said breathlessly, hardly daring to believe her own eyes. "It's water. Lots of it."

"Looks good, doesn't it?" Travis asked.

She glanced at him briefly, taking the time to notice the half smile curving his mouth as he watched her. A slow curl of something warm and liquid unwound inside her, and Lisa had to force herself to turn her gaze back on what had to be the most beautiful pool of water she'd ever seen. Standing at the crest of yet another hill made of sand, she stared down at the shallow valley below. And in the heart of that valley lay an honest to goodness oasis.

For some reason, she'd never considered them real. She'd thought of them as products of Hollywood, created when filmmakers needed a lush spot for the ever popular love scene. Yet there it was, sparkling in the vast expanse of brown, like an emerald tossed into the dirt.

Pale light kissed the horizon, signaling the rising of the sun, warning of the heat to come. But below, in that blessed valley, tall, slender palms grew in a semicircle around the pool of blue water. The silky fronds rustled merrily in the breeze and sounded to Lisa like applause—as if even the trees were welcoming her. Grass, actual grass, lined the banks leading down to the water's edge, and dozens of bushes and plants thrived here, in the middle of nothingness.

After days of living in a beige world filled with fear and exhaustion, just the sight of the oasis was enough to make her heart swell with relief.

"It's wonderful," she said, and heard her voice crack.

"Even better," Travis told her, "we're officially in El Bahar now."

She turned her head to look at him again. "You mean…"

He grinned. "We're safe."

Safe. They'd actually made it. Escaped her captors. Survived the desert. Tears stung Lisa's eyes, but she blinked them back. Ridiculous to cry now that it was all over. The time for tears would have been in the cave. Or when she was struggling to keep up with him as they crossed the sand. But to get all misty now, when their troubles were behind them made absolutely no sense.

The last few days crowded together in her mind. Images of Travis, guiding her through the darkness, arguing with her, feeding her, protecting her, rose up in her mind, one after the other. She owed him so much more than she could ever repay. How does a person go about thanking someone for their life?

Especially, how did *she* go about it, since she hadn't exactly made his job any easier.

"I can't believe it."

"You can check the map if you don't believe me." His voice teasing, he looked at her as if he knew exactly what she was thinking.

"It's not that," she told him with a smile, letting her gaze slide from his to the desert landscape behind them. It felt as though she'd been born in this desert. And though she'd never admit this out loud to anyone, there had been times when she'd doubted that she would ever leave it. Yet here they were. What was that old saying? "Bloodied, but not beaten?" Lisa smiled to herself and took her first easy breath since the morning she'd been kidnapped.

They'd come so far, she and Travis. In more ways than one.

She'd only known him a few short days, but in some ways, Lisa felt closer to this man than to anyone else she'd ever known. Amazing how a few days of intense living could make you feel so…attached to someone. Looking up into that rugged face with its strong lines and sharp planes, Lisa's heart turned over. He'd literally saved her life. He'd pushed her to find her own limits and then helped her surpass them.

"You did it," she finally said, staring into those chocolate eyes that were now so familiar to her.

His grin slowly faded as he shook his head. "No, princess, *we* did it."

She laughed shortly and heard the irony in the sound. "We, huh? Awfully generous, Captain America." She shifted her gaze back to the cool, green grass below them. Easier to admit this part if she wasn't looking at him. "You practically had to save me in *spite* of me."

He took her upper arm in a firm grip and turned her around to face him. Heat pushed through her bloodstream at his touch, quickening her breath, staggering her heartbeat. Her stomach did another slow flip-flop, and Lisa wondered if she would ever feel that sensation again once they'd gone their separate ways.

His thumb rubbed her skin before he released her, and Lisa didn't even want to think about the immediate loss of warmth.

"Don't be so hard on yourself," he said. "You stood up to it. Way better than some I've seen."

She'd like to believe that, Lisa realized. For once in her life she'd like to believe that she'd accomplished something on her own. Strange. Three weeks ago her biggest accomplishment to date had been arranging an impromptu dinner party for seventy-five of her father's closest friends. And she'd been pretty proud of herself for it, too.

Now, though, she'd been put to the test and she'd passed. She'd survived a kidnapping and a hostile desert. She'd eaten a snake, slept in a cave and managed to keep up with a professional warrior on a forced march. And though heaven knew it hadn't been easy, she'd made it.

A sense of pride filled her, and Lisa marveled at it. It had been so long since she'd been proud of herself for anything.

"We'll rest here today," he was saying, and Lisa pushed her thoughts aside to listen. "Head for the city when the sun goes down. If we're lucky, we won't have to walk the whole way in. Might run into one of the El Baharian desert patrols." He slung his weapon over his shoulder and held out a hand to her. As she took it, he folded his fingers around hers and said, "But for now, how about we go on down there and scoop up some of that water?"

An hour later Travis leaned back against a date palm and laid his weapon on the grass beside him. For the first time since this whole thing had started, he felt relaxed. Now that they were in El Bahar, he knew that even if there were pursuers in the desert somewhere behind them, they would never risk crossing the border to cause trouble.

Mission accomplished, he thought, and wondered why he didn't feel more relieved about that. He should be quietly celebrating. Hell, they were about to go their separate ways—at last. Two days ago he'd been able to think of nothing else. But now, watching Lisa at the water's edge, only a foot or two away, things were different. In the soft hush of early-morning light, she knelt on the grass, using his water-filled Kevlar helmet as a wash basin. Drawing his knees up, he rested his hands on them and watched as she lifted first one arm, then the other, smoothing fresh water along her skin.

His body tightened and his hands clenched into fists. Yep, it was a good thing the mission was nearly over, he told himself. He was starting to get *way* too fond of this woman. If someone had told him he'd be feeling like this a few days ago, he would have thought they were nuts.

But damned if she hadn't gotten under his skin. Her fierce stubbornness. Her dogged determination to not be beaten. Her willingness to argue at the drop of a hat—and the fact that he didn't intimidate her in the slightest. He admired her—and he hadn't expected to.

Not one of the spoiled rich girls he'd grown up around could have stood up to the past few days. They'd have wilted under the pressure. But Lisa'd only gotten stronger. Like steel tempered under fire, she'd faced the worst and come out better for it.

His gaze narrowed on her as she cupped her hands and splashed water on her face and neck. Lifting her chin, she stared up into the already brassy sky and let water droplets slide down her throat and beneath the neckline of her dress. She sighed and he felt it.

Damn it, he felt that sigh right down to his bones.

It was the first time he'd really seen her in daylight—and he had to admit, at least silently, that she was made for sunshine. Her blond hair, even as wet as it was now, looked like gold, and her fair skin was—

Travis frowned as a quick jolt of anger pulsed through him. In a few long strides he was kneeling down beside her.

She glanced at him, smiled and said, ''It feels so good to wash all of this sand off that I...'' Her voice trailed off as she looked into his eyes. "What is it? What's wrong?"

"You tell me," he ground out and half turned her until he could see at close range what he'd only just spotted. On her shoulder, a large purple bruise discolored her skin, and she flinched as his fingertips smoothed over it gently.

"Oh, that."

He hadn't seen it before. But then, since the moment they met, they'd been in the dark. Either at night, or in the cave. "Yeah, that."

"It's nothing. Just a bruise."

"They hit you?" he asked unnecessarily, fighting the urge to run back the way they'd come, find the SOBs and give them a few bruises.

She shrugged out from under his touch and looked over her shoulder at him. "Just one of them. Generally they treated me pretty well, considering. This was just the one time."

"Once is enough."

"Exactly my thoughts," she told him, and gave him a brave smile that tore at his heart. And she hadn't said a word of complaint about this, hadn't whined or asked for sympathy, despite the fact that her shoulder must have been hurting. There was a slender thread of iron in this woman, making her so much more than she seemed. Travis pictured her, alone, scared and facing down her captors. He was willing to bet she'd given as good as she got. Hell, she'd bitten him, and he was rescuing her. Maybe this was the only physical bruise she carried, but how many others stained her heart? Her soul? And she hadn't let them stop her, either. A swell of pride filled him.

He reached out again, giving in to his instincts, and this time caressed her cheek with his fingertips. Her eyes closed as he touched her, and he felt her tremble shake through him, too. Trouble, his brain shouted, but thankfully, his body wasn't listening. His blood felt as if it was boiling in his veins. Every breath staggered in and out of his lungs, and his heart pounded hard enough to shove through his rib cage. He wanted her. Needed her. Here. Now.

The slide of his fingers across her skin sent shafts of pure, white heat slicing through him and it was all he could do not to grab her, pull her close and cover her mouth with his. But despite the rush of need choking him, there was still a small, rational voice in the corner of his mind screaming at him to back off. This wasn't real. None of this. It was a world apart from reality. Like this oasis in the middle of a desert, his time with her was a spot of glory in the middle of an everyday life. And soon, they'd be back in civilization. Back to the real world—where he and the princess, under normal circumstances, would never have met.

He pulled back, but Lisa reached up and caught his hand in hers, holding it to her face, stroking her fingers along his. "Travis…"

"This'd be a big mistake," he said, his gaze shifting from her eyes to her mouth and back again.

She licked her lips, and his insides tightened even further. Which didn't really seem possible.

"It doesn't feel that way right now," she told him, and her voice was soft, welcoming.

"It will by tomorrow." He knew it. And if he had one active brain cell, he'd break this off and walk away now. While he still could.

She turned her face into his palm, then looked at him again. "All my life, I've worried about and planned for tomorrow. For once I'd just like to claim today and let tomorrow take care of itself."

An invitation.

One he couldn't have refused.

Even if he'd wanted to.

Pulling her closer, Travis bent his head. His gaze locked with hers, he moved in slowly, deliberately, giving her time to change her mind. Praying she wouldn't. Seconds ticked past. Closer. He inhaled her scent, warm and wet and woman. Closer still. Just a breath away now and he could almost taste her. She tipped her head back and leaned in toward him. Her blue eyes looked deeply into his, and Travis swore he could see straight into her soul.

Then their lips met, his eyes closed and thought stopped. Sensations poured through him, swamping him with the force of a tidal wave and he rode that swell, loving the ride. Gathering her tightly to him, his arms came around her as he deepened the kiss, parting her lips with his tongue, sweeping into her warmth, tasting her. She sighed into his mouth, and he took that small breath for his own, swallowing it and tucking it away inside him as though he might need that extra breath later.

Her tongue entwined with his, and she reached up, wrapping her arms around his neck, scraping her fingers across his nape. He shuddered at her touch, wanting more, needing more. Breaking the kiss, he dragged his lips along the line of her throat, tasting sand and fresh water and her soft, smooth skin. It fired his blood anew and sent desire pumping through him.

She moaned and tilted her head to one side, offering him access.

"Travis," she whispered, and her voice broke on his name. "Don't stop."

"Don't worry about that," he promised. Hungrily he moved his hands over her body, and she arched into his touch, silently urging him on. His fingers found the side zipper on her dress, and in an instant he'd pulled it down and slipped one hand beneath the torn yellow fabric. He cupped her breast and she gasped as the same, nearly electric shock of pleasure jolted them both. Her bra was nothing more than a bit of lace and a couple of straps. No match for a Marine.

His thumb caressed her hardened nipple through the lacy material, and she sighed his name, fueling the fires within. She filled him. His mind, his heart. All he could see and feel was her. This woman. This incredible woman who did things to him he never would have thought possible. Need roared up inside him, demanding to be fed.

He'd never known anything like it. Her passion simmered inside him, but it was more than that. He couldn't name it and didn't want to bother to try. It was enough that he could fill his hands and his heart with her.

Hands fumbling, mouths tasting, they pulled at each other's clothes in a frenzy to mate. To feel skin against skin, heat to heat. And when they were naked, he laid her back on the grass in a patch of shade thrown from the surrounding date palms.

A desert wind sighed across them, carrying the scent of the far-off sea and the heat of the sun. Travis speared his fingers through her hair, loving the feel of the silky, wet strands sliding over his skin. He cupped her face, turning her gaze to meet his. Reading the passion in her eyes, he dipped his head to hers and claimed another kiss. He took her, reveling in the feel of drowning in her warmth.

Lisa reached up and wrapped her arms around his neck, pulling him closer. She wanted to feel all of him pressed to her. His broad chest, sprinkled with a dusting of dark hair, was tanned and muscular. Soft and rough, hard and smooth, their bodies moved together, scraping flesh to flesh. Her fingers trailed down his back, loving the feel of him beneath her hands.

His callused palms moved down her length, stroking, caressing until Lisa writhed beneath him, lifting her hips, arching into him. Her legs parted in eager anticipation and when he touched her center, she groaned aloud.

Too much, she thought, her mind racing. It was all too much. Sensations escalated. Fire. Heat. A dazzling of sparks shooting through her blood. She looked into his eyes and saw a passion she'd never seen before. Five times she'd been engaged and yet she'd allowed none of her fiancés to touch her like this. There'd been no sparks. No magic. No hunger for more than the occasional kiss and cuddle.

She'd thought there was something wrong with her. Assumed that she was frigid. Accepted the fact that she lacked that certain something that made a woman want to be touched, explored, desired.

But there hadn't been anything wrong. She simply hadn't been with the right man.

Here, in this unlikely place, with a man who'd risked his life to save hers, she'd finally found him. And herself.

He dipped one finger into her heat and Lisa cried out, "Oh, Travis."

"I want you, darlin'," he said, his voice a whispered hush. "But—"

"*But?*" she repeated, suddenly terrified that he would stop touching her. That he would pull away before she knew the rest. Before she could finally experience what she'd waited all her life to feel. Had she finally found the right man only to have him turn from her?

"I don't have any protection," he said on a disappointed groan that shook her to her bones.

Her eyes flew open, and she stared into the chocolate depths looking down at her. "Protection?" Her brain had become so fuzzy she'd forgotten something that no woman should ever forget.

"Condoms." One corner of his mouth lifted into a sad smile. "Not exactly standard equipment for a recon mission."

Her body was tingling. His finger stroked that most sensitive piece of flesh and she quivered in his arms. Desperation rose up inside her. He couldn't stop. *They* couldn't stop. She had to finish this. Had to ease the ache building inside.

"It's okay," she murmured, lifting her hips into his hand, driving his finger deeper. "It's safe. I'm healthy."

"Me, too," he assured her, slipping another finger into her depths and stroking her body from the inside.

"Oh…" she sighed, licked her lips and asked, "Then what're we waiting for?"

"Am I glad to hear you say that," he said, and moved to cover her body with his.

Kneeling between her thighs, he shifted his hands to her bottom and lifted her hips high enough to ease his entry.

Lisa felt cherished, adored, and for that feeling she would risk anything. She tipped her head back into the grass, stared up at the lightening sky, then closed her eyes, the better to concentrate on what was about to happen to her.

He entered her body with one, swift, sure stroke and she gasped at the intimate invasion. So hard. So powerful. Like nothing she'd ever known before. And *so* worth waiting for. Her body ached and she felt herself stretching to accommodate him. After a few seconds ticked past, though, she began to wonder why he wasn't moving.

She opened her eyes to find him staring at her, irritation glittering in his dark-brown gaze.

"What is it?" she asked breathlessly. "What's wrong?"

"You're a virgin," he said flatly.

She smiled to herself, rocked her hips and took him deeper inside before saying, with some satisfaction, "Not anymore."

"You should have told me."

Ridiculous to be having this discussion now, she thought and moved again, twisting her hips this time until she saw a muscle in his jaw twitch as he tried for control.

"Could we—" she reached out to let her fingertips trail along his chest until that wall of muscle trembled "—talk about this...*later?*"

He groaned, clenched his teeth and nodded. "Right. Later. For sure."

"Oh, for sure."

He moved, rocking his hips, pushing himself so deeply inside her that she was sure she felt him touch her soul. He leaned over her, brushing his mouth over hers, then shifting to take first one nipple then the other into his mouth.

Lisa groaned, giving in to the spiraling whirl of feelings coursing through her. She felt as though she were racing through the darkness, headed for a glimmer of light that hung just out of her reach. Every aching muscle in her body strained for it. Tension built in a rush. He pushed her higher and higher, and when Lisa thought she couldn't stand the suspense any longer...the fireworks began.

The tingling deep inside built into a shower of sparks that cascaded through her, splintering the imagined darkness, covering her in bright, glorious color. So much more than she'd ever expected. So much better than she'd hoped. And it was all because of him. This one man who'd crept into her heart and carved his name there.

He felt her body climax, and the contractions shimmered through him, urging him to completion. And it was completion, he thought, staring down into those lake-blue eyes of hers. It was a homecoming. To a place he'd never been before.

To a place he never wanted to leave.

Her gaze locked with his as he emptied himself into her, and when he murmured her name, she cradled him in her arms and softened his fall.

Seven

He wasn't sure how long they lay there, but it was long enough for the sun to shift and the skimpy shade to swing wide of them. The sun poured down from a clear, empty sky and bathed them both in a heat that burned.

Rousing himself, Travis held on to her tightly and rolled them off into the shade again. The cool of the grass pressed against his back as he stared up at her, lying flat on top of him. "So," he said, "it's later. Talk."

She stretched and damn near purred, rubbing her legs and upper body against him until he felt himself go hard and ready again.

Okay, this wasn't going to work. If he expected to talk to her, then he'd better keep some distance between them. A couple thousand miles ought to do it.

He set her to one side, rolled away and snatched up his clothes. Then, tossing her dress and underthings to her, he said flatly, "Talk."

She sighed and he got the message. She plainly didn't want to have this conversation. But she should have told him. Maybe it would have stopped him from making love to her. Maybe not, but she should have said something.

Throwing her a quick glare over his shoulder, he yanked on his clothes. "Why didn't you tell me?"

"It's not exactly something I advertise, you know."

Damn, she didn't even look embarrassed to be lying naked in the dappled shade. For a recent ex-virgin, she was getting the hang of this sensuality thing real quick. Which brought him right back to the question at hand.

"How could you be a virgin?" he demanded, throwing his hands wide as he turned for another eye-popping look at her. "Do you live in a city filled with blind men?"

One corner of her mouth lifted. "Thanks. I think."

"Oh, it was a compliment, believe me." He

pulled his socks on, then reached for his combat boots. "But I don't get it. Have you been locked up in a convent or something?"

He heard her clothing rustle as she dressed and tried to keep from imagining her breasts as she hooked her bra.

"Of course not."

"Then what the hell were you waiting for?"

"It's not that I was *waiting,* exactly. The point is," she was saying, "I just never... *wanted* sex. I've never met anyone who—I mean I never wanted them to—I sort of figured I was frigid."

"Hah!" He couldn't help it. The short, sharp laugh shot from his throat before he could choke it off. He tied up one boot, then looked at her. Her pale skin looked tempting beneath that scrap of lace—and just a little pink. He'd rolled her out of the sun just in time. His hands itched to hold her again. His mouth watered at the thought of tasting her, and other parts of his body stood up at full attention. *"Frigid?* Honey, if you were any hotter, you'd have melted me."

A smug smile curved her mouth as she tugged her dress over her head. The worn fabric hid her body from him, and Travis figured that was just as well. Keep them both out of any more trouble. They had plenty enough already.

"So, it was... good."

It wasn't a question and yet it was.

"Beyond good," Travis said, and knew it for the understatement of the century. "But you know that."

"Yes, I do. What I don't know is why you're making such a huge deal out of this," she said. "We're both grown-ups. We made a choice—which I for one, don't regret for a single minute."

"This isn't about regrets."

"You could have fooled me."

"I didn't say I regretted anything."

"Then for heaven's sake, Travis, what exactly are you saying?"

He pushed one hand across the top of his head, stared off into the distance for a long moment before turning to glance at her briefly. "The plain truth is," he continued, tugging on his other boot and tying it up, "this changes things."

"Like what?" she asked. He turned around again to look at her.

"First off," he started, and it pained him to even say the words, "I'm thinking that if you were a virgin, you weren't 'safe.'"

"As a virgin," she pointed out, "I was perfectly safe. I've hardly been able to contract any diseases, now have I?"

"No," he agreed, "but you may have just contracted a baby."

She blew a puff of air at him and waved her hand dismissively. "Please. Women try for years to get pregnant. One time is hardly going to do the trick."

"I'm willing to bet lots of 'happy couples' have told themselves that."

"You're worrying over nothing," she told him, and yanked the zipper of her dress up.

"And you're not worrying at all," he countered.

"What would be the point?"

"Excuse me?"

"Well, whether I worry or not, the damage is done, so why worry ahead of time?"

"And how comfortable is your head, stuck so firmly in the sand?"

One pale-blond eyebrow lifted. "I'm not going to let you spoil this for me."

"Spoil it?"

"That's right. I've waited all my adult life for this experience, and now that I've had it, you're not going to ruin the memory of it."

"Well pardon the hell outa me."

"It won't be easy," she told him, giving him a look that could have fried bacon, "but I'll try."

He snatched up his weapon, slung it over his shoulder, then pushed himself to his feet. Staring down at her, Travis's gaze flicked over her thoroughly, from the top of her still-damp head to the soles of her feet. And it was all he could do not to grab her up and start the magic all over again.

But he called on years of training and withstood the urge. Barely. This was *so* not good. He'd finally met the woman who not only electrified his body but touched his heart—and she was farther away now than ever. There was no future here. He knew it. And so, he suspected, did she.

Marines and debutantes just did not mix.

"Listen, princess—*Lisa,*" he corrected, "you're my mission, not my date. I screwed up here and—"

"Oh, thank you very much," she snapped, scrambling to her feet so that she could glare right into his eyes. And it was quite a glare.

"All right," he admitted, "that came out wrong."

She folded her arms over her chest and tapped her foot in the sand. "Was there a *right* way to say that?"

"Probably not," he muttered, wondering how this mission had gone so wrong so completely? From the minute he'd slipped into that shack to free her, it seemed as though everything had gone against them. Missing their ride. Having to hide out. Hiking across the desert. And now this. But this he had no excuse for. This he'd done all on his own.

And as much as he knew it had all been a mistake, he still couldn't find it in himself to regret it. But what now? Walk away as though nothing had happened? Hell, yes. That was really his only choice. He didn't fit into her world any more than she would fit into his.

Lisa clung to what was left of her pride and wrapped it tightly around her slightly bruised heart. Well, this was just what a girl wanted to hear the minute her lover put his clothes on. She'd waited years for this moment only to have the one man who turned her blood into fire tell her he was sorry it had happened. Perfect.

Tears burned at the backs of her eyes, but she refused to let them fall. Through sheer will and determination, she held them back. It was bad enough knowing that he thought of their time together as a mistake. She wouldn't make her humiliation any worse by turning into a teary female.

Instead, she fell back into comfortable, familiar territory and shut off the emotions clamoring to get out. Over the years, she'd had plenty of practice at hiding what she was feeling. Her father had never approved of ''scenes.''

''Why don't we just pretend none of this happened?'' she offered, though her body still hummed from his touch.

''That won't solve anything.''

''There's nothing to solve.''

''And if there's a baby?'' he demanded. ''Will you ignore that, too?''

She flushed at the direct hit and supposed she'd deserved it. But wasn't this what he wanted? Wasn't he looking for a way to distance himself? Well, there it was…being handed to him on one of her father's silver platters. You'd think he'd take the opportunity and run with it.

"*If* there's a baby, and that's a big if…" There wouldn't be, she told herself firmly. The gods simply weren't that cruel. "…I'll take care of it."

Now it was his turn to flush. In anger. She watched color race up to fill his cheeks and spark like fire from his eyes. His hands fisted at his sides, and she had the distinct feeling that he wanted to punch something. Badly.

"Just like that," he said through gritted teeth. "You'll take care of it."

"Yes." Oh, she knew what he was thinking—and it showed how little he really knew her. He'd assumed that she would hustle herself off for an abortion. But Lisa would never be able to do that. Not that she didn't sympathize with women who were forced to make such a heartrending decision. She did. But for herself, she simply wasn't capable of ending a life just to make her own more comfortable.

No, if she was pregnant, then she would be a mother. The word slammed into her mind and made her knees quake just a bit. She'd always wanted children. Although she had to admit that her fantasy of a family had always included a husband. Still, as she'd so recently discovered, not everything turned out the way you wanted it to.

"You're a real piece of work, you know that?" he muttered darkly and took a step closer.

That stung, but she didn't let him know it. Lifting her chin, she met him glare for glare. "Then it's lucky for you that you're almost rid of me, isn't it?"

"Princess," he said, his gaze flicking over her, "you have no idea."

Her breath hitched, and a small twinge of pain shimmered inside. But she didn't have to worry about him seeing it reflected in her expression. He'd already turned his back on her. She watched him stalk across the grass and climb the sand hill that surrounded this little valley. At the crest he sat down, pulled his weapon across his lap and stared out into the distance.

Her lover was gone.

Her guard dog was back.

And inside, Lisa wept.

The desert patrol spotted them an hour later.

Travis was all business as he briefed the king's men on the situation, then climbed into the back of the Jeep, putting himself as far away from her as possible. Lisa smiled and said all the right things, but her mind was working independently of her speech. Every thought was of Travis and what would happen now. Would he disappear the moment they hit the American Embassy? Would he even remember her a month from now? Would he want to?

The Jeep hit a rut in the road, and her back teeth jarred together. Reaching out, she grabbed hold of the edge of the windshield and braced herself. Too late, of course. Just as she'd been too late to protect her heart from Travis Hawks.

The marble foyer of the embassy felt cool and the sleek elegance of the building brought home the fact that they were back in civilization. The El Baharian soldiers had called ahead, letting the embassy know they were coming in.

Travis stood back as the Ambassador himself scuttled forward to greet Lisa. The man barely spared Travis a glance as he said, "Miss Chambers, I'm delighted to see that you're well and safe."

"Thank you, Mr. Ambassador," she murmured, but her soft voice echoed in the vastness of the place.

How sophisticated she sounded, Travis thought, remembering how she'd screeched at him out in the desert. But then, that was a different Lisa from this one. And damned if he didn't already miss that other woman. The one he'd come to know. To...care for.

He shook his head and told himself he'd had too

much sun. It wasn't affection he felt for her. It was just the kind of camaraderie that developed between people when they shared a tense situation. They'd survived together. But they sure as hell didn't belong together.

"Sergeant…" the Ambassador tacked a question mark onto that single word.

"Hawks, sir," he answered. "Travis Hawks."

"Of course," the little man said. "The other members of your team are waiting for you. If you'll follow my secretary…" He waved one hand to indicate a tall man in his forties.

"Thank you, sir," Travis said and started after the secretary, already heading down a long hallway. He didn't look back at Lisa. He'd learned long ago that looking back only made things worse. Better to keep his gaze fixed straight ahead. On the future that wouldn't include Lisa Chambers.

"Gunnery Sergeant Hunter thought you'd be hungry first," the man in front of him said. "If you go through that door there, you'll find the kitchen."

Food. Drink. Sounded good. The only thing that would make it better was if Lisa was with him. But she'd probably have servants trotting a meal up to her in no time. "Thanks," he said with a nod, then pushed through the door.

"Well speak of the devil and in he walks," Deke shouted with a wild laugh.

"He sure looks like he's been to hell and back," J.T. agreed as he hurried over to slap Travis's back with a solid thump of welcome.

"Never thought I'd be glad to see your ugly faces again," Travis told them, shaking hands with the best friends he'd ever had.

"Hawks," Jeff Hunter said from across the room.

Travis snapped the other man a quick look. A Gunnery Sergeant, Jeff was the Senior NCO and the man in charge of their recon team.

The man's stern features dissolved into a grin. "We're damn glad to see you, Travis."

"Likewise, Gunny." He dropped his pack unceremoniously to the floor, tossed his weapon to Deke and headed for the other man. Shaking the hand he offered, Travis asked the question that had been haunting him for a few days now. "The Marine who got hit on the chopper? How is he?"

"Don't worry about him," Jeff said with a smile. "Took one in the shoulder and he may even get some liberty to recuperate. He wanted me to thank you for getting him a trip home."

"That's good news, Gunny," Travis said, feeling a rush of relief push through him.

"Could have been worse if you hadn't waved us off," Jeff told him, meeting his gaze and holding it for a long minute. "You made the right call."

"Thanks. Just glad it worked out." Sort of, he added silently.

"Man," J.T. was saying, "it must have been pure torture putting up with little miss rich—"

One hot look from Travis cut that phrase off before it could be finished. "She did all right," he said, shifting his gaze from one to the other of the Marines standing around him. "She stood up to it. She really came through."

"So did you," Jeff said, and gave him another slap on the back strong enough to stagger a slighter man. "And now that that's all taken care of, you hungry?"

"Gunny," Travis said with feeling, "I could eat one of those camels we passed on the way in. Hide, hump, hooves and all."

"Not necessary," Jeff told him. "We may be in El Bahar, but the embassy is American territory. Take a look at what the chef cooked up for you and Miss Chambers."

Travis looked over at a gleaming stainless-steel countertop that was piled high with enough food to make a fair-size banquet. His mouth watered as he muttered, "Fried chicken, potato salad, watermelon, strawberry shortcake and chocolate chip cookies." He glanced at Jeff. "Is Lisa—Miss Chambers being fed now, too?"

"As we speak."

"All right, then." He sighed heavily, pushed his friends out of the way and said, "I've died and gone to heaven, fellas. If this is a dream, don't wake me up."

Eight

Everyone was asleep.

The muted roar of the jet's engines pulsed just below the chorus of snores reverberating from the front few seats. Travis pushed himself from the plush leather chair and walked down the length of the richly appointed plane toward the galley.

His worn, dirty boots sank into the thick, sky-blue carpet, and his gaze flicked over his surroundings with interest. Lisa hadn't even had to request her father's private jet. Mr. Chambers, on hearing that his only child was safe, had dispatched his plane to carry her, and the recon team that had saved her, home. And Travis had never seen such accommodations.

Charcoal-gray leather captain's chairs were scattered around the front of the plane and three of them were fully reclined, allowing the Marines to snooze on their way home. An overstuffed couch hugged one wall of the plane. On the other wall a desk was outfitted with a fax machine, computer and printer. A mahogany bar took up most of the wall at the front of the jet, and he'd been told that the door in the rear led to a bedroom complete with queen-size bed and master bath.

He shook his head, hardly able to believe that people actually lived like this. And at that thought, a flash of himself, traveling in military transport planes rushed up in his mind, and he almost laughed aloud at the comparison. But the urge to laugh died as quickly as it came when he realized that the plane was a tangible example of just how little he and the princess had in common.

Travis's back teeth ground together, and he told himself it didn't matter. What they'd shared was over. As it should be. The fact that he wished it wasn't didn't mean a damn thing.

He quickened his step, headed for the galley, just past the desk. He didn't feel like sleeping. He'd done plenty of that at the embassy. And since Lisa was back in the bedroom, and his friends were snoring loudly enough to wake the dead, coffee seemed like just the right ticket.

As he came around the corner, Travis stopped short and felt every nerve ending in his body go on full alert.

Lisa stood there, looking as different from the woman he'd come to know as night was from day. Gone was the torn, dirty dress and the tangled mass of blond curls. She wore the clothes her father had sent to her. Some sort of filmy, light-blue dress with a skirt tight enough to drive a man crazy, thinking of ways to peel it off her. The pale-blue spike heels she wore brought her much closer to his own height than she had been the past few days and did absolutely amazing things for her legs. Her shining blond hair was pulled back from her face with a diamond clip that glittered like chips of ice in the overhead lights. There was no spark of irritation shining in those blue eyes anymore—now there was only a cool sophistication that he simply had no idea how to relate to.

But even as that last thought registered, the expression in her eyes shifted, changing, and just for an instant she was his princess. The woman he'd known so intimately in a setting that should have killed them both. In a heartbeat, though, that change was gone and she was a beautiful stranger again.

''I, uh,'' he said, trying to find a way to cover his

own reaction to her, "I didn't know you were back here. Just came for some coffee."

Nodding, she picked up a delicate china cup, set it on its matching saucer and filled it from the nearby glass carafe. Steam rose from the surface of the coffee cup as she handed it to him. But that heat was nothing compared to what sizzled between them as her hand brushed his.

She jerked back quickly, sloshing some of the inky black liquid over the cup's lip. "Sorry," she murmured, picking up a linen napkin and handing it to him.

"No problem," he said. After blotting up the mess he tossed the napkin aside. He allowed his gaze to sweep her up and down, and he felt the sharp jolt of need slam home in his gut. Well, he'd just have to get used to ignoring that, he told himself. There was no help for it now. They were on their way home. Back where she lived a life of luxury on Park Avenue and he...*didn't*.

And just to drive himself totally insane, an image of her naked, lying on the banks of the oasis, leaped into his mind. The memory was so clear he could almost feel the silky softness of her skin. A sudden tension crashed through him, and Travis immediately let that vision go. No peace there, he reminded himself.

It was stupid of him to feel so uncomfortable

around her. When two people had gone through what they had, side by side, they should be able to talk to each other civilly, for Pete's sake. Determined to prove to both himself and to her that it was possible, he leaned one hip against the tiled counter, took a sip of coffee and watched her as he commented, "Quite a plane."

Oh, yeah, Hawks. That was brilliant.

"My father likes it," she said, picking up her own coffee.

"So do the guys," he said wryly.

The other men's combined snores drifted toward them, and Lisa smiled briefly. "It is comfortable for long trips."

"It's got military transport beat down to the ground, I'll give you that."

"Bad, huh?"

He shrugged. "War's hell, but it still beats transport."

A smile tugged at the corner of her lips and set up an answering tug deep inside him. Damn, she got to him like no other woman ever had. And he'd been a fool to let it go as far as it had. Now he'd be paying the price for letting down his guard.

Yep, when she got back home and resumed her life, partying, going to lunch and forgetting all about him, Travis had the distinct feeling that he was going to be haunted by dreams of her. By thoughts of what might have been. He could wish it were different, but as his grandfather used to say, "If wishes were horses, beggars would ride."

"So," he said, his voice overly loud in an effort to quiet the voices in his mind, "how's it feel to get back to reality?"

Lisa lifted her chin, took a deep breath and looked up at him. He felt the solid punch of her gaze right down to the soles of his feet.

"The desert felt more real."

Lisa meant it. Looking into those chocolate eyes of his, she realized just how much she'd missed seeing them in the past twenty-four hours. Since entering the city of El Bahar, she and Travis had been kept separate, through accident or design. She wasn't sure which.

All she was sure of was that she'd missed him. Missed arguing with him. Missed the way he smiled. The way he seemed to stand so much taller than any other man she'd ever met. Missed knowing that he was there. By her side. Ready to protect and defend.

The men in her world wore three-piece suits, showed up at the "right" parties and bought and sold Fortune 500 companies before breakfast. Yet none of them carried themselves with the kind of self-confidence Travis did. None of them would even have risked lunch for her sake, let alone their lives.

And, she thought with an inward groan, none of them were capable of starting a flash fire in her bloodstream, either.

He'd touched her in so many ways. In a few short days Travis Hawks had managed to march into her life, her heart and her soul. And she was pretty sure there'd be no getting him out again.

Which was going to make for a very lonely life.

"You did great out there," he was saying, and she pushed away her thoughts to concentrate on what little time she had left with him. "In the desert, I mean," he finished.

Pride swelled inside her briefly, but she pushed it back down again. It was only through his and God's efforts that she'd ever made it out of the desert alive. Even now the memory of fear was fading, along with the sense of accomplishment she'd experienced in keeping up with her rescuer.

Here, in the safety of her father's jet, surrounded by the luxury she'd grown up in, all of it seemed so far away. So unreachable. Even Travis. He was right here in front of her. And yet she knew that the moment he'd seen this stupid plane, he'd distanced himself further from her. She'd watched the Marines' reactions to the jet. Seen the awe in their faces. And she'd seen cold, hard realization come into Travis's eyes and knew that she'd lost him. For good.

Better now to pretend she'd never had him. She laughed shortly and shook her head. "Thanks, but I think we both know that without you it would have been a different story."

"Yeah, but you weren't trained how to survive that kind of thing."

"True enough," she agreed, and plastered a wide, phony smile on her face. "But you should see me at a designer's show. I'm known as the fastest draw of a credit card on the eastern seaboard."

"Cut it out."

The snap in his voice had her blinking in surprise. "What?"

He set his coffee cup down with a clatter, then reached out and grabbed her upper arms. Lisa felt the hot, hard strength of him pouring down into her bones, and she wanted to sway against him. To bring back the memories of their time together. To relive it. To experience the magic again. But his features were just as tight as his grip, so she swallowed those feelings back.

"Don't start pretending again."

"Pretending?"

"Yeah," he said, and loomed over her, his face just a breath—or a kiss—away. "Don't start trying to play the dimwit rich girl. Not with me. Don't pretend to be less than you are."

"Who's pretending?" she asked, and pulled free

of his grasp. The sudden lack of warmth from his hands chilled her and made her just a little bit lonelier than she had been. But she knew she'd better get used to that. "You called it from almost the moment we met. You said I was a spoiled princess. You said all I had going for me was daddy's money."

He winced.

"No point in backing down now," she continued, saying aloud what she knew he'd been thinking. "We are who we are, Travis. You're Daniel Boone and I'm...I'm..." She shook her head. "I don't know who I am anymore."

"Well I do," he said tightly, bending down low so that they were eyeball to eyeball. His voice came in a rush of hushed anger that rolled over her, pushing his words deep inside her. "You're Lisa Chambers. And that's a helluva lot more than I gave you credit for being. You're tough and beautiful and strong and so damn sexy I want you again, right here."

Her knees wobbled and her stomach pitched.

"You've pissed me off and you've made me proud," he said, and darned if she didn't feel tears burning the backs of her eyes. She couldn't ever remember hearing someone tell her they were proud of her before. And the words acted like a salve on a wound she hadn't known she carried. She blinked those tears back quickly but apparently not before he'd seen them.

Straightening up, Travis took a half step back from her, and she wanted to tell him not to go. To stay close. Because when he was around, she felt like the kind of person she used to dream of being.

"Look," he said, reaching up to shove one hand across the top of his head. "We've been through a lot together, that's all. So don't put yourself down, cause I know better."

She swallowed hard and wished she could throw her arms around him.

"And there's something else," he said, making Lisa's breath catch in her throat.

What? Was he actually going to say something about a future? Would he tell her that he cared? Did she *want* him to care? Oh yes. Yes, she did. Because as strange a thing as it was to admit, she'd fallen in love with the hard-core Marine with the slow, Southern slide in his voice.

She wouldn't have thought it possible to love so suddenly. So completely. So surely. But it was there. Within her. Nestled like a nugget of pure-gold knowledge. Travis Hawks was the one man in the world for her. Hopefully, he felt the same.

"What's that, Travis?" she asked.

He glanced back down the wide aisle as if to assure himself that his friends were still asleep. When he was satisfied, he turned his gaze back to her and said quietly, "Until I know for sure that you're not pregnant, I'm going to be a part of your life whether you like it or not."

Every bit of air left her body. Not in a rush. It slipped out, like air leaking from a balloon. And just like that, her tidy little vision of a cozy cottage built for two dissolved.

Disappointment gave way to anger and anger to rage. In seconds it was pumping through her bloodstream, looking for a way out. How could she have been so stupid? Why was *he* so stupid? Didn't he see that they belonged together? Didn't he feel the same magic when they touched?

"*That's* what you had to tell me?"

"Yeah," he said, surprise etched on his features as he recognized the fury in her tone. "What'd you think?"

She hadn't been thinking at all, she told herself. She'd been dreaming. Wrapped up in a ridiculous little dream in which he loved her. Hurt and anger simmered inside until it came to a boil, making every breath a superhuman effort. She trembled with the force of it and still had to fight back tears of disappointment and frustration.

Which only made her angrier.

"What I *think*, Travis Hawks," she said, every

word dropping like an icy stone, "is that *you* are an idiot!"

"Huh?"

She pulled her right foot back, then slammed the toe of her brand-new shoe into his left shin.

"Ow! Hey!"

He grabbed for his injured leg, and Lisa limped past him as if he were a stone statue. Her toes throbbed, but the pain was worth it. She only wished she'd been able to kick as high as his thick head.

Nine

They were met in D.C. by Lisa's father, a three-star General and of course the media. There were far fewer reporters than Lisa had expected yet more than Travis was comfortable with.

As the plane's door swung open, cameras flashed frantically in the night. A strobe light effect accompanied Lisa as she walked down the stairway to the tarmac. Her gaze shifted automatically to her father. Alan Chambers impatiently checked the time on his Rolex, then muttered something to the General beside him before starting forward to meet his daughter.

Right behind her, Lisa heard Travis and his friends taking the metal stairs with hurried steps. Apparently they were more eager to get back to the real world than she felt at the moment.

"Lisa." Her father's booming voice came, loud enough to be picked up by the television cameras cordoned off more than thirty feet away.

She flicked a quick glance at the reporters, then looked back at her father. Tall, black hair streaked with gray, Alan Chambers was an imposing figure. At least, he'd always intimidated her. Not that he didn't love her, she thought, defending him. He did. In his way. But he was a busy man, with his sights set on a seat in the Senate.

"Hi, Dad," she said as he came close enough to wrap her in a brief, tight hug. She inhaled his familiar scent: fine cigars, breath mints and woodsy aftershave. And just for a minute she wished that hug would go on. That her father would hold her and tell her everything would be all right. That she wouldn't miss Travis even before he was gone.

But he patted her back awkwardly, then stepped away, holding her at arm's length, where, she thought with an inward sigh, he'd always kept her. Still, his smile was warm and his eyes shone as he said, "Honey, how are you?"

"I'm fine. Really." A little bruised around her heart, but at least it didn't show.

"I can't tell you how worried I was," he was saying, his gaze lifting to look at the Marines assembling behind her. "No more shopping trips for a while, okay?"

She gave him the smile he expected, even though he wasn't looking at it. "Good idea." Then, steeling herself, she half turned and said, "Dad, I'd like you to meet Travis Hawks. He's the man who brought me out of the desert."

Travis stepped forward and shook the man's hand, barely glancing at Lisa. "Sir."

"Sergeant, good to meet you." Her father's gaze drifted past Travis to the others. "Good to meet all of you. I want to thank you for rescuing my wayward daughter."

Travis frowned slightly but was careful not to show it. He'd expected Lisa's father to be just a bit more glad to see her. But then, Mr. Chambers might be the private type, preferring to do his celebrating out of the glare of the media. Travis couldn't blame him any for that. The continuous flicker of camera lights was annoying.

"Marines," the General spoke up next. "Well done."

"Thank you, sir," Jeff replied, snapping to and returning a salute.

"Indeed," Mr. Chambers said. "The General,

here, informs me that you've all been given two weeks of leave."

The men grinned.

"And to make sure you understand how grateful I am, I'd like you all to be my guests at the Sheraton. Take some time to relax, enjoy yourselves."

Lisa's gaze shot to Travis, and he felt the power of it slam home to his gut. Two more weeks with her. Was that a good or a bad thing? Probably a little of both.

"Thank you, sir," Jeff said, glancing at Deke and J.T., "but if it's all the same to you, I think the team would rather take the two weeks with their families."

Mr. Chambers looked shocked for a second or two, as if he was a man not used to hearing the words *no, thanks.* But to give him his due, he recovered quickly enough, nodding sharply at Jeff before fixing a steady stare on Travis. "I'm disappointed," he said, "but of course I understand. However, I would appreciate Sergeant Hawks staying in town a few days at least. As the man most directly responsible for my daughter's rescue, I'd like to thank him personally."

Travis opened his mouth to turn him down. First off, he didn't answer to Alan Chambers. Second, he didn't want or need thanks for doing his job. Besides, staying in D.C. meant staying near Lisa, and that probably wasn't a good idea. Leaving now would be for the best, he knew.

No point in hanging on to something that was already dead and buried, right? But then his gaze caught Lisa's. In those lake-blue eyes he read regret and goodbye. A jolt of something sad and sweet pinged around his insides. Before he could stop himself, he said, "Be happy to, sir."

"Excellent," her father crowed.

Her eyes softened just a little, but before Travis could figure out exactly what that meant, her father had grabbed him and turned him toward the flashing cameras. Dropping one arm around Travis's shoulder, Mr. Chambers drew Lisa in close on his other side. Then he gave them each a squeeze and ordered, "Smile now, you two."

Travis felt like a bug under a magnifying glass. And the ache in his heart could have been the pin, jammed through his body, keeping him in place.

How easy it was to slip back into old patterns.

After more than two weeks in a desert, where Lisa's strength of will had been her greatest weapon in the quest to stay alive, she was right back where she started. Here, in this mint-green room, her will wasn't needed or wanted. Here she was what her father expected her to be.

"Thank you, Patti," she said as the maid set a

breakfast tray down on a nearby table. Amazing. A few days ago she had been crouched in a cave eating a snake. Today there was steaming coffee and toast on a silver tray.

"Oh, you're welcome, ma'am," the woman said on her way out the door again. "We're all so glad you're back home safely."

Lisa forced her lips up a notch or two into what she hoped would pass as a smile. It was simply the best she could do at the moment. Fatigue dragged at her. Through snatches of sleep, Travis's image had haunted her. His eyes, his smile, his touch. And finally, staying in that wide, empty bed had just been too much for her.

From her vantage point on the plush window seat, she'd watched the sun rise, brushing pale color across the sky as it wiped away the last of the stars. In the desert, the sunrise had been followed by quiet, the promise of blistering heat and a day spent in hiding. Here, the city was coming to life, cars and people rushing down the avenue, everyone in a hurry to get somewhere they would hurry home from in a few hours.

And tomorrow would be the same. Within a few days her life would return to normal. She'd pick up the threads of her everyday routine and go on as if nothing had ever happened to disrupt it. Travis would be gone, back to duty. And she would be…here.

She should be happy. Or at least relieved. She was safe. Home. Frowning to herself, she stood up, crossed to the tray and poured herself a cup of coffee. Holding the cup between her palms, she walked back to the French doors leading onto the small balcony. Stepping outside, she shivered as an early-morning breeze sailed past, tugging at the hem of her sapphire-blue silk robe. She took a sip of the hot coffee, walked to the rail and stopped.

Restlessness clawed at her. The familiar felt strange now, and she found herself thinking fondly of that desert trek. Here she was what she'd always been. Alan Chambers's daughter. An attractive woman who knew how to throw a good party.

With Travis she'd discovered another Lisa. A Lisa she'd thought had faded away years ago. There in the desert, when they were struggling to survive… counting on each other…helping each other…she'd felt *alive* for the first time in way too long.

And in Travis's arms she'd discovered what it was like to really love.

But now it was over, and the man who'd touched her as no one else ever had was probably counting the minutes until he could get away.

Setting her coffee cup down on the wide railing,

Lisa gripped the scrolled metal in both hands. The cold of the black iron seeped into her bones until she felt as chilled outside as she did within. Pulling in a long, deep breath, she threw her head back and stared at the lightening sky as she tried to adjust to the heaviness in her heart.

"You'd better get used to it," she muttered. "Once Travis is out of your life, that feeling's going to be with you a long time."

Hearing the words aloud made her question them, though. Frowning, she thought, why *should* she let him go? Who said she *had* to go back to being the woman she'd been before all this started? Slowly, thoughtfully, she straightened up, shifting her gaze back to the stream of cars out on the avenue. Blindly she watched as motorists flicked off their headlights in deference to the brightening sun. But she wasn't seeing the traffic at all. Instead, she looked inward and found the memory of a pair of chocolate eyes that watched her with desire and admiration.

Her heart twisted, and a slow, sweet ache unwound through her. She missed him. She missed who she was when she was with him. And darn it, she didn't want her old life back. She wanted a new life. A new start. With Travis.

"I'm not going to lose him," she said, her tone strengthening with each word. "I won't." Her grip on the railing tightened until she wouldn't have been surprised to find the cold black metal snapping in her hands. Resolve filled her. Excitement fluttered in the pit of her stomach. And anticipation dried her mouth and made her heart beat wildly.

She could do this.

She could convince Travis that they belonged together.

Sure he was stubborn. But she could be just as hardheaded when it came to something she really wanted. All she'd need was time. But all she had were a few short days.

"This was a mistake."

Travis slapped one hand against the wall and leaned into the wind rushing past him through the opened window. Air-conditioning might be popular with most people, but he was a man who needed fresh air. It kept his head clear and helped him focus. And God knew, he needed all the help he could get at the moment.

He had to figure out how to dig himself out of the hole he'd leaped into.

The quiet of his hotel room strained on his nerves. But he was in no mood for the artificial company of the television set. If Jeff and the guys had stayed in town, it might have been easier to stay distracted. But as it was, all he could think about was Lisa. And that wasn't going to do him any good.

He glared down at the stream of traffic on the streets below and envied the people in those cars. At least they were on familiar turf. Going about their business. Getting things done. Not him.

"Nope," he muttered. "Travis Hawks *should* be hightailing it back to Texas, but instead he's hanging around to spend time with a woman he might have made pregnant."

But even as he said it, he knew that wasn't the only reason he was still here, where he so clearly didn't belong. He wasn't thinking about some phantom child. It was Lisa's face that stayed in the front of his mind. Her laughter. Her touch. Her sharp tongue and hard head.

His gut tightened and his breath clogged in his lungs. This was his own damned fault. He'd let her in. Allowed her to become important. To matter. Pregnant or not, Lisa Chambers had made her way into his heart and he didn't have the first clue about how to get her out.

The worst of it was, he wasn't at all sure he *wanted* her out. Oh, he knew there was no future for them. They were miles apart in every way imaginable. And if he hadn't known it before, he would have had to acknowledge it the moment he'd seen the media greeting their return from El Bahar. Her father was news. And by association so was she.

She hadn't grown up with a silver spoon in her

mouth. Hell, she'd had the whole damn set of flat-ware. They were from different worlds. She'd never be satisfied with his, and he had no interest in trying to belong in hers.

"And that," he muttered darkly, "is that."

Nodding sharply, he pushed away from the window, stalked over to his duffel and grabbed a red T-shirt with the USMC emblem emblazoned across the front. Yanking it on, he shoved his arms through the sleeves, pushed the tail of the shirt into the waistband of his jeans and headed for the door.

Now that he'd made up his mind, all that was left was to tell Lisa. He owed her that. He owed *himself* that.

He'd go see her right now. Tell her to her face that he was leaving. No doubt she'd agree. Hell, she'd probably been thinking about this all night, too. Now that she was back where she belonged, he was sure she'd come to the same conclusions he had. So it was best to get this whole thing over with and behind them as quickly as possible. Of course, he'd call in a couple of weeks to check out the pregnancy threat. But God willing there would be no baby and they could simply fade from each other's lives.

And maybe in a few dozen years he'd be able to look back on his time with her and not suffer the ache that pounded through him with every beat of his heart.

Travis grabbed the brass knob and gave it a vicious twist. He pulled the room door open and instantly forgot every last one of his well-intentioned plans. Instead he stared into a pair of lake-blue eyes and felt himself drowning in them.

"Hello, Travis," she said, her voice skating along his spine.

And just like that, the roller-coaster ride that was Lisa Chambers, took off again.

Ten

One look into his eyes was all it took. Her knees wobbled and her stomach pitched and rolled. Lisa took a long, deep breath and hoped for balance. It didn't come. Just looking at him was enough to turn her insides to oatmeal.

"What are you doing here?" he asked, and his voice sounded a shade less than welcoming, despite the gleam in his eyes as he looked at her.

She swallowed back her disappointment. Somehow she'd half expected him to sweep her up into a romantic embrace and kiss her the way he had at the oasis. But his stony expression told her that was a vain hope. It was all right, though. Because no matter what he said, she felt his desire for her shimmering in the air between them. He couldn't disguise it any more than she could. And that was something to hang on to.

"Well, it's nice to see you, too." Without waiting for an invitation—because heaven knew it might not be forthcoming—Lisa slipped past him and into the room. She heard him close the door behind her and, just for a moment, she indulged another hope that he'd come up behind her, wrap his arms around her middle and pull her flush up against him. She wanted to feel his warm, solid strength again. Needed to recapture the sensations she'd experienced all too briefly in that faraway desert.

But naturally none of that actually happened.

"I was just coming to see you," he said.

She flinched at the distance in his voice. Ordinarily those would have been good words. But said in that tone, Lisa was sure that if she let him keep talking, she wouldn't like what he had to say.

"Well then," she spoke up quickly, filling the brief silence before he could. "This is what I call good timing."

"Lisa—"

"Travis..." She turned around quickly to face him and, for the space of a single heartbeat, lost herself in the warmth of his gaze. Yet, as tempting as it was to stay lost, she saw in the tension of his stance that he was already preparing himself to say goodbye. And she couldn't let him do that. "I came to take you sight-seeing."

He frowned. Obviously, he hadn't been expecting that. Slowly he folded his arms across his impossibly broad chest. "Sight-seeing?"

For a moment or two she faltered. She should have thought of this. He was a Marine, for Pete's sake. He might have been in D.C. any number of times. Funny, this had seemed like such a good idea a couple of hours ago. Now, she felt...foolish. So just to make things worse, her brain shut down and her mouth took over. "I thought you might like to see some of Washington while you're here. Unless you've been here before, of course." Great, she thought absently as she watched her hands waving about, keeping time with the flood of words. Now she *looked* foolish, too. "Because you know, if you have been here before, then you probably aren't interested. But if you haven't, you really should see some of the city, and I could show you because I've lived here my whole life and—" She finally ran out of breath, thank heaven. Now if only the floor would open up beneath her so she could fall into a black hole.

When she stopped talking, a long minute of strained silence ticked past. Lisa kept her gaze locked with his, as if she could will him into agreeing. And even as she tried, a part of her recognized that if Travis Hawks didn't want to do something, he couldn't be intimidated into it. Wasn't that one of the things she admired about him?

Most of her life the men she met were all eager to do whatever she asked, in hopes of getting in good with her father. Travis, though, couldn't care less who her father was and had more than once voiced his low opinion of "spoiled princesses." Which was why, she told herself, his opinion of her mattered so much.

He reached up and moved both hands along the sides of his head. Lisa watched the play of muscles beneath his faded T-shirt. Her mouth went dry, and a warm curl of something achy and delicious settled low in her belly. Really, he was the most amazing man.

"I was coming to see you," he said, his voice rumbling through the silence like an out-of-control freight train, "to say goodbye."

She winced at the jab of pain those words caused. And the warmth she'd felt only moments ago turned to ice. He was leaving? Already?

"Travis—"

"No, let me say this," he said, stepping close enough that she would have sworn she could hear his heartbeat thundering in time with her own.

"Whatever this is between us? It's no good. You know that, right?"

"No, I don't."

"Damn it, Lisa..."

"Damn it, yourself," she said quickly, letting the words tumble from her mouth in a rushed attempt to head him off at the pass, so to speak. "There's something *magical* between us, Travis, and you know it. We shouldn't waste it. We should be enjoying it."

"It isn't real," he argued and another quick slash of pain shot through her. "It was the danger. The fear. The whole experience of being out in that desert together. It was just circumstance, Lisa."

"No. I don't believe that, and I don't think you do, either." What had happened so briefly between Travis and her had been the most real thing in her life. And she wouldn't let him throw it away so easily.

His features went, if possible, even stonier. If she hadn't known better, she would have thought he was a statue, carved from unforgiving granite.

"What I believe," he said, "is that my world and yours just don't mix."

"They don't have to."

"Yeah, they do. Or they'll collide, and the crash will be something spectacular."

"So to avoid that, you'll run."

He stiffened, and she gave herself a mental point for scoring a direct hit.

"I'm not running."

She glanced at his sneaker clad feet and snorted a short laugh. "Heck, Travis. You've even got your track shoes on to make a little extra time."

"I'm trying to do what's right."

"You're wrong."

"I don't think so."

"And what about me maybe being pregnant?" She had to throw that one in. Lisa still didn't believe that she would prove to be pregnant. After all, one time was one time and what were the odds? She'd probably have a better chance at winning the lottery. Yet she was running out of ammunition and the war wasn't over yet. "What happened to your vow to stay close until we knew?"

He scowled at her, and she knew she had him. Scraping one hand across his jaw, he inhaled sharply and blew out the air in a rush of exasperation. "I'll call you in a couple of weeks and—"

"I won't answer the phone."

"Damn it."

"If you want an answer to that question, Travis," she said, playing her last card, "you'll have to stick around long enough to find out."

"When will you know?"

She shrugged as if she wasn't sure, when in reality, she knew very well that she'd find out one way or the other by the end of the week.

"Why are you doing this?" he asked.

"Why are you *not?*"

"I'm trying to do what's right."

"So am I," she told him and looked up into his eyes.

He grabbed her shoulders, and she felt the hot, strong imprint of each of his fingertips as if he were branding her skin right through the silk of her blouse. Tendrils of excitement and desire spiraled through her body, at direct odds with the near panic rising up in her brain.

"You're crazy, you know that?"

"I can live with that," Lisa said softly, smiling up at him. She'd won. She saw the surrender in his eyes, felt it in his touch. He'd be staying. For a while, at least. And somehow, in the time he was here, she'd have to convince him that they belonged together.

"You're so beautiful."

Lisa blinked. "What?"

"Beautiful," he repeated, and shifted his gaze over her features slowly, lovingly.

Lisa's stomach jittered, and a flush of heat raced through her bloodstream. "I am?"

"Oh, yeah," he said, one dark eyebrow lifting. "And you know it."

All right, so she'd primped a little before coming to see him. What woman wouldn't? After all, she hadn't exactly looked her best out in the desert. Lisa ran the flat of her hands down the front of her charcoal-gray slacks, then fidgeted with the gold chain belt at her waist. Her pale-pink silk blouse suited her, she knew, with its scooped neck and three-quarter-length sleeves. And the small but elegant diamond heart she wore around her neck had belonged to her mother.

She reached up now to finger it nervously.

He lifted one hand from her shoulder to stroke his fingertips along her cheek and sent shivers skipping giddily through her veins. So fast, she thought. So incredibly fast. She'd hardly known him a week, and yet it felt as though her soul had been waiting for him all her life. Lisa didn't understand how this could have happened. And so quickly. Maybe it was the tense situation they'd shared back in the desert. Maybe fear and danger and the need to depend on each other for survival had compressed months of living into a few short days. But it didn't really matter how it had happened. The simple fact was she had absolutely no doubts.

She loved Travis Hawks.

For the next few days Travis spent almost every waking moment with Lisa. And leaving her every night was getting more and more difficult. His body ached to join hers again. His hands itched to touch her, and the taste of her still lingered on his tongue. Desire chewed at his soul until it was all he could do to keep from grabbing her.

And damned if she wasn't enjoying it. He could see it in the way she moved. The way she talked. The way she gave him those long, smoldering glances from beneath lowered eyelids. She touched him all the time. A stroke on the arm, a pat on the cheek. She threaded her arm through his and walked close enough beside him that he swore he felt her body heat pouring into his, making the fires inside burn even brighter.

He was living in a constant state of hunger. His nerves were frayed and his control was slipping. A few more days with her and he'd throw all of his high-minded intentions out the window and toss her onto the nearest bed. All that kept him strong was the knowledge that to make love to her again would only make things worse. As it was, his heart was ragged from the knowledge that he'd be leaving her soon. That their lives would probably never again connect. That these few dwindling days with her were all that he would ever have.

And as he struggled to keep his passion in check, he fed his brain with images of her, so that years from now he'd be able to pull them out, like pictures from a photo album. He told himself that one day he'd be able to remember her without the pain of losing her. But even he didn't believe that.

They traipsed through the Smithsonian, strolled the streets of Williamsburg, Virginia, and visited Ford's theater. They went on a White House tour, saw Congress and the Senate, and now today they were at the mall.

Grassy hills were filled with tourists, snapping pictures of each other and buying stupid souvenirs at the stands plopped along the greenbelt like squatting bugs in the road.

Hand in hand they passed the POW/MIA booth and when his step faltered slightly, Travis felt her hand tighten around his in silent support. Farther along the path, surrounded by leafy trees, stood The Wall. Just a scrape of stone etched into a rise in the ground with thousands of names scrolled across it, the Vietnam memorial was simple yet powerful. At the Korean War memorial, though, Travis stopped dead.

His gaze locked on the small squad of soldiers, frozen in time. Lisa's hand in his was warm, alive and he welcomed her strength as he studied the faces of the statues. Young men, eyes alert for trouble, they moved through a marsh, weapons ready. Behind them a gray granite wall was etched with hundreds of faces, giving the impression of ghosts ready to step out from beyond whatever veil separated them from this world.

Travis's jaw clenched. Every professional soldier felt a kinship with those still missing. Like an empty chair at a dinner table, their absence was never forgotten. Silently he said a brief prayer for the lost men and women who had never come home—then took another moment to be grateful that he had. He looked at Lisa then, standing so close, and found her gaze fixed on him. Understanding and compassion shone in her eyes, and his heart swelled painfully in his chest.

"You're really something, princess," he whispered, knowing it wasn't enough. But how did you find the words to tell a woman how much she meant to you when at the same time you were trying to distance yourself from her?

She leaned into him, her shoulder-length blond hair lifting in the soft wind. "It's not so hard to understand what you would be thinking right now."

"It's this place," he said, tearing his gaze from hers long enough to sweep the surrounding area. "It's good to see it. To see all the people here. To know that no one's been forgotten." It was more, of course. Monuments to the fallen, remembrances of past bravery, made him proud to be who and what he was. And knowing she, too, was proud, touched him.

"You won't be forgotten, either," she said, and

the tone of her voice drew his gaze back to her. "Not by me. Not ever."

Before he could think of a response, she let go of his hand and started walking. Spring sunshine fell across her like a blessing. Her white slacks and red, long-sleeved shirt looked fresh and bright. Her blond hair gleamed in the sunlight, and the sway of her hips tightened his body and stole his breath.

This was nuts and he knew it.

They'd been together for days now. And every night, when he was lying alone in his bed, in that empty hotel room, he told himself to leave town. To get out while he still could. Yet every morning he waited for her, looking forward to his first glimpse of her. How was he going to live without her? How would he face the coming years knowing that he wouldn't be able to look into those eyes of hers, hear her laugh or feel her touch?

He was a damn fool for staying around as long as he had, and it wasn't getting any easier. If he had any sense at all, he'd hop the first plane to Texas, spend some time with the family, then rejoin his squad. Face the next mission.

But even as he thought it, he knew none of that would be enough to help him forget Lisa Chambers.

Two days later Lisa moved through the crowd but kept her gaze on Travis. Her father's house was filled with the rich and mighty, gathered together for a formal dinner party in Travis's honor. Tuxedos, designer gowns and enough jewelry to give a cat burglar a heart attack crowded the room, but she saw only one man. Wearing his dress blue uniform, Travis Hawks stood out from the rest of the people like an eagle in the midst of a flock of pigeons. Though obviously uncomfortable in his surroundings, he stood tall and gorgeous, looking like a poster of For God and Country. While the men around him discussed financial statements and tax shelters, he quietly stole the attention of every female in the room.

And she was no exception. Smiling at the familiar faces she passed, she nodded appropriately at all the right times, mouthed a few pleasantries and all the time concentrated on keeping her heart from breaking. She hadn't been able to reach him. Despite what she knew they shared, Travis was going to leave. She sensed it in him. Knew their time was almost over…and couldn't come up with a plan to stop him.

"Oh, Lisa," a female voice cooed, "you simply *must* tell me everything about that gorgeous man."

She glanced at Serena Hathaway, forced a smile and resumed her role as hostess.

Travis didn't know how they all stood it. He'd

never been so bored in his life. These people, standing around pretending to be interested in whatever anyone else was saying, made mingling an art form. He felt as out of place as a thief in church. But Lisa, he told himself, fitted right in here. This was her world, and it couldn't have been explained any more clearly to him.

She looked beautiful, of course, in a forest-green, floor-length dress that clung to her slim figure with a lover's caress. Her hair was swept up on top of her head and held in place by a clip with diamonds. More sparklers winked at her ears, and he was willing to guess the diamond necklace she wore cost more than he'd make in his entire career.

Yep. As much as he hated being here, it was a good thing he'd come. Seeing Lisa in her element, he realized just how far out of his reach she really was. Now maybe he could make his heart believe it.

"Ah, Travis," her father said, coming up behind him and slapping one arm around his shoulder, "you don't mind if I call you Travis, I hope."

"No, sir," he said, and noted that though the man was talking to him, his gaze was shifting past him to others in the room.

"I'd like a word with you in my study."

Nodding, Travis followed him, relieved to have a distraction from his thoughts of Lisa, even if only for a minute. He stepped into a distinctly masculine room filled with bookshelves. Maroon leather chairs crouched before a now-cold fireplace, and crystal bottles of amber liquor glistened from the top of a polished bar. The smell of cigar smoke lingered here, and even as he had that thought, Alan Chambers stepped behind a wide, mahogany desk, lit a cigar and offered one to him.

"No, thank you."

The other man puffed a bit, sighed, then walked over and sat down in one of the chairs, indicating Travis should join him.

He studied his cigar for a second, then said, "I wanted to thank you again personally for everything you did for my daughter."

"Not necessary, sir," Travis told him. "I was just doing my job."

"Of course. But still, it must have been difficult dealing with a woman so…" He let the sentence just hang there, as if he couldn't find the proper word to end it.

Annoyed, Travis supplied, *"Brave?"*

Chambers blinked, then laughed shortly. "Well now, there's a word not often used to describe my little girl."

Irritation shot through him, but he tamped it down. After all, this was Lisa's father.

"Now," the man went on, "I'm the first to admit

that my girl's the woman to call if you want an affair handled correctly. But Lisa? In a desert? No, no. If not for you, well, I wouldn't like to think what might have happened.''

Remembering her tenacity, her sheer will, Travis said firmly, ''She would have found a way to survive.''

The man actually chuckled again. And this time Travis took offense.

''Mr. Chambers, sir, I have to say you don't know a thing about that woman.''

''I beg your pardon?''

''It's *her* pardon you ought to be begging. That's a hell of a woman out there, and she deserves better from her own father.''

''Now see here…''

''No, sir,'' Travis said, standing up, ''I see plenty. I see a man so wrapped up in making his next million he doesn't see what's right under his nose. A daughter to be proud of. To love.''

''Who the hell do you think you are, Marine?''

''I know who I am, Mr. Chambers,'' Travis said through clenched teeth. ''And I know who Lisa is. It's you I can't figure out.''

The older man rose from his chair, but was still forced to look up to meet Travis's gaze. Anger flashed briefly in Alan Chambers's eyes. ''It's been a long time since anyone's spoken to me like that.''

"Then maybe it's time, sir," Travis said, refusing to back down on this one. He'd seen Lisa at her worst, and he was willing to bet that she'd done a damn sight better in that desert than her father would have in the same situation. "Lisa's strong and capable and smart."

"Is that right?"

"Damn straight. I'm not saying she's perfect. She's got a hard head and a temper to match. But she made me proud out in that desert. And you should be proud of her, too."

"Interesting."

"Yeah?"

"You're in love with my daughter, aren't you?"

Stunned, Travis stared at the man as if he was suddenly speaking Greek. "What?"

"Answer the question, Travis," Lisa said from the doorway.

Both men spun around to face her as she slipped through the door and closed it behind her.

"How long have you been there?" Travis demanded.

"Long enough to know I want to hear you answer my father's question."

He looked from Lisa to her father and back again. Emotions churned inside him, but he'd be damned if he'd let himself be cornered. Those blue eyes of hers locked on him, and he felt the slam of their punch right down to his bones. But he couldn't give her what she wanted.

If nothing else, being in this house tonight had taught him that much.

"The answer's no, Lisa," he said softly, nearly choking on the lie.

Eleven

Lisa flinched as if he'd struck her. Pain blossomed inside her and spread on a slow-moving tide of misery. Amazing how much power one small word could carry. Her gaze locked with his, she fought to draw breath. She stared into his eyes, and even from across the room she saw regret shimmering in those brown depths.

"You're lying," she whispered, her voice breaking on the words.

His features twisted briefly. "Lisa—"

"Why are you lying?" she asked, not really expecting an answer. He didn't disappoint her. He didn't say anything, simply stared at her through eyes that looked as pained as she felt.

"Honey," her father spoke up, and she jumped, startled. She'd almost forgotten he was in the room. And frankly she didn't care. All that mattered at the moment was Travis and making him admit that he cared for her. She couldn't be wrong about this. She couldn't be. She'd felt the passion in him. The tenderness. It was more than desire between them and they both knew it.

"Let him go," her father said. "Don't make another mistake. Five engagements are enough for anyone."

"Five?"

She stiffened and met Travis's stunned gaze squarely. She probably should have told him about those engagements herself. "Yes, five." Slanting a quick glance at her father, she frowned at him, then looked back at the man still watching her. "I tried," she said, hoping to explain to him what she'd only recently discovered herself. "Tried to be what everyone expected me to be. But they were no different than my father."

"Excuse me?" The older man blurted.

She ignored him, focusing her gaze on Travis. Willing him to understand. "They wanted me for a decoration. An asset at parties. They didn't care who I was or what I thought. Not really. They saw the

Chambers name and that was enough for them.'' She took a step closer. "Don't you see, Travis? I wanted, needed to be more. And with you…I am.''

"Five broken engagements are nothing to be proud of,'' her father said tightly.

She winced, but before she could speak in her own defense, Travis turned on the man.

"You're her father, for God's sake. Shouldn't you be on *her* side?''

"I am,'' the man insisted.

"Then God help your enemies,'' Travis said bluntly. "Don't you think it's better that she had five broken engagements rather than five divorces? Can't you be proud of her for recognizing a mistake and taking steps to correct it?''

Lisa's heart filled until she wouldn't have been surprised to see it fly from her chest. She'd never been defended so nobly. She'd never seen anyone stand up to her father. And watching Travis in action made her love him all the more.

"Sergeant, you are out of line,'' her father muttered.

"Mr. Chambers, you're probably right. So to remedy that, I'll be leaving.''

"Don't go.''

He looked at her. "It's no good, Lisa. It wouldn't work.''

"Isn't it worth a try?" she demanded, ignoring her father's blustering.

Travis stalked across the room in a few long strides and paused when he reached her side. Lifting one of his hands, he touched her cheek and gave her a half smile that tugged at the corners of her heart. "Trying wouldn't change the facts." Shaking his head, he said softly, "Goodbye, princess."

And then he was gone.

When the door was closed again, her father spoke up. "You're better off without him."

"Better?" Head pounding, heart aching, her eyes swimming with tears, she whirled around to face the man who had never seen the real her. "Better how, Dad? Is it better for me to stay here in this house, running your life, arranging your parties?" She lifted the hem of her dress and marched across the room, not stopping until she was within arm's reach of him. "What exactly is that better than? Having my own life? A husband? A family?" She sucked in a gulp of air and tried to ease the ache inside her. But it was too big. Too all encompassing to be shoved aside. Lisa reached up and rubbed away a solitary tear. She didn't have time to cry. Didn't have the luxury of indulging a bout of self-pity.

Looking up at her father, she studied his perplexed expression and realized that she hadn't been entirely fair to him, either. After all, if she'd never stood up and demanded that he take notice of her…the *real* her…then how could she be angry that he hadn't?

"This isn't all your fault, Dad," she said, nodding to herself, "I gave up my dreams because it was easier to be what you needed me to be."

"Your dreams? You mean teaching?"

"Yes," she said, reaching out to lay one hand on her father's arm.

"You couldn't have earned a decent living on a teacher's salary," he reminded her.

She smiled and shook her head. "That all depends on what your idea of decent is, doesn't it?" She looked up at him and silently admitted that she'd blamed him too long for the things that had gone wrong in her life. If she wanted a new start, a new life, then she would have to go out and make it on her own. "I love you, Dad," she said, watching him closely enough that she caught the flicker of emotion in his eyes and was pleased. "But I can't be just your daughter anymore. I have to find a place for myself."

He studied the ash tip of his cigar for a moment or two, then asked, "With him?"

"Oh, yes."

"Humph. Well, the man's got guts, I give him that."

"Yes, he does."

"Stood right up to me and called me on my own carpet."

"I know." She smiled. "Pretty impressive, huh?"

"Yes," he said, reaching for her and pulling her close for a hug. "But not as impressive as my daughter."

Lisa closed her eyes, wrapped her arms around his middle and hung on, savoring the sweetness of this one perfect moment. Amazing what a little honesty could do for a person.

"I do love you, honey," he said, his voice soft as a caress. "I always have."

"I know that, Dad." But, oh, how good it was to hear the words.

He gave her a pat, cleared his throat, then leaned back to look down at her. "So. Just how do you plan on convincing that man to see things your way?"

Oh, she had some very definite ideas on that. But they weren't plans she felt comfortable sharing with her father. So rather than go into specifics, all she said was, "Trust me, Dad. I'll make him an offer he can't refuse."

The ache in his chest would go away eventually. Twenty or thirty years ought to take care of it. Travis scowled at the man in the mirror and snatched up his shaving kit. Stomping back into the bedroom, he shoved the kit into his duffel, then tossed the whole bag onto the nearest chair. It hit with a thud, which did nothing to ease the tension clawing at his insides.

"Nice job, Travis. Tell her father off, then leave her to deal with the mess." Yeah, he'd handled that really well. Shaking his head in disgust, he paced the room like a prisoner on death row looking for a chink in his cage.

But there wasn't one.

He kept seeing her face when he'd said goodbye.

Pain. It had shimmered over her, through her and then reached its grasping hands out for him. The bite of her pain was still stronger than his. His back teeth ground together, he shook his head in an attempt to dislodge that last portrait of her, and walked to the window. Throwing it open, he leaned into the wind, feeling its full force.

She'd get over it, he told himself firmly. Hadn't she been engaged *five* times already? *Yes,* a voice inside whispered. But then it reminded him that she'd been a virgin until that sun-filled morning with him at the oasis. She'd waited. For him. For love. Just as she would wait again.

And one day…she'd find love again. Then someone else would touch her as Travis had. Someone else would swallow her gasps and lose himself in her eyes. And that knowledge ripped what was left of his heart from his chest.

He closed his eyes against the starry sky and saw her in memory, her naked body dappled with the shade of the palm trees. His body tightened, his mind drifted back and he could almost feel her skin beneath his hands. The warm smoothness of her. The silky slide of his callused palms across her flesh. His mouth went dry, and he knew that if he tried, he could still taste her on his lips.

But why up the torture level? He scrubbed both hands across his face as if he could somehow wipe away his thoughts.

A knock on the door brought him lurching around to glare at the intrusion. Vowing to get rid of whoever was standing on the other side of that door, he stalked across the room, yanked it open and snarled, "What?"

"Ah, you've missed me," Lisa said, and pushed past him into the room.

His breath caught hard in his chest like a cold ball of lead. "Go home, Lisa."

"What would you say if I said I *was* home?"

"I'd say you're nuts. This is a hotel."

"I meant, being here with you."

"I know what you meant and you're wrong."

"Am I?" She turned around to look at him.

She'd changed out of that party dress, but this

outfit was just as alluring. A sleeveless top scooped low at the neck and clung to her breasts before skimming her rib cage and disappearing beneath the waist of her skirt. And the hem of that short, tight black skirt stopped at midthigh, exposing her shapely, stocking-clad legs to full advantage.

She wore high, spindly heels that made him wonder how she could keep her balance, and when she cocked her right hip, he watched the muscles in her legs shift with mouthwatering fascination.

Oh, he was in for a hard time now.

Still, he called on years of Marine training to shut off his emotions and focus on the job at hand. And that job was getting her the hell out of his room before he did something stupid like make love to her again.

"Yeah," he said tightly, "you're wrong. You don't belong with me. So, do us both a favor and go home. Find yourself fiancé number six somewhere else."

She blanched, and he gave himself a solid mental kick. But being kind wasn't going to get rid of her, and damn it, she *had* to go.

"I thought you understood. About my engagements," she said. "You told my father—"

"I do understand," he said, despite his better judgment. He wouldn't hurt her any more than he absolutely had to. "But you have to understand something, too. I can't be who you want me to be."

"And who's that?" she asked, folding her arms beneath her breasts and pushing them up until he saw the tops of them rising just above that scoop-necked blouse.

He swallowed hard. "The man you need. A man who's comfortable at a party like the one tonight."

"If that's what I wanted, I would have married one of those five fiancés."

True, he told himself, but couldn't take comfort from it. Because it changed nothing. It fixed nothing.

"We're too different, Lisa."

"No, we're not."

"Hell, you could put my family's house inside your father's and still have room for the garage."

"Do you think I care about that?"

"*I* care."

"Then you're an idiot."

"So find yourself someone who's not."

"I don't want anyone else."

"Damn it, Lisa, don't make this harder than it has to be."

"Oh," she said, locking her gaze with his, "I'm going to make it a lot harder." Then, before he knew it, she was peeling that blouse up, up and off.

His heart hammered in his chest. His body went on full alert. "What do you think you're doing?"

"I think," she said, "I'm seducing you."

Next came the bra. She undid the front clasp, and his mouth went dry as she shrugged out of the lemon-yellow silk, baring her breasts to him. Her nipples peaked, and all he could think of was tasting them, suckling them, drawing them deeper and deeper into his mouth until she was writhing beneath him, begging him for the release only he could give her.

But he couldn't. *Could* he?

She reached around to her back, slid the zipper on her skirt down, then let the damn thing fall to the floor. His heart stopped.

Flat-out stopped.

She wasn't wearing underwear, heaven help him. Just a slim black garter belt that rode her hips, slid low across her abdomen and held up the stockings that clung to her upper thighs.

Travis felt sweat break out on his forehead. He reached up, rubbed one hand across the back of his neck and reminded himself to breathe. But he knew if he could just get his hands on her, he wouldn't even need to breathe. Lisa. All he needed was Lisa. Damn it. His entire body seemed to be pulsing to a throbbing need that was crouched low inside him, waiting to pounce. When he thought he could speak again, he lifted his gaze to hers and lied as best he could. "This isn't working."

She smiled, a slow, knowing smile that women have been giving men for centuries. Then her gaze dropped to his crotch. "Seems to be working fine."

Caught by his own body's reaction to her. He exhaled heavily, narrowed his gaze on her and said, "Think you're pretty smart, don't you?"

"Hmm." She planted her hands at her hips and— the only word for it—sashayed toward him. Then she reached out with one hand and let her fingertips slide down his chest, scraping against the fabric of his T-shirt. "As a matter of fact, yes. I guess I do."

He could smell her. Her perfume swam in his head until his thoughts were nothing but a blur of need and hunger. He'd have to be a dead man not to respond to her. And he sure as hell wasn't dead. One more night, he thought. One more night with her. Was that so much to ask?

Travis grabbed her. One arm snaking out to wrap around her waist, he yanked her to him and held her tight against him.

"Travis…"

"I want you bad," he muttered, sliding one hand up her body to cup one breast. His thumb and fore-finger tweaked her nipple, and when she shivered, he felt as though he'd just been awarded a medal.

"You can have me," she said, tipping her head back to look him dead in the eye. "That's what I've been trying to tell you. We can have each other. We can have it all.''

''Don't want it all,'' he murmured, lowering his head to hers. ''Just want you.''

And then he kissed her and felt everything else fall away. Nothing, no one, was more important than this moment. She wrapped her arms around his neck and clung to him. And still it wasn't enough. He needed to feel her. Be a part of her. Slide himself so deeply into her that even apart they would be together. Dropping his hands to her bottom, he lifted her, and she wound her legs around his middle.

Hunger roared inside him, demanding to be fed and he surrendered to it. Thoughts, desires, emotions clamored in his brain but all he could focus on was the feel of her. He slid one hand farther along her body and touched her damp heat.

She jolted in his grasp, but he held her tightly. Taking her mouth with his, he savored the taste of her, the glory of her, while his hands explored her secrets and drove her along the high road to passion. She twisted in his grasp, moving into his touch, trying to take more of him inside her.

His tongue entwined with hers, tasting, taking, giving. She moaned gently and broke the kiss, letting her head fall back, allowing him access to her throat. She arched into him, pressing her breasts to his chest, moving her hips in time with his touch and sighing when his teeth nipped at the base of her neck.

"I love you, Travis," she whispered, and the words shot into his heart with the accuracy of a sniper's bullet.

Breathing hard, he lifted his head, looked directly into her eyes and admitted, "I love you, Lisa. Too damn much."

She smiled. "It's never enough, Travis. I'll never have enough of you. Be with me. Be inside me."

Man, he wanted that more than anything, but he still didn't have any protection. But then why should he? He'd planned on being all noble.

As if she could read his mind, she smiled, reared back in his arms and slowly, tauntingly, slid one hand down her body. Like a lover, she touched herself, skimming her fingertips across her breasts, along her rib cage, to the edge of that garter belt.

His throat closed up just watching. "What're you…"

She slipped her fingertips beneath the black lace belt and when she pulled them free, she was holding two small, foil packages.

His heartbeat thundered. "Two, huh? You were pretty sure of yourself."

"Uh-uh," she said, shaking her head. "Sure of you."

He nodded, grabbed the condoms from her and

then dropped her unceremoniously onto the bed. Laughing, she bounced on the mattress and watched him as he quickly stripped off his clothes. Then he ripped open the small package, fit the condom to himself and joined her.

Lisa smiled up at him and said, "Give me a minute and I'll get these heels and stockings off."

"Leave 'em on," he ordered, and dipped his head to take first one nipple then the other into his mouth.

She cried out and moved into him, offering herself up to his ministrations. Pleasure, deep, soul-satisfying pleasure rushed through her, and she sighed and gave in to it. Her mind blanked out. All she could think of, all she could feel, was Travis. Now. Always. She couldn't lose him. Not after this. Not when they were so clearly meant for each other.

He touched her, dipping one finger into her heat, and Lisa's hips lifted. That slow, deep tickle built within and she fostered it, moving into his touch, trailing her hands up and down his back. She wanted him. Needed him.

His thumb brushed an especially sensitive spot, and her legs fell open. Eagerness rushed through her blood and fed the desire already nearly choking her. His mouth. His hands. He suckled her and she gasped, feeling the drawing sensation right down to the soles of her feet. Too much, her brain shouted, but her body refused the warning. It would never be too much. Never. Her lungs heaved for air that wouldn't come. Her blood pumped through her veins, liquid fire.

"Travis," she said, lifting her hips higher off the bed, "I need...I need you. Now."

"Me, too, baby," he said, lifting his head long enough to kiss her firmly. Then he moved to kneel between her legs, and she watched as he stroked her center. A quickening started low in her belly. A flutter of expectation. A rush of urgency. When the first eruption began, he pushed himself inside her and she clung to him, wrapping her legs around his hips, pulling him deeper, closer.

He whispered her name, and it sounded like a prayer.

She looked up into his eyes and welcomed his kiss that joined them completely. His hands captured hers, fingers locking, gripping.

And then they were tumbling off the edge of a cliff, together.

Twelve

"**W**hat do you mean you're still leaving?"

Travis sat up and looked at her. "This didn't change anything, Lisa."

Pain blended with fury. Just a half hour ago this man had held her, made love to her and even, for one brief moment, actually admitted his love for her. Now *this?* Lisa swung her hair back out of her eyes, pushed herself up and, clutching the sheet to her chest, demanded, "Then what will, Travis?"

He shook his head and stood up. Lisa couldn't take her gaze off him. In the lamplight pooling around him, his broad shoulders, muscular back and narrow hips shone golden, as if he were an impossibly gorgeous sculpture. But then he moved, shattering the image, and the look on his face when he turned toward her was too full of apology to be anything but real.

"That's the trouble. Nothing will."

"I don't accept that." She wouldn't. Couldn't. Darn it, she hadn't waited for love this long just to find it, then have it snatched away.

"You have to," he said, grabbing up his pants from the floor. Tugging them on, he glanced at her. "Hell, princess, you saw it yourself tonight."

"What do you mean?" She pushed one hand through her hair, angrily shoving it out of her way.

"That party. Those people." He threw his hands up and laughed, a short, raspy sound that held no humor. "I mean, your father's got an actual *ballroom* in his house."

"*His* house," she reminded him quickly. "Not mine."

"Doesn't matter," he said. "Don't you get it? That's what you're used to." He laughed again and shook his head. "I'd never be able to give you marble floors and private jets and chefs. I can't give you chauffeurs and designer dresses." He looked at her for a long minute, then added, "And I won't offer you less."

"You think I care about any of that?"

"*I* care. That's the point."

Panic reared its ugly head. All her life her father's money had mattered. Everyone she'd ever met had been suspect. Did they want to know her for herself or for the Chambers name and fortune? Now, it was coming down to the money again. Only, this time the man she loved *didn't* want her because of the money.

"But none of that matters to me, Travis. I'm not interested in what you *can't* give me." She clambered off the bed, dragging the sheet with her and wrapping it around her naked body like a makeshift toga. Clutching it to her breasts with one hand, she reached out with the other and laid it flat on his chest. She concentrated briefly on the steady pound of his heart beneath her palm, then said, "I just want to know if you love me."

He caught her hand in his and squeezed it gently. Then, lifting it, he kissed her knuckles before releasing her again. Taking a step back from her, almost as if he didn't trust himself to be too close, he said, "Yes, Lisa. I love you."

Hope sparked to life in her heart, then winked out again a moment later when he kept talking.

"But I'm not going to ask you to marry me."

She opened her mouth to argue, but he cut her off.

"Because," he said, his gaze locked with hers,

"one of these days you'd regret giving up everything you've ever known for the kind of life you'd have as a Marine wife."

This couldn't be happening.

He *loved* her.

He'd admitted it.

And still she was going to lose him?

No. She wouldn't let her father's fortune be the deciding factor in her—their—happiness. She wouldn't let this be the end. "Travis—"

"I've already got a flight out. I leave tomorrow." The words tasted dry and bitter, but he forced himself to say them. This was for the best, he told himself. For both of them.

He didn't want to wake up one morning a few years from now and see regret in her eyes. Better he deal with the pain now, than wait until they had a few children. Children.

Baby.

His gaze shot straight to her eyes. "I'll call you in a few days."

"Why?"

"To see if—"

"Oh, yes," she said, and her voice sounded wounded, distant. "You have to do the right thing, don't you? Can't have a pesky pregnancy turning up without you knowing about it."

"Lisa…"

"What if I am pregnant?" she asked, lifting her chin into that defiant tilt he'd come to know so well in the desert. "What then, Travis?"

He didn't know. He just hoped to God she wouldn't be. Then neither of them would be forced into a marriage that could only end badly. It tore at him to think of leaving her…of never seeing her again. But what else could he do?

"We'll talk about that if and when it happens," he said.

"An answer for everything." She brushed past him, headed for the clothes she'd discarded such a short time ago.

He watched her as she let the sheet drop, and felt the hard, solid punch of desire again when he got another eyeful of her in that garter belt. But desire would die eventually if it was smothered by a blanket of resentment. And damn it, she *would* resent him. Sooner or later she would start thinking about what she could have had if she hadn't fallen in love with a Marine.

Two weeks ago he hadn't known she existed. Now the thought of living without her was almost enough to kill him. Who would have guessed that love could strike so quickly, so completely?

In just a few minutes she was dressed and facing him. Her expression was frozen. Only her eyes were alive and they glimmered with a pain he knew he'd caused. Travis fought down the urge to grab her and crush her to him. His arms ached, and an empty sensation opened up around his heart. The years ahead of him stretched out for an eternity that he knew would be filled with memories of her and the haunting images of what might have been.

"I'm not going to argue with you about this any longer, Travis," she said, and he heard goodbye in that short speech.

A part of him wanted her to argue. To find a way to talk him out of this decision. Yet a small, rational corner of his mind was grateful that she'd accepted it. Because her not fighting the inevitable would make this so much easier. Even though it killed him to know that she, too, was going to walk away.

"I thought you were different," she said. "I thought that this time it would be about me. Not my father's money—*me.*"

That hit him hard. "I don't give a good damn about your father's money."

"Wrong, Travis. That's all you care about." She walked across the room and stopped alongside him. Looking up into his eyes, she shook her head, and when she spoke again, her tone held an iciness he'd never heard from her before. "When we should be celebrating our love, we're saying goodbye. Why? Because my *father* has money."

He hissed in a breath through clenched teeth. "I'm doing this for you, Lisa."

"Uh-huh. Tell yourself that on those cold, lonely nights in your future, Travis. Maybe it'll help."

Then she left, quietly closing the door behind her. Silence crowded in around him. The shadows in the corners seemed to reach out for him, as if they were going to drag him deeper into the darkness. And then he knew. Nothing could help him through all the lonely nights to come.

Through delays and layovers and more delays, Travis's military transport flight took him hours longer than it would have, had he flown on a regular airline. And through it all his brain worked, taunting him, punishing him. Images of Lisa stayed with him, and he knew this was just the beginning. She'd never be out of his heart. His soul. Walking away from her had been like taking a knife and hacking off a limb. The ache went bone deep. Not even stepping out of the plane and into the hot Texas wind was enough to lighten the black mood riding him.

He called home to alert the family that he was on his way. Then he got a ride to the nearest car rental agency and within an hour he was driving down the road, headed home. But for the first time in his life, he didn't want to be there. His heart was in D.C.— and he never should have left.

His hands tightened on the wheel and squeezed. All he could think about was Lisa. Holding her, loving her, losing her. How she'd looked at him through wounded eyes.

"Damn it." He let go of the wheel just long enough to slam his fist against it. "I'm an idiot." That fact went down hard. But it was so true he couldn't deny it any longer. She'd risked everything. She was willing to give up everything. For *him*. And he'd looked her dead in the eye and told her it wasn't enough. He squeezed that steering wheel tightly enough to snap it in two. "Hell," he muttered, "I'm lucky she didn't shoot me."

But then she hadn't had to. The pain in her eyes had stabbed at him, doing far more damage than any weapon could have done. And there was only one cure for it. As he realized what he had to do—what he *needed* to do, a sense of urgency filled him. His heartbeat accelerated. His breathing quickened. Now all he had to do was convince Lisa.

Pulling into the drive, he listened to the scrape and rustle of the gravel beneath the tires, then parked the rental car behind his brother's truck. Judging by the three other cars clustered in the drive, the whole family had gathered to say hello. Well, he thought, scrambling out of the car, they'd just have to wait their turn. First things first.

Grabbing his duffel out of the back seat, he

headed for the two-story Victorian where he'd grown up. Sunshine yellow with sage-green trim, the old place looked familiar, comfortable. It had withstood tornadoes, brush fires and more than a hundred years of hard living—not to mention him and his brothers.

The door flew open when he was halfway across the yard, and a grin he couldn't stop creased his face as he watched his sister race down the steps toward him. He dropped his bag and grabbed her up into a tight hug.

"Sarah, it's good to see you," he said as he swung her around before plopping her back onto her feet. Shifting his gaze to the house again, he asked, "Where's Mom?"

"Inside," she said, smiling. "Along with everybody else."

"Good. That's good." He nodded, grabbed up his duffel bag out of the back seat, then dropped one arm around his sister's shoulders. "I've got something to tell all of you."

"Yeah?" she asked, tipping her head back to look up at him. "What's that?"

"Not yet," he said, shaking his head. "First I have to make a phone call."

"Interesting."

"You have no idea." Already thinking ahead, Travis tried to come up with just the right words, just the right apologies that would convince Lisa to give him another chance. And if she wouldn't take his call, then he'd just fly back to D.C. and camp out on her father's doorstep until she *had* to talk to him.

"So who is she?"

"How do you know it's a she?"

"Oh, please." Sarah laughed and broke away from him, taking the five steps to the porch at a run.

His older brother, John, appeared in the doorway and held the screen door open for him. Grabbing the duffel, he said, "Been a while, little brother."

"Too long." He shook his brother's hand, then grinned as Lucas stepped into the hall, fists up, bobbing and weaving on the balls of his feet.

"Okay, Travis, I've been practicing, and this time I'm gonna win."

"Later." Ignoring his brothers and sister, he walked on into the living room, looking for his mother. God, it felt good to be back here. Here, where nothing changed. Where family was everything. And here is where he wanted Lisa.

"Hello, honey," his mother said and walked across the polished wood floor to collect a hug.

"Hi, Mom." His arms went around her, lifting her clean off the floor until she squealed, slapped his shoulders and demanded to be set down.

Her short, black hair was windswept and tousled.

Her sharp, brown gaze locked on him even as she smiled and shook her head. "You're too thin. But I can take care of that."

"I've been looking forward to your cooking for weeks," he said. "And as soon as I make a phone call, I'll be ready for everything you've got."

"A phone call? To whom?"

"Lisa. Mom, you're gonna love her. She's funny and smart and way too good for me."

"Is that right?"

"Oh, yeah." He shoved one hand across the top of his head and moved to the phone. "Now all I have to do is convince her that I love her."

He picked up the receiver as his mother said, "Why don't you go on and get something to eat first?"

"This can't wait," he told her with a grin, but took a long deep breath, hoping for the scent of his mother's special pot roast. That grin dissolved into a thoughtful scowl. He could have sworn he smelled Lisa's perfume. That mingled scent of citrus and flowers seemed to be everywhere, now that he noticed. But that wasn't possible—so clearly, he was way further gone than even he'd thought. His mind was conjuring up her scent just to torture him.

Shaking his head, he dialed *O* and asked for directory assistance. Then he waited.

"What's the matter, Travis?" Sarah asked.

"Nothing."

His sister laughed and his mother warned, "Sarah…"

Lucas and John grinned at him, and Travis had the distinct feeling that everyone here was in on a joke but him. "What's goin' on?" he demanded, and an instant later heard the answer to his question.

"Frances," a too-familiar female voice called from the kitchen, "something's wrong."

"What city please?" a voice in his ear inquired, and slowly he hung up the phone and turned around.

Travis swallowed hard and fought down a rush of expectancy. He shot his mother a look, but she only shrugged, smiled and dropped into a chair. Footsteps tapped against the floorboards, and he watched Lisa hurry down the hall from the kitchen.

She wore faded blue jeans, a denim shirt and sneakers. Her blond hair was in a ponytail that danced with her every step, she had his mother's apron tied around her middle and a wooden spoon in her hand.

He felt as though someone had punched him in the stomach. All the air left his body, and he had to try twice just to say her name. "Lisa?"

She ignored him, staring directly at his mother. "Frances, everything's ruined. The stew's boiling over and the bread's black."

"I'll be right there," his mother assured her as

Lisa whirled around and marched back down the hall. When she was gone, Frances looked up at her son. "I could go help…unless, of course, *you'd* like to offer your services instead."

With his family's laughter bursting out around him, Travis stalked down the short hallway, pushed through the swinging door and stepped into the large, square, pale-blue kitchen. He wasn't crazy. She really was there. In his house. At the stove. And she wasn't looking at him.

Grabbing her, he turned her around, keeping both hands at her shoulders. Those blue eyes of hers stared up at him, and he'd never been so glad to see anyone in his life. But he fought down the elation streaking through him to get a few answers first.

"What are you doing here?" he demanded.

"At the moment," she said, with a disgusted glance at the stove behind her, "burning dinner. But I'll learn."

"That's not what I meant."

"I know." Lisa stared up at him and tried to keep her heart from bursting right out of her chest. It hadn't been difficult to decide how to handle this. The moment she'd left him in that hotel room, she'd gone home, packed a bag and commandeered her father's jet for a ride to Texas.

His family had welcomed her, and she'd kept herself busy, telling herself she'd done the right thing.

She'd known that the only way to fight Travis's stubbornness was to ignore it. But ever since she'd arrived, doubts had plagued her. What if he'd only been being kind before? What if he'd claimed to love her as a way to ease dumping her? What if she'd made a colossal fool of herself and now was facing humiliation in front of his family?

Now, though, staring up into those chocolate-brown eyes, she saw everything she'd hoped to see and knew she'd done the right thing. She felt the almost electrical charge of warmth skittering through her from his hands directly down to her bones. He loved her.

So, keeping her voice as steady as she could, she took the plunge and said simply, "I came to marry you."

"I don't recall asking," he said, but a shimmer of light in his dark eyes gave her the courage to keep going.

"No, you didn't," she said, lifting both hands to lay her palms on his chest. His heartbeat thundered, and she felt her own quickening to beat in time. "Because you're a hardheaded man."

"I want to do right by you."

"Then marry me."

A muscle in his jaw twitched, then his features cleared and darkened again in an instant. "Are you—"

She had to think about that for a minute, then realized exactly what he was asking. "I don't know," she said, knowing that this was definitely the time for honesty. "But this isn't about a baby. This is about us."

"Yeah, it is."

"Good. We agree."

He shook his head, his gaze moving over her face like a warm caress. "I'm damn glad to see you, princess," he admitted, then added, "in fact, I was just trying to call your father's house to tell you I was going to come back to collect you."

"You were?"

"Oh, yeah." He reached up and cupped her cheek in his palm. "You're too deep inside me, Lisa. You're a part of me. I can't lose you."

She sucked in a gulp of air and blew it out again in a rush. "You won't lose me. I love you."

"I love you, too, princess. But are you sure about what you're doing here? I'm a Marine. That's all I've ever wanted to be. I'm no stockbroker."

She actually laughed and, oh, it felt good. "I don't want help with my portfolio." Fisting her hands in his T-shirt, she pulled him closer and kept her gaze locked with his as she said, "I want you to marry me because you need me."

"I do."

"You want me."

"I do."

"And you love me."

He smiled—a slow, wicked smile that curled her toes and made sensuous promises she planned to hold him to.

"Oh, yes, ma'am. I do."

"You keep practicing those two little words, all right?"

"I guess I can do that," he said, dropping his hands to her waist and pulling her flush against him.

Sliding her palms up his chest, she wrapped her arms around his neck, looked up at him and said, "You stole my heart, Travis. Out in that desert you claimed it, whether you meant to or not."

He bent his head, resting his forehead against hers, and released a long breath he hadn't known he'd been holding. For the first time since leaving D.C., he felt…whole again. "You can't have your heart back, princess. But you can have mine. It's belonged to you from almost the first moment I laid eyes on you."

With the stew erupting on the stove and black smoke still curling from the oven, Travis kissed his princess. And the moment their lips met, he knew, deep in his soul, that he was finally the richest man in Texas.

* * * * *

Look for Maureen Child in our
DYNASTIES: THE CONNELY'S series.

is proud to introduce

DYNASTIES:
THE CONNELLYS

*Meet the royal Connellys—wealthy,
powerful and rocked by scandal,
betrayal...and passion!*

TWELVE GLAMOROUS STORIES IN SIX 2-IN-1
VOLUMES:

WILD ABOUT A TEXAN
by
Jan Hudson

JAN HUDSON

a winner of the Romance Writers of America RITA®
Award, is a native Texan who lives with her husband in
historically rich Nacogdoches, the oldest town in Texas.
Formerly a licensed psychologist, she taught psychology
at university for over a decade before becoming a full-
time author. Jan loves to write fast-paced stories laced
with humour, fantasy and adventure, and with bold
characters who reach beyond the mundane and
celebrate life.

This one is for all the loyal readers
who have been asking for and eagerly awaiting
Jackson and Olivia's story.

Also, special thanks go to Carolyn Lampman
for SSS/IS and to Buddy Temple, former Texas
Railroad Commissioner.

Prologue

He woke suddenly, his heart hammering against his chest. He rolled over and reached for her, but the place where she had lain was empty. Something told him that she was long gone, but Jackson strode through the suite shouting her name. The only sign that she had been there was the second champagne glass beside his on the nightstand.

Cursing, he grabbed the phone and called her room.

"Miss Emory has checked out, sir," the operator told him.

"Checked out? When?"

"I don't know. Would you like the desk?"

"Yeah."

He cursed some more while he waited, turned the air even bluer when he found out that it was ten o'clock in the morning and she had a three-hour head start on him.

Ten o'clock? He never slept that late. Then he remembered that they hadn't done much sleeping the night before. God, he hadn't been able to get enough of her. He'd never met anyone quite like Olivia, never experienced such a powerful connection with any woman. He'd known from the minute he saw her at the first prewedding shindig that she was a special lady. And he'd known that he wasn't the only one aware of the chemistry between Irish Ellison's bridesmaid and Kyle Rutledge's groomsman. Everybody had seemed to notice.

Trouble was, he hadn't been able to get Olivia alone; they had always been surrounded by people— and she had seemed to prefer it that way. In fact, she'd been feisty as a fractious filly when he'd tried to move in on her and cut her from the herd, telling him in no uncertain terms to get lost. But Jackson hadn't let that stop him. God may have shorted him a bit on brains, but he'd made up for it with luck and determination. And Jackson was determined to have Olivia Emory, sass and all.

He had already been making plans to take her back to Texas with him, and damned if she hadn't run off. Well, she wasn't going to get away from him that easy. She couldn't run far enough or fast enough.

Snatching his tuxedo pants from the bedpost, he yanked them on and pulled on his dress boots. He let loose another string of oaths when he couldn't find the studs to his shirt. He grabbed a Dallas Cowboy jersey from a drawer and dragged it over his head as he made for the elevator.

Outside, when Jackson flagged a taxi, he saw that snow was really coming down hard. The cab driver

earned his extra twenty bucks, but the few minutes
he shaved off the ride to the Akron airport didn't help.
Jackson discovered that Olivia's plane had left two
hours before he had arrived, and now the runways
were shut down. A mean snowstorm was moving in,
and all the major airports in the area were closing. He
tried to charter a plane or a chopper, but everything
was grounded until the storm passed.

The ride back to the hotel was slower, and Jackson
felt as if somebody had broken both his ankles and
thrown him in a hole. He was miserable. Truth was,
he had fallen for Olivia Emory—fallen *hard*.

Strange that he'd zeroed in on her. Even though
she was a beautiful woman, she wasn't the type he
usually chose. Olivia was a bright lady with a string
of letters after her name, and he was dumber than a
barrel of horseshoes—coming from a family of smart
go-getters, he'd figured that out when he was just a
kid. And he'd never cared much for women who
played hard to get; there were too many willing ones
to put out the effort to chase one.

She was rare. He'd known it instantly.

He had watched her relentlessly the entire weekend
of his cousin Kyle's wedding, for, despite her words,
he'd known sure as the dickens that she felt the same
sparks sizzling between them that he did. Still, she
wouldn't even let him hold her close when they
danced at the wedding reception. She acted prissier
than Miss Culbertson, his third-grade teacher.

They were waltzing with a yard of daylight between them when everything suddenly changed. She
started to shake, then plastered herself against him.

"Dance me over to the side door," she'd said. "And let's get out of here."

"Are you sick or something?"

She shook her head.

He didn't question the shift in her attitude again. He chalked it up to his famous good luck—or maybe his charm had finally worn her down. He had danced her to the exit; they left. They found a quiet supper club a few blocks away where they ate and drank champagne and talked.

And laughed. God, how they had laughed. He'd loved the way she laughed, deep and throaty. Sexy as hell. He told every funny story he could think of just to hear the sound of it. Then the banter changed to plain conversation. He couldn't remember when he'd enjoyed just talking to a woman so much.

Back at the hotel, he'd kissed her in the elevator. When the door opened at his floor, they had gone to his suite together as if it were the most natural thing in the world. Making love with her had been unbelievable. Beyond his wildest dreams.

Now she was gone. He was heartsick.

And colder than a well-digger's butt.

It was freezing outside, and it finally dawned on him that he wasn't wearing a coat. Damn, if that woman hadn't turned him inside out!

He hadn't even taken his room key with him. When he stopped by his desk for another, the clerk handed him an envelope.

"What's this?" Jackson asked, frowning.

"A message for you, sir."

Jackson ripped open the envelope and squinted at the contents. The words danced and blurred; he cursed, crushed the paper in his fist and strode to the elevator.

He was going to D.C. even if he had to hire a bulldozer to get there.

One

This is a mistake, Olivia thought as she sat on the back pew of the Dallas church filled with white flowers and wedding guests.

She should never have let her friend Irish talk her into coming to her sister's wedding. Weddings were a jinx. If she had simply driven straight to Austin and not stopped by Irish's house, she wouldn't have been in this predicament. But she had, and she was.

The moment she saw him waiting at the altar with his brother and the others, she'd known that she'd been lying to herself for the past year and a half. Her insides twisted and her throat tightened. The feelings were still there. Just the sight of him churned bittersweet longings deep within her.

Suddenly, the floral fragrance turned cloying, the crowd oppressive. Her survival instincts, honed from years of experience, screamed at her to flee.

Just as she started to rise, the music swelled and every eye turned toward the aisle. Too late. The first bridesmaid appeared in the archway.

Olivia felt her skin prickle, and she knew that he'd spotted her. She tried not to look at him, but her gaze lifted as if responding to a command, and their eyes met. For a moment they stared at each other. Her defenses crumbled; music and people disappeared; time was suspended.

Then he grinned and winked one wicked dark eye. Who else but Jackson Crow would flirt with a woman in the middle of a wedding? He would probably still be flirting with women at his own wedding.

Damn him. Damn his strength, and damn her weakness. And her stupidity for coming today. Another person might offer all sorts of excuses, but Olivia couldn't hide behind the comfort of denial. She was a psychologist—or soon would be. Like the proverbial moth to a flame, she'd come to the wedding because she wanted to see Jackson again.

With tremendous effort, she forced herself to pay attention to the bride's entrance, to the wedding ceremony. Eve Ellison, Irish's younger sister, was exquisite in her simple satin and lace gown. Matt Crow, Jackson's younger brother, looked at his bride with such tenderness that Olivia felt her eyes sting. Irish, radiant with the recent news of her pregnancy, was matron-of-honor, and Dr. Kyle Rutledge, her plastic surgeon husband, was a groomsman.

Despite her best efforts, Olivia heard little of the vows. Her attention vacillated between watching Jackson and glancing anxiously toward the exit. She didn't want to disturb the ceremony by leaving, but she didn't want to face Jackson either. As soon as the church cleared, she would sneak out a side door, take a taxi back to Irish and Kyle's house, and—

Rats! She didn't have a key to the house.

"You may kiss the bride."

She glanced up from the tissue she had shredded in her lap to find the couple in an embrace and Jackson staring at her. She stuffed the shredded scraps into her purse and clutched the small bag with both hands.

"Ladies and gentlemen, may I present Mr. and Mrs. Matthew Crow."

The couple beamed; the crowd stood; laughter and applause broke out. The organ began to play, and the wedding party started down the aisle. As Jackson and Irish approached, Olivia studied one of the stained-glass windows and tried not to hyperventilate.

She waited until every single guest had cleared the pews, then hurried to a side door and flung it open.

There, leaning casually against a wall, stood Jackson Crow.

"Going somewhere, darlin'?"

"I—I'm looking for the ladies' room."

Looking amused, he stepped to one side, revealing the sign on the door behind him. "There it is. I'll wait for you."

"No need," she said with forced gaiety. "I know that you have best-man duties, photographs and such."

"I'll wait."

Once inside, she delayed as long as she could, using cold compresses on her face, then reapplying the lipstick she'd nibbled away during the service. Finally, with no other reasonable options, she straightened her shoulders and opened the door.

A lazy smile broke over his face as his gaze scanned her. "You're a sight for sore eyes. Do you know how long and hard I looked for you after you left Akron in such an all-fired hurry? Where'd you get off to?"

"I went home to Washington."

"I mean after that. I was in D.C. by midnight, and you'd already hightailed it for parts unknown. I did everything but call out the hounds to find you."

"I went to visit a friend in Colorado—not that it's any of your concern."

"Damn right it's my concern. After that night—"

"I'd rather forget that weekend, Jackson. I...I don't know what possessed me to— Well, I'm ordinarily much more sensible. It must have been the champagne. I'm not much of a drinker, and—" Realizing that she was blathering and that he was amused at her discomfort, she stopped and drew a deep breath. "I would appreciate it if you would be a gentleman and forget that night ever happened."

A slow grin lifted one corner of his sensual mouth, a mouth that had haunted her for months after their encounter. She still remembered the taste of it, the feel of it on—

"Not likely, darlin'," he said in a slow drawl as he ran a knuckle along her jawline. "Even though my mama did her best to raise a gentleman, nothing's wrong with my memory."

Her spine started to unravel, then Olivia caught herself and stiffened her resolve. She wasn't going to fall into his trap again. There wasn't room for a man in her plans. Certainly not a man like Jackson. If she hadn't been so terrified when she'd spied her ex-husband across the dance floor, she would never have left with Jackson that night. But she'd been so shocked to realize that Thomas had found her that she'd acted impulsively, thinking only of escape and of Jackson as a heaven-sent protector.

"You might as well forget it," she snapped. "There will never be a repeat performance. Now, if you'll excuse me…" She tried to push past him, but he blocked her way.

"Not so fast," he said, pinning her between his arms and the wall. "Now that I've found you again, darlin', I'm not about to let you get away this time."

A door opened down the hall, and Jackson's grandfather stuck his head out. "Jackson—" He gave a little hoot. "Might have known you'd have a pretty woman cornered somewhere. 'Scuse me, ma'am, but, Jackson, you'd better get in there or your mama's gonna skin you alive."

"I'll be there in a minute, Grandpa Pete."

"Please go ahead," Olivia said.

"I'm afraid if I leave you might cut and run."

Jackson's grandfather, known to everyone as Cherokee Pete, ambled toward them. Well into his eighties, he was still ramrod straight, and merriment danced in his dark eyes. With his long gray braids, he reminded Olivia of Willie Nelson in a tuxedo.

"Well, as I live and breathe," Pete said, "if it isn't Olivia Emory. How are you, young lady?"

She smiled and held out her hand. "It's Olivia Moore now, and I'm fine, Mr. Beamon."

"Moore?" Jackson said sharply. "Are you married?"

"None of that Mr. Beamon stuff," Pete said, both he and Olivia ignoring Jackson's question. "Despite this monkey suit, I'm still just plain Cherokee Pete. Get along, Jackson. I'll take care of Olivia until you're through with the picture taking."

Jackson didn't budge. "Are you married?"

She started to lie. Lying would have solved a multitude of problems, but something in his tone wrung the truth from her. She sighed and shook her head.

"Then why the name change?"

"It's a long story."

"I've got time."

"No, you ain't," Pete said. "Jackson, get going. You can jaw about this later." After Pete shooed his grandson away, he tucked Olivia's arm through his. "Little lady, how about you and me mosey on over to the reception? There's plenty of room in that fancy limousine out front, and I'll be the envy of every man in the room if I show up with such a beautiful woman on my arm. You wouldn't deprive me of that pleasure, now would you?" He patted her hand and smiled in a manner so charming and infectious that she couldn't help but return it.

"You're a shameless flirt, Pete Beamon. Now I know where your grandsons get their charm."

His grin widened and he winked. "Taught 'em everything they know. Come along, Miss Olivia. On the way to that highfalutin restaurant they reserved, you can tell me why your name is Moore now. I'm a mite curious myself. So you didn't get remarried?"

"Not likely. Even though I've been divorced for

three years, I just decided to take back my maiden name.'' That wasn't precisely the truth, but she'd decided that it was the simplest explanation. Actually, Moore was a name she'd picked from a phone book in Durango.

Pete nodded. ''Decided to scrap the name of the sorry scoundrel you got shed of.''

''How did you know my ex-husband was a sorry scoundrel?''

''Just stands to reason. If he amounted to anything, you'd still be married to him. If you ask me, he was a blamed fool to let go of a woman like you.''

If he only *would* let go, Olivia thought as they neared one of the limousines waiting at the curb.

''Glad to know you're single,'' Pete said as he helped her into the car. ''Seems Jackson's taken quite a shine to you, and I've got a proposition to make.''

''A proposition?''

''Yep. Nothing I ever wanted more than for my four grandsons to find a good wife and settle down to raising a family. I was mighty tickled when Kyle hooked up with Irish and when Matt and Eve got together, though both of those pairs had some rough spots, let me tell you. That makes two down and two to go. Now it's about time that Jackson, being the oldest, got himself hitched to that very particular woman he finally found. I can tell he's ready.''

''Ready?'' Olivia felt her chest clutch and her face go warm. ''Who's the very particular woman?''

''Why,'' Pete said, ''you are.''

''*Me?*'' Her voice went up an octave.

He nodded. ''Irish speaks very highly of you, and I can tell Jackson's taken with you. He was like a bear with a sore paw when he lost track of you. Scoured the woods good for your whereabouts, kept looking for the longest time. Hired a passel of people to help, too. In my book that makes you a special lady. Now, here's my proposition. If you'll marry Jackson, I'll give you two million dollars on your wedding day.''

Dumbstruck, Olivia could only gape at Pete. She knew that the old man, despite his folksy talk and simple ways, was enormously wealthy and could well afford what he was offering. She just couldn't believe that he was actually making the offer. Finally she managed to stammer, ''Two *million* dollars? Ma— *marry* Jackson? *Me?* You're kidding.''

''Nope, I'm dead serious. I just handed Eve her two for marrying Matt.''

''But, Pete, that's ludicrous! I certainly wouldn't marry your grandson for two million dollars.''

The old man sighed. ''Well, truth to tell, Jackson would be a handful for any woman to put up with— not that he's lacking in character, you understand. He's a fine boy. But he's the oldest, and I'd like to see him under the steadying hand of somebody who could see through all his hoorah. It's past time for him to give up his wild ways and settle down. You strike me as the perfect person to tame him, you being a psychologist and all. Irish tells me that you're a real smart lady.''

''Too smart to want to marry Jackson Crow. I'm not interested in taming him, nor am I in the market for a husband, thank you very much.''

"Now don't you decide too quick. Take some time and think about it. It would mean a lot to me to see that boy happy. Why, I'll even up the ante to five million if need be."

Two

Jackson didn't wait for any of the family. As soon as the photographer snapped the last picture, he took off like his tail was on fire. He must have broken every speed limit between the church and the restaurant on Turtle Creek, but he didn't care. He aimed to find Olivia fast. The notion that she might skip out again had him in a cold sweat.

For the life of him, he couldn't figure out why she had affected him so, but something about Olivia had turned him seven ways to sundown. Even after a year and a half, he still thought about her all the time. Maybe he'd built her up into some kind of goddess with no good reason. Maybe if he spent a little time with her he'd find that she was just an ordinary woman, nothing like the person he remembered.

Maybe—

But when he walked into the reception and saw Olivia standing with Grandpa Pete, all the maybes disappeared. Just looking at her made his heart swell in his chest until it hurt, and he felt a big grin spread over his face. Lord, she was beautiful. Long legs, lush body, lips that begged to be kissed and big bedroom eyes that he wanted to dive into.

Beautiful, absolutely. But there was something else about her that grabbed him by the throat, something he couldn't quite define or understand. It was the kind of thing that some people wrote poems about, except he couldn't write a poem if his life depended on it. Every time he was around Olivia, an old memory popped up. She reminded him of a bird he'd once encountered. A blue jay.

When he'd been about ten or eleven years old, he'd received an air rifle for Christmas, something he'd been begging for. He'd half listened to the usual lecture about safety, thinking he knew just what to do. After all, he'd been shooting Scooter Franklin's rifle for nearly a year. Feeling very mature and full of himself, he'd gone into the woods behind Grandpa Pete's store with the rifle and hung a target on a tree.

When the paper bull's-eye had been shot to shreds, he looked around for another target. He tried a few pine cones on a fence post. Easy stuff. That's when he spied the jay. Without half thinking, he took aim and pulled the trigger.

The bird fell to the ground, and Jackson had rushed to view his prey. But the jay wasn't dead; it was only wounded, and it flapped around the ground with a bum wing. Suddenly feeling like a dirty dog for what he'd done, Jackson had tried to pick it up, thinking to take it somewhere for help. The bird wouldn't let him near. It pecked and squawked and fought him until Jackson's hands were bloody and he was in tears. Finally, he'd taken off his shirt and thrown it over the jay to capture it. Held close, it had calmed.

Grandpa Pete had fixed the injured wing and kept the jay in a cage on the porch until it was able to fly again.

Jackson had put the air rifle in the back of his closet and never picked it up again. He never forgot that panicked, injured bird, needing help but instinctively fighting for survival against him.

Olivia had that same fierce way about her, as if *she* were fighting for survival. Had she been badly injured in some way? He was almost sure of it. Everything in him ached to gather her close, to calm her and hold her till she healed.

A crazy notion, he supposed. After all, she was the psychologist. He was just a lucky stiff who had more money than sense and who, to keep from being called a goof-off, built and ran a fancy golf club for his buddies in the millionaires' club.

Still, he wasn't going to let her get away. She might not know it, but she needed him.

He strode toward her.

Play it cool, Crow. Play it cool, he told himself. Don't scare her off.

She looked like a startled doe when he took the wine glass from her fingers and handed it to his grandfather.

"Let's dance," he said, drawing her into his arms.

"There's no music," she said, pushing against his chest. "The band is still setting up."

"I'll hum until they start." He pulled her back to him. "What do you want? Waltz? Fox-trot? Tango? I do a mean tango."

Laughing, she stepped out of his arms. "Jackson, you're still a piece of work. Behave."

He winked. "I'd rather misbehave with you."

"Jackson!" she whispered. "Your grandfather." She gestured with her eyes, indicating someone was behind her.

"Grandpa Pete's gone."

She glanced around. "Where did he go? We were talking."

He shrugged. "No telling. But Pete's sharp. He knows when three's a crowd. If you won't dance with me, would you like a drink? I see that the bar is open."

"Just the wine I didn't get to finish."

"That's easy." He signaled a waiter with a tray of champagne glasses and plucked two from the load he carried. He handed one glass to Olivia.

"Thanks," she said, ducking her head to study the bubbles rather than look at him.

He touched a bit of dark hair at her shoulder, letting the shiny strand curl around his finger. He couldn't help touching her. "You've cut your hair."

She nodded. "Just a little."

"Have you lost weight?"

"Just a little."

He lifted her chin and ran his thumb over the sexy dimple there. "Why did you run away from me?"

"I didn't run away."

"Could have fooled me."

"I didn't run away. I left."

"Why in such a blamed hurry?"

"I explained that in my note. I had to catch my flight home."

"But you didn't stay home. You disappeared off the face of the earth. I know because I looked everywhere for you. Your roommate Kim didn't know where you were. Not even Irish, your best friend, knew where you were. I thought Kyle might strangle me when I interrupted his and Irish's honeymoon trying to find you."

"I told you that I went to visit a friend in Colorado. I had a sudden opportunity for a job, so I went."

"And left no forwarding address?"

She shrugged, then, looking as if she would like to bolt any minute, she chugalugged her champagne.

Back off, Crow, he warned himself. Instead of pressing her, he smiled and held out his untouched glass. "Want another?"

She shook her head.

"Irish didn't tell me you were coming to the wedding. Is this your first time in Texas?"

"I've been in Texas once or twice, and I didn't know about the wedding. I was just passing through Dallas and decided to call Irish and Kyle, and you know Irish. The next thing I knew I was their houseguest and getting dressed for the ceremony."

"Passing through?" he asked, trying to sound casual.

She nodded.

There was a long silence while he waited for her to expand on her comment. Finally he asked, "Going where?"

"To Austin."

"Austin?" He waited again for her to elaborate.

"Yes," was all she said.

Getting information out of her was harder than trying to put socks on a rooster.

"Jackson, my man," a deep voice said as a big hand clamped his shoulder. "Might have known you would try to monopolize this lovely lady. Olivia, it's good to see you again. I'm Mitch Harris. We met at Irish and Kyle's wedding. I understand that you're going to be working with Dr. Jurney at the University of Texas. That's great, really great. Looks like we'll be neighbors. May I be the first to welcome you to our capital?"

Rankled that Mitch seemed to know more about Olivia's plans than he did, Jackson scowled and said, "Get lost, Mitch. This is a private conversation."

Mitch only grinned and shook him playfully by the nape. "Now, Jackson, is that any way to talk to your governor?"

"You're not *my* governor. Hell, I didn't even vote."

And, blast it, Olivia's eyes widened as if she were impressed with the big lug who was standing there looking as smug as a packed-pew preacher.

"Of course I remember you, but I didn't realize that you were the governor," she said, extending her hand to Mitch.

"I wasn't when we met. Hadn't even decided to run then. I was just inaugurated this past January."

"Congratulations, Governor."

Mitch kept holding Olivia's hand a lot longer than necessary, which burned Jackson good. "The only reason Mitch got elected," Jackson said, "was that he used to play a little pro football. People didn't know he got his brains scrambled from all the hits on the field.''

"Jackson!" she exclaimed, clearly shocked by his comment.

Mitch only chuckled. "Actually, I think it was mostly because my opponent got caught in a scandal a week before the election. Nobody was more surprised that I was, but I won, fair and square.''

"Oh, I'm sure you're being modest," she said.

"No, he's not," Jackson said. "Mitch Harris hasn't got a modest bone in his body. And if you don't get lost, good buddy, I'm going to revoke your golf privileges at Crow's Nest.''

"Are you trying to get rid of me?" Mitch asked.

Jackson shot at him with his index finger. "You got it in one, Gov.''

Mitch laughed. "Then I guess I'll be moving along. I'll talk to you about that other matter later, Jackson. Olivia, it was good to see you again.'' He slipped a card from a case in his breast pocket and handed it to her. "Give me a call when you're settled, and I'll show you around, take you to dinner. Austin has some of the greatest restaurants in the state.''

If Mitch hadn't walked away right then, Jackson would have decked him. Instead, he jerked the card from her hand, tore it in little pieces and dropped them in a nearby flowerpot.

"Jackson! Why did you do that?"

"Do what?"

"Don't be dense! Why did you tear up Mitch's card?"

"'Cause I don't want you calling him. Stay away from the man. He's dangerous. Let's dance."

She didn't budge. "Dangerous?"

"Yes. He dyes his hair, lies about his golf handicap and wears boxer shorts with little smiley faces all over them."

She tried to keep her lips pressed together, but she finally lost the battle with a laugh. "Jackson, aren't you ever serious?"

"More than you know, darlin'." He pulled her close and breathed in the sweet smell of her. "I'm real serious right now."

"Olivia!" came a feminine squeal from a few feet away.

Olivia pushed away from him, and her face lit up. "Kim!" She held out her arms and they hugged like long lost sisters. "It's been so long. You look great!"

"And so do you. Why didn't you write? We were worried about you."

Olivia shrugged. "Sorry, but you know me. I hate writing letters. It's so wonderful to see you again. Irish tells me that you've had an exciting offer with the state department. Let's go powder our noses and catch up on all the news."

And slick as a whistle, she was gone. Jackson could hardly follow her into the ladies' room—though he considered it. His good manners finally got the upper hand, and he turned away, looking for Mitch. He and his old friend had a little business to discuss.

He hadn't even considered Mitch's outrageous request earlier, knowing that, sure as shootin', he would end up humiliated. He was painfully aware of his limitations. Now things had changed. Jackson told himself that he was letting himself in for a lot of grief, but in spite of the risks, he was going to take Mitch up on his offer. Somehow he would manage to keep from looking like too much of an idiot. After all, he'd been fooling folks for years, and Olivia was worth the gamble.

Olivia and Kim talked nonstop for twenty minutes or more. Finally Kim said, "I hate to leave you, but I promised my folks that I would be right back. Irish invited me over for breakfast tomorrow. We'll spend the morning gabbing." Kim hugged her. "Gosh, I've missed you two." With a wiggle of her fingers, her friend left.

Olivia lingered, repairing her makeup and stalling her return to the reception. She'd loved catching up on all the news with Kim. She'd missed her vivacious young friend. Although Kim was more than a decade younger than Olivia, the two of them, along with Irish, had been housemates in Washington and had become very close. Kim had been in college and working part-time for Congresswoman Ellen Crow O'Hara, Jackson and Matt's older sister and Kim's aunt by marriage. Olivia had been working on her doctorate in psychology and trying to get her life back on track after her divorce. Irish, who had inherited the old house they lived in, was working as a cosmetic consultant and trying to get her life back on track after a terrible mugging in New York that had ruined her modeling career.

The bonds that Olivia forged with the two women had saved her sanity. They had become the sisters she'd never had, the closest thing to a family that she had left. Her mother had died when she was ten. Her older brother had left home the day he turned eighteen, and God only knew where he was. Her father, a prominent cardiologist in Palm Springs, had disinherited her when she divorced Thomas, not that severing ties with her father was any great loss. He was a tyrant whose abuse had driven her mother to suicide, her brother to the streets and her into a terrible marriage to a man who could have been her father's clone.

"Olivia?"

She glanced up to see Irish's beautiful face smiling in the mirror. "Irish, the wedding was lovely. Eve looks so happy."

"She is happy. But you look awfully sad."

Olivia shook her head and tucked her lipstick into her purse. "No, I was just reminiscing about the good times we had in Washington at your old house."

"We did have some crazy times there, didn't we? But come on, the bride and groom are about to cut the cake, and Jackson is wearing a hole in the floor outside. He sent me in after you."

"Irish, I really don't want to get involved with Jackson. I'm simply not ready for any kind of meaningful relationship with a man. I've been stung too many times."

"Oh, don't worry about Jackson. I don't think *meaningful relationship* is in his vocabulary. In fact, someone like him might be good for you. You need to cut loose and have a little fun. Come on."

Olivia had no choice but to rise and rejoin the party.

* * *

Despite her resolve to keep her distance from Jackson, he was at her side almost constantly, and she'd been enjoying herself. He was a wonderful dancer, and she told him so as he whirled her around the floor.

"Thanks," he replied. "I majored in dancing and poker at college."

She laughed. He was such a cutup. "Where did you go to school, and what did you really major in?"

"I have several alma mammies, and my major changed from semester to semester. Academics never interested me the way it did my brother and sister and cousins. I wouldn't have even gone to college if it hadn't been for Grandpa Pete putting the screws to me."

"I recall Irish telling me something about a deal your grandfather made with each of you. He paid for your education, then gave you a million dollars when you graduated?"

"Yep. Then we had five years to double the million. If we did it, he sweetened the pot. My sister sank her million into an ingenious invention by her boyfriend, who's now her husband. Matt started Crow Airline and struck it rich. Kyle made a killing as a plastic surgeon to the stars in California. My cousin Smith, Kyle's younger brother, started a computer company when he was in college and made his fortune."

"And you?" Olivia asked. "How did you double your money? I assume that you did."

"Yep. My biggest talent has always been my luck, so I bought a million dollars worth of lottery tickets."

She stopped dead still, astonished. He did a fast

shuffle to keep from trampling her toes. "*Lottery tickets?* You're joking."

"Nope. If you think about it, I had great odds. Won eleven-million dollars."

"You won?"

"Absolutely."

She shook her head. "Jackson Crow, you're crazy."

He grinned down at her. "Absolutely." He pulled her close and whirled her around the floor again. "I'm crazy about you, Olivia Emory."

She stiffened. "Moore."

"Sorry. Moore. I'm glad you're rid of that bozo's name."

She'd told him the same story about her name change that she'd told his grandfather. Amazing how easily she'd learned to lie, especially when her life had come to depend on it. She had changed names two or three times since she'd last seen Jackson. Her ruse must have worked, for she hadn't seen or heard from Thomas since he'd tracked her to Akron and crashed Irish's wedding reception.

"Relax," Jackson whispered in her ear, drawing her close.

"Pardon?"

"You suddenly went stiff as a post."

"Sorry. I must be getting a bit tired."

"Oh, hell, I'm the one that's sorry. I've been dancing your feet off for an hour. Only way I figured I could hold you and stay decent in front of my mama and daddy. Let's go sit down, and I'll get you something from the buffet. Oh, shoot, Mama's waving at us. You mind visiting with my folks some more?"

"Not at all. I like your parents. They're very nice."

"They're curious is what they are."

"About me? Why?"

"Let's just say that they're sizing you up as a future daughter-in-law."

Her breath caught. "A what?"

He chuckled and kissed her nose. "Don't worry about it, darlin'. I'm a long way from being ready to make that trip down the aisle."

Olivia was cordial with Mr. and Mrs. Crow and chatted amiably with them for a few minutes. She really did like his parents, but when Jackson left for the buffet table, she excused herself politely and stole away. Distance was what she needed. Distance from Jackson Crow. She had no plans to take up with him where they left off in Akron. If she hadn't become so frightened when she'd spotted Thomas across the room, she wouldn't have thrown herself at Jackson and dragged him from the reception.

She retreated to a courtyard outside the elegant inn, a spot lush with tropical plants and hanging baskets. She sat on a stone bench, hoping to make herself invisible behind the ficus tree growing beside the seat.

She felt foolish, a woman hiding like a child to avoid a confrontation, but she'd spent so many years fleeing and hiding, simply to survive, that the response was as conditioned as those of Pavlov's dogs. Instinctively, whenever she felt threatened, she ran.

Jackson Crow posed no physical threat to her—at least she didn't think so. Yet, she seemed to have a penchant for picking abusive men. She'd thought Rick, her college fiancé, was a kind, caring person until the first time he'd lost his temper. And her ex-husband Thomas—

She shuddered.

Olivia had sworn off any sort of significant relationship with men. She didn't have the emotional stamina for it—at least not now. And maybe not ever.

Her brief fling with Jackson had been a mistake, just as she knew that rekindling their affair would be a mistake. She sensed that although Jackson played the clown on the surface, he was a deeply intense individual underneath. The first time their eyes met, she had responded with a visceral feeling that stunned her. The first time he'd kissed her, she'd gone up in flames. The first time they had made love, she'd been lost.

Those feelings were still there.

Jackson Crow was Trouble. She was glad that they would be living over two hundred miles apart.

Holding a heaping plate of food in each hand, Jackson scanned the room.

Mitch Harris strolled up. "Lose something?"

"Yeah." Ignoring Mitch, his gaze scanned the clusters of people again. Where in the dickens had she gone now?

"You thought any more about accepting that appointment to the Railroad Commission?"

"I've had other things on my mind."

Mitch chuckled. "Yeah, I noticed. Beautiful woman."

Jackson glared at his friend. "Keep your mitts off her, Mitch. I mean it. This one is special. If you try to move in on her, I'll break both your legs and all your writin' fingers.''

"I got the message earlier, my friend. Jackson, I really wish you'd take that spot for Bledsoe's unexpired term. Things are getting backed up over there. I need to make an appointment this week, and you're my first choice. You're sharp, and I don't know of anybody any more fair-minded than you are.''

Jackson snorted. ''You're laying it on a little thick, aren't you?''

"No, I'm serious. You know the oil business backward and forward, and I know you keep up with the other areas that the commission regulates. I think you'd be perfect for the job.''

"Actually, I have been thinking some about it. I'd have to move to Austin, wouldn't I?''

"Be a devil of a commute if you didn't. Come on, Jackson, it's not permanent—just till the next general election. I know you like Austin, and remember, we've got some fine golf courses in the area.''

"None of them as good as Crow's Nest—the first tee is only ten yards from my front door. Austin's golf courses aren't the big drawing card for me.''

"Ah,'' Mitch said, grinning, ''but we're soon going to have a drawing card that no place else has. The lovely Olivia.''

Jackson answered with a slow grin of his own.

"Tell you what, if you'll agree to take the appointment, I'll show you which way Olivia went.''

"Buddy, you're on.''

Three

Olivia drove down the tree-lined street on Austin's west side, then turned into the driveway. She bumped over the cracked asphalt that had been heaved upward by live-oak roots and pulled to a stop in her space beside the garage apartment in the rear yard. She waved to Dr. Tessa Jurney, who was sitting on the side porch of the main house.

Grateful to be home and doubly grateful that it was Friday, she climbed from the oven of a car. Sweat trickled from her hairline, and her sleeveless shift stuck to her back from the car's leather seat. She blotted her face and neck with a paper towel from the roll she'd learned to carry with her.

"Come have a glass of iced tea," Tessa called. "You look as if you're about to melt."

"I melted a long time ago," Olivia said as she

walked toward the porch of the two-story house, an elegant white clapboard from the thirties. "Is it always this hot?"

"At this time of year? Always. People around here say that there are two seasons—summer and August. Thank goodness August is finally over. September is a bit better, especially toward the end, and October is glorious." She poured a glass of tea from the pitcher and handed it to Olivia.

Olivia took a long swallow, then rolled the cold glass over her forehead. "The first thing I'm going to do when I get a pay check is to have my car's air conditioner fixed. I never needed it in Colorado, so it wasn't a problem. Even though the car's getting old, it has never given me a moment's trouble. I didn't even know the air conditioner wasn't working until I headed to Texas."

"I'll be happy to loan you money to—"

"No." Olivia held up her hand. "Absolutely not. You and Ed have already done too much for me— helping me get this job and letting me live in your apartment for practically nothing. No loans, but thanks, anyhow."

"At least drive Ed's car for a while. He'll be in Atlanta for ten more days, and it's just sitting idle in the garage."

With the temperatures still soaring into the nineties, it was murder to be stuck in a car without air-conditioning. But Olivia hated to be a mooch. She wasn't accustomed to having to depend on the generosity of others or doing without conveniences—at least not until she left Thomas with nothing but the Lexus she still drove, her clothes and what few personal items she could hurriedly throw into the car. She couldn't even count on her father—he'd disinherited her when she walked out on Thomas, even though she'd been frightened for her life. In the past few years, Olivia had learned to survive on a lot less than she was accustomed to—and been a thousand times more content.

For two years Dr. Tessa Jurney had been her major professor in graduate school at American University in Washington, D.C. Tessa and her family had moved to Texas shortly before Olivia had been forced to flee, but they had kept in touch with a card or a phone call now and then. Tessa and Irish were the only people who knew the whole story—or at least most of it— about her past. Olivia had always meant to finish her doctorate, but with Thomas after her...well, things had gone on hold for a while. Tessa had pulled the strings that had allowed her to complete her degree.

"How are your classes going?" Tessa asked.

"Wonderfully. I have some really bright students in the two undergrad classes I'm teaching, and I'm enjoying my seminar with Dr. Bullock immensely— even though we have lots of reading to do. I just came from three hours in the library."

As Tessa refilled their glasses, a truck stopped in front of the house across the street. The name of a furniture store was scrolled across the side.

"Looks like our new neighbors may be moving in soon," Tessa said.

"Um. Do you know who bought the house?"

"No. Jenny and her friends are hoping that it's a family with a 'really fine' son in her age range."

Jenny was the Jurneys' thirteen-year-old. They also

had a son, Bill, who was sixteen. Both were good kids. Part of Olivia's deal for living in the apartment was to be close by for Jenny and Bill on evenings when the Jurneys went out or the occasional weekend when Tessa and Ed were out of town. Jenny and Bill were at that awkward age when they were too old for sitters and too young to be alone—especially for an entire weekend.

A luxury car pulled to a stop behind the truck and a long-legged blonde got out and hurried up the walk of the Spanish-style home.

"The owner, you think?" Olivia asked.

Tessa shook her head. "Looks like a decorator to me, and I'd venture that no expense has been spared. I priced a chair at that furniture store last year. It cost more than Jenny's braces. The braces won."

The two of them did some more speculating as the delivery men toted couches and tables and chairs up the front walk. In the two and a half weeks that Olivia had been living in Austin, the new-neighbor question had been an ongoing saga. The Sold sign went up the day after Olivia arrived, and there had been a parade of repairmen and plumbers and landscapers coming and going.

It was a beautiful home, Olivia had thought with a tiny twinge of envy as she'd watched the painters apply a coat of warm cream to the stucco. She loved the red tile roof and the sprawling hacienda style with the walled courtyard. A beautiful home indeed, but her little apartment suited her just fine—and she was thankful to have it. Although it was furnished with castoffs as Tessa had warned, the rooms were really quite charming, especially after Olivia had done some painting and spent a couple of weekends scouting garage sales and resale shops. She'd actually enjoyed going "junking" as Tessa called it—and gotten some darned good bargains.

She smiled at the notion of Michelle or Dani or any of her other chichi California pals buying used goods in someone's garage or at a Goodwill shop. Olivia had come a long way from California, and she wouldn't go back for anything. She much preferred the peacefulness of her life now—the friends she'd acquired since she left that life.

"Something amusing?" Tessa asked.

"I was just thinking about how much I like Austin—and going to garage sales. Want to go junking again tomorrow?"

"Can't. Jen has a soccer game that I promised to attend."

Another big truck stopped across the street.

"Moving van," Olivia said. "Looks like Jenny's suspense will soon be over. I hope for her sake that a really fine guy is moving in."

Olivia was brushing her teeth Saturday morning when a knock came at her door. Probably Tessa, she thought. She rinsed and hurried to the door, wiping her hands on the seat of her shorts.

Her heart stumbled when she opened the door. Jackson Crow leaned against the jamb, a big grin on his face and a cup dangling from his index finger.

"Mornin'," he said, tugging the brim of his straw cowboy hat.

"What are you doing here?"

He held out the cup. "Came to borrow a cup of sugar."

"Sugar? You came a long way for a cup of sugar. How did you find me?"

"Irish gave me your address. A cute little redhead with braces told me you lived up here. Jenny, I think she said her name was. Say, is that coffee I smell? I'd give fifty dollars for a cup of coffee right now."

Olivia sighed. "Okay, come on in, but you can't stay long. I'm going junking."

"Is that like slumming?"

"Not even close."

He tossed his hat on the sofa and followed her to the kitchen alcove where she poured a mug of coffee for him. "Sugar? Cream?"

"One sugar. No cream. Say, this is a nice place you've got here."

"Thanks. I like it."

"Cozy," he said, standing so close that she could smell the faint scent of his aftershave.

She tried to act casual, as if Jackson's dropping in was an everyday occurrence, but she was so nervous that she spilled sugar all over the cabinet before she finally got a spoonful into the coffee. Why did he have to stand so close? She handed him the mug and stepped back. Unfortunately, the alcove was so small that she bumped into the stove and couldn't retreat any further. His presence filled the compact area as he raised the mug to his mouth and swallowed.

"Ah, that hits the spot. You make a great cup of coffee. You don't happen to have any leftover eggs or a biscuit or something, do you?"

"No," she said, yanking open a cupboard, "but

here's a granola bar. You can take it with you. Now, if you'll excuse me, I have to leave."

"What's the hurry?"

"I told you that I was going junking. If I don't hurry, all the good stuff will be gone before I get there."

"Get where?"

Olivia sighed. "I'm going to hit several garage sales first. I have a list from the paper."

"Garage sales? Well, I'll be darned. You don't strike me as the type." He stuck the granola bar in his pocket, refilled his mug with coffee and said, "Tell you what, I'll go with you." He started for the door, grabbing his hat on the way. "Which one do you want to hit first?"

Olivia tried every way she could think of to dissuade Jackson from accompanying her, but he was unyielding. The last thing in the world she wanted was to spend the morning with Jackson Crow and his extraordinary smile.

Well…not the last thing.

Actually, her spirits had seemed remarkably high from the moment he'd arrived at her door. Just seeing a familiar face, she supposed. But spending time with him wasn't wise. She wasn't going to allow herself to get involved with Jackson. Thank goodness he lived several hours away.

"Why are you here?" she asked as they walked down the steps of her apartment.

"I came to see you—to borrow a cup of sugar."

She rolled her eyes. "No, I mean, why are you in Austin?"

"Business."

"Shouldn't you be tending to it?"

He grinned as he slipped on his sunglasses. "It doesn't start until Monday. I have the whole weekend free. Want me to drive?"

"No, thank you. I'll drive. You navigate." She thrust the folded newspaper and map into his hands and jerked open her car door before he could play the gentleman.

"We're lost!" Olivia said.

"Aw, naw. Why don't you turn left right up here?"

Fuming, she whipped into a convenience-store lot and jerked the newspaper and map from his hands. "We're lost! I thought you were going to navigate."

"I told you that I was better at driving than navigating."

After studying their location and their destination on the map, she realized that they were several blocks away from the garage sale that she'd marked with two stars. "That's where we're going!" She poked a spot on the map. "You've been taking us around in circles." She thrust the papers at him, counted to ten, then pulled out and turned to the right. This was the third time they'd been lost that morning. She could almost believe that Jackson was deliberately trying to make her angry.

"Sorry, sugar," Jackson said, turning his smile up to high. "I'll make it up to you. I'll take you someplace special for lunch. You like Mexican food?"

"I love it, but I'd love finding a desk that I can afford even more. I really need one. Darn it, if we had been there five minutes sooner, I could have bought that one on Elm Street."

"The leg was broken. It wasn't a good deal. We'll find a better one, trust me. At least you got a bargain on that toaster. Two bucks ain't bad."

She laughed as she pulled to a stop at the address she sought. "You're the one who got the bargain. I can't believe that you were arguing over fifty cents. Me, I can believe, but *you?* I thought you told me that you'd never been to a garage sale."

"Haven't. But Grandpa Pete has trading days on the grounds of his store in East Texas. People have been coming to set up tables and booths there for as long as I can remember. They rent space from him and sell everything from used pots to goats. I learned dickering there, learned from a master. No finer horse trader than Grandpa Pete."

"Seems strange. I thought your grandfather was a millionaire."

He laughed. "Billionaire's more like it, but he's just plain folks. We all are. Nothing makes him madder than for one of us to start acting uppity."

"Uppity?" She smiled at the old-fashioned term.

"Those are Grandpa Pete's words," he said as they climbed from the car and headed for the goods displayed along a driveway.

Olivia spotted it immediately—a small Queen Anne writing table that had been painted a ghastly shade of green. With a little work—no, make that a lot of work—it would be beautiful. And perfect for her apartment.

"Like it?" Jackson asked.

"I love it," she whispered. "Under that awful paint is a very nice piece of furniture. It's exactly what I've been looking for—better actually."

"Great. Let's get it."

When she looked at the price tag, she sighed. "I think the owner knows what's underneath the paint. It's sixty-five dollars. Even though it's a steal at that price, I can't afford it. I was hoping to find something for about twenty-five."

"Maybe we can dicker a little."

Jackson knew the outcome before Olivia said a word. Damned if she didn't have tears in her eyes. It about tore his heart out. He'd buy her a hundred ugly green desks if she wanted them, but she was such an independent female, he knew better than to try. He'd found out early in the morning that she didn't intend to take a penny from him, and if he didn't hush about it, she'd turn around and go home right then. He'd kept his mouth shut after that.

But, damn, he hated to see that wistful look on her face as she ran her fingers over the top of the table.

"No go, huh?"

Olivia shook her head. "I could only get her to come down fifteen dollars. You're not considering buying that ratty thing, are you?"

He held up the stuffed armadillo that he'd been looking at to kill time. "I might. I kind of like old Jake here. He has character, don't you think? Grandpa Pete would love him, and he's got a birthday coming up soon. Let me see if I can do a little dickering for him. And these beach towels." He grabbed a couple of towels from the display table. "I saw a lamp over there that you might check out, too."

While Olivia was examining the lamp, Jackson made a quick offer to the plump little woman running the sale. She looked at him kind of funny, but she shrugged and agreed to the deal. He whipped out his wallet, paid her, and made his way back to Olivia with Jake and the towels under his arm.

"Wait till you hear about the package deal I made. Fifty-six dollars for the desk, old Jake, and the towels."

"Fifty-six doll—" She raised an eyebrow and eyed him suspiciously. "Exactly how much was that dreadful animal?"

"Too much. But I made a deal with her—twenty-five for the desk, twenty-five for the armadillo, and six for the towels." He shot her his brightest, most sincere grin. "Grandpa Pete's gonna love this guy."

"Why don't I believe you?"

"Trust me. I know my grandfather's taste. He'll be perfect for his museum display at the trading post. It's full of what you might call *unusual* stuff. My mother says it's beyond tacky."

"Irish told me about your grandfather's place, including the stucco teepee she stayed in. No, I mean that I'm not sure that I believe you got my table for twenty-five dollars."

"Ask the lady," he said with a sweeping gesture toward the seller.

And darned if Olivia didn't do just that.

He could have kissed the garage-sale lady when she said, with a perfectly straight face, "That was our deal. Twenty-five for the desk, twenty-five for the armadillo, six for the towels. You have a way to haul the desk?"

"We'll be back after lunch with my pickup," Jackson told her, scooting Olivia away before she could question the woman further. If he wanted to pay twenty-five dollars for a mangy four-dollar armadillo, well…it wasn't any skin off anybody else's nose.

In the car Olivia insisted on giving him money for the desk. He didn't argue.

"It's hotter'n blue blazes in here," he said. "Crank her up and turn on the air conditioner. How about we get some lunch now? You know how to get to Congress Avenue?"

"Of course. But the air conditioner is broken."

"What's wrong with it?"

"I don't know. I'm going to take it in on the fifteenth and find out."

"Why wait until the fifteenth?"

"Payday."

He bit his tongue and didn't say a word. He wouldn't be surprised if she insisted on paying for her own lunch.

She did.

"Sorry, darlin', but I've got my pride. I invited you to lunch. I pay."

He watched the struggle play at the corners of her beautiful mouth, then she said, "Thank you. The food was great. I loved the tortilla soup."

"Best in town. Austin has some great places to eat. How about dinner tonight?"

"I don't think so, but thank you. Jackson, I really don't want to get involved. I've told you that."

"Involved? You gotta eat, I gotta eat—why not? You have another date?"

She shook her head. "No, and I'm not likely to. I want to start stripping the desk, and I have some reading to do for my classes. I'm very busy. Thank you, but no."

He didn't plan to give up without a fight, but he let it go for the moment.

Olivia had been completely out of her mind in allowing Jackson Crow within fifty yards of her, certifiable to agree to his accompanying her to the garage sales, completely nuts to go to lunch with him. Driving home with him sitting in the passenger seat was torture. She hadn't forgotten one moment of their night together in Ohio, the way his mouth felt on hers, the way his hands—

"Watch it!"

She skidded to a stop, realizing that she had nearly rear-ended a UPS truck. Her splayed hand slapped her chest, and she sucked in a noisy gasp. "Oh, dear Lord. I'm sorry. I didn't see him. I didn't see him. I swear I didn't. I'm sorry."

"No harm done, sugar. Don't worry about it. Want me to drive?"

She shook her head, then eased around the truck. Once past, she stole a glance at Jackson. He was sitting relaxed in the passenger seat, one elbow out the window, one booted foot crossed over his knee, calm as could be. If Thomas had been riding with her, he still would have been cursing her stupidity. And she couldn't imagine Thomas, or any man she'd ever known, spending a Saturday morning going junking with her. And enjoying it.

Yes, it was a good thing that Jackson lived so far away. Even for a woman who had sworn off relationships, a man like him would be hard to resist.

She pulled into the Jurneys' driveway. "Where is your pickup? I don't see it."

"It's in the garage."

She frowned. "Which garage? Is it being repaired?"

"Nope. It's running fine. It's in my garage. Ready to go get the desk?"

"I don't understand. Where is your garage?"

"Over there." He pointed to the house across the street.

Four

"**Y**ou're living *there?*"

Jackson grinned as he leaned against the side of her car and looked toward his new home. "Yep. Moved in last night."

A sick feeling uncoiled in the pit of her stomach. "But why?"

"Well, the house was ready and the guys had my stuff on the truck, and I have to start work Monday, so it seemed like a good time."

"No, I mean why *there?*"

"I needed a place to live, and it was for sale. I really like the place. Wanna come look around?"

"Jackson Crow, stop being obtuse! Why did you pick a house across the street from where *I* live?"

"Lucky, isn't it? You know I've always been lucky. Did you know that they used to call me Lucky when I was in school?"

"Jackson, don't try to feed me any of that baloney! You didn't just *happen* to buy a house there! You're deliberately trying to make my life miserable."

"Oh, sugar, don't be mad at me. I'll swear on a stack of Bibles a mile high that I never intended to make your life miserable. After I let Mitch talk me into taking a government appointment and agreed to come here, I must have looked at two dozen houses. This was the one I liked the best. Honest. Cross my heart and hope to die." He drew a big *X* across his chest and affected an expression of pure innocence.

She narrowed her eyes. "When did you buy it?"

"Oh, about two or three weeks ago."

"Exactly what date?"

"Hmm, let's see." He stuck his fingers in his back pockets and looked skyward. "Seems to me I signed the papers the day after Matt's wedding. As I recall you were still in Dallas visiting with Irish and Kim. You hadn't even moved to Austin yet. Ready to pick up your desk now?"

She sighed. "I suppose so."

"Good. Let's go get my truck."

He touched the back of her waist to guide her, and she almost jumped out of her skin. Why was it that a hundred men could make such a simple, polite gesture without her even noticing, and yet Jackson's most casual touch could send her soaring?

This was not good.

Living in such close proximity was going to be a problem, but she could hardly order Jackson to move from his house, and she certainly couldn't afford to leave her apartment.

"Look," she said as she strode down the driveway,

"if you're going to be my neighbor, we're going to have to establish some rules here."

"Absolutely, darlin'. You come up with a list, and we'll discuss it later in the week. Say, would you mind stopping by a grocery store with me while we're out? I wasn't kidding about needing sugar. My cupboards are totally bare. I don't even have a jar of peanut butter or a box of Froot Loops in the house."

"Poor baby."

He ignored her sarcasm and flashed that grin again. "I'll bet you don't even eat Froot Loops."

She tried to stay exasperated; she really did. But there was something so endearing about Jackson that her exasperation kept dissolving as fast as she could shore it up.

"What sort of appointment did you accept from Mitch?"

"I'm the newest member of the Texas Railroad Commission. The title is kind of confusing. We don't have much to do with railroads—at least not anymore. Mostly we regulate the oil and gas industry. Three people were elected to head the commission, but one of them got caught with his hand in the cookie jar and resigned. Mitch talked me into filling out his term until the next general election."

"So how long will that be?"

"Oh, a year or so. Isn't that about how long you're gonna be in town?" he asked.

Her eyes narrowed. Was that a smile or a smirk on his lips? "Why can't I believe that this is a coincidence? When did the governor ask you to take the position?"

"About six weeks ago. Long before you came to Texas—though if I'd known you were going to be living in Austin, I'd have already been here to greet you. Want a tour of my house?"

"Maybe some other time. I'd like to pick up the desk and get busy on it. It will have to be stripped."

"I'll help," he said, a slow grin spreading over his face as he gently hooked his arm around her neck. "Stripping is one of my specialties."

Olivia scraped the last blob of bubbly green goop from the table and wiped it down with a rag. Under all that paint, she'd found solid walnut. It was going to be beautiful. She dropped the rag on the newspapers layered over a shady section of Tessa's driveway and picked up a steel wool pad to finish the process.

She hesitated a moment in her task, and her eyes went immediately to the male tush in tight jeans sticking out from under her car hood. Make that two taut male tushes. One was Jackson's, the other was Bill Jurney's. Jackson had insisted on tinkering with her air conditioner, and no sooner had he lifted the hood than the teenaged Bill joined him. It must be a male thing Olivia supposed. Jackson and Bill seemed to have bonded already, laughing and talking and taking a trip to the auto parts store for various doodads. Bill, who had obtained his driver's license only a few weeks ago, now practically worshipped the long-legged Texan who seemed to know all about cars.

"I believe that's got it," Jackson said. He stood and glanced toward Olivia. When he caught her watching him, he winked. "I think we fixed it. How's the stripping coming along?"

"I'm almost finished with this step. I still need to stain it. Did you really fix my air conditioner?"

"Think so. Bill, crank her up and let's see if she's cooling now."

After running the engine for a few minutes, Jackson pronounced the job done and closed the hood. Still wiping his hands on a rag, he strolled over to where she worked. "Say, that's looking great. Need any help?"

"You've done more than enough if you've repaired my car and saved me from melting in this Texas heat. Thank you so much. You're a godsend, but I must insist on paying for all the parts you used."

"No problem. Like I told you, it's just being neighborly. The parts didn't come to more than ten dollars, and I had some spare coolant. Bake me a chocolate pie some time, and we'll call it square."

"That's a deal." Of course she'd never baked a chocolate pie in her life, but she could certainly follow a recipe—or buy one from the bakery.

Jackson insisted on helping with the desk, and having two people working did make the staining go faster. He helped her move it into the garage and stayed for the first coat of varnish.

"I can't believe that's the same piece of furniture you got this morning," he said. "It looks real nice."

"I'm pleased with it." She cleaned her tools, then snapped off her rubber gloves and laid them aside. "I'll put another coat of varnish on it tomorrow."

Jackson glanced at his watch. "Looks like I've got just enough time to go clean up before dinner. I'll be back in a shake."

"Oh, I can't go out with you. Tessa has a meeting, and I promised to grill hamburgers with Jenny and Bill and a couple of their friends."

"I know." He winked. "Bill told me. I'm invited, too, and I'm bringing the ice cream."

During the cookout and afterward as they sat in lawn chairs in the backyard, Jackson charmed Bill and Jenny and their friends the same as he charmed everyone else. Jenny and the Dobson twins, Erin and Edie, from down the street were absolutely moon-eyed over him and giggled through the evening as only thirteen-year-old girls can giggle. Bill and his friend Greg glanced at each other and rolled their eyes at the girls' behavior, but they hung on to every word of Jackson's account of camping and white-water rafting in Idaho.

"That's awesome," Greg said.

"Yeah," Bill added. "How old were you when you went the first time?"

"Oh, my brother Matt and my cousin Smith were about your age, maybe a year older. Kyle and I were two or three years older than that, in college as I recall."

"Wow," Bill said, "what a great way to spend the summer."

"Yeah," Jenny added wistfully. "I'd love to go."

"Oh, Jen, get real," her brother said. "You'd be scared to death."

"I would not!"

"Hey, pardners," Jackson said quietly. The squabbling stopped immediately. "Tell you what. We can't go white-water rafting down the Salmon, but we can go tubing down the Guadalupe." He turned to Olivia. "Ever done that?"

"I don't even know what you're talking about, so I suppose I haven't."

Both Greg and the Dobson twins were familiar with tubing, so they explained how you used an inner tube from a truck tire to sit in while the current of the shallow river swept you along.

"It's loads of fun," Erin said. Or was it Edie? Olivia still couldn't tell them apart. "But we haven't been in *ages*."

"We'll all go one weekend soon," Jackson said, "if your parents say it's okay."

"Go where?" Tessa said, joining the group.

"Hi, Tessa," Olivia said. "I didn't hear you drive up. Jackson is promising to take the kids on a tubing trip."

"Only if you go, too," Jackson told her.

"Oh, I don't know about—"

"Please, Olivia," Jenny said. "Please, please, please. It will be such fun!"

When the twins and the boys added their own pleas, Olivia threw up her hands and conceded. "But only if your parents agree."

"I'll agree," Tessa said, beaming.

Olivia shot her a dirty look, but Tessa only beamed wider. From the moment Tessa had met Jackson earlier in the afternoon and heard an abbreviated—and sanitized—version of their past history, Olivia knew that Tessa had matchmaking on her mind.

"We'll see," Olivia said.

"How about next weekend?" Jackson asked to the delight of the kids. "If we wait too long, the season will be over."

"But there are seven of us, eight if Tessa comes."

"Count me out," Tessa said. "I don't swim—or tube, but you can use my SUV."

"No problem," Jackson told her. "I'll have one of the guys bring a van from the club."

"What club?"

"Crow's Nest," Jackson said. "My golf club and lodge in East Texas."

"Crow's Nest?" Tessa said. "I believe my husband Ed has been there on golfing weekends with his company."

Jackson nodded, but didn't comment further.

"Come on, kids," Tessa said, "it's time to break up the party. Bill, would you and Greg walk Erin and Edie home? Night all!" She shepherded Jenny inside, and the others walked away, leaving Olivia and Jackson alone.

"I have to say good-night, as well," Olivia told him. "Thanks again for fixing my car and helping with the desk."

"You're welcome."

She turned to leave, but he fell into step beside her. "I'll walk you to your door."

"It's just up those steps."

"I know, but my mama always told me to see a lady to her door."

The stairs were too narrow to walk abreast, so she led the way, excruciatingly aware of him close behind her. Once on the landing, she turned nervously toward him. "We're here!"

"So I see." He reached up and unscrewed the glaring light bulb.

"Why did—"

"Bugs."

Before she could protest, he kissed her.

His mouth was warm and wonderful, his arms strong and secure.

Pushing him away was difficult. But after a minute or two, she finally found the resolve to do so.

She drew a shuddering breath and said, "That's one of the rules we need to establish. No kissing."

His arms stayed wrapped firmly around her. "No kissing?"

"No kissing."

"Not even a little one like this?" He touched the end of her nose with his lips.

She shook her head.

"Or this?" He pressed his mouth against one eyelid, then the other.

"No."

"What about this?" he whispered beside her ear before his tongue traced the inner shell.

She sucked in a gasp as white-hot flame flared inside her. "Absolutely not!"

"Oh, sugar, I may just die if you won't let me kiss you." He bent and captured her lips once again.

Her knees sagged, and she clung to him, trying to conjure up the resolve that had escaped her once again.

She might have kissed him forever if Jackson hadn't broken it off and said, "Night, darlin'. Sleep tight."

He turned and sauntered down the stairs; she stood welded to the spot, feeling as though she'd been hit by a lightning bolt.

Five

The sun was barely up when Olivia started sanding. She hadn't slept worth a darn all night, so she'd finally given up and gone downstairs to work on the desk. She'd rehearsed exactly what she planned to say to Jackson scores of times, tossing and turning between each version of her speech. While many—if not most—women would be delighted with his attentiveness, she had no intention of being anything other than a friend to him.

There would be no more kissing, no more…anything else. She intended to finish her dissertation, do her internship, then go into practice. Having another man in her life didn't figure into her plans. She had learned her lesson. She intended to be totally self-sufficient and goal oriented.

Despite her determination to disregard Jackson, her gaze kept drifting to the house across the street.

Nothing stirred.

She wiped down the desk with a tack rag and glanced over again. Still nothing.

She was almost finished with the varnishing when Jackson's pickup pulled into his driveway. Where in the world had he been so early?

Not that it was any of her business—nor did she care where he'd been. She directed her focus to the stroke of her brush down the table leg.

"Mornin'," a deep voice said.

Olivia glanced up to find Jackson standing a few feet away. She hadn't even heard his footsteps. The man moved like a wraith, even in boots.

"Good morning," she answered. "You're up early."

"Early? Darlin', I've already played nine holes this morning."

"Of golf?"

"Yep. Promised Mitch. I beat him nine out of nine holes, so he was ready to quit. Tell you the truth, I was glad. I was hoping you'd be up by now. Had breakfast?"

"No, but—"

"Good. Me neither, and my stomach's about stuck to my backbone. Let's go grab a bite at the Magnolia Cafe. They make the best gingerbread pancakes you've ever eaten and omelets that nearly float off the plate."

"I don't think so, but thank you. I'll have a bagel when I'm finished here."

"Looks like you're about done to me. And they have bagels at the Magnolia. They have anything your

heart desires, but I never could pass up their gingerbread pancakes.''

She tried to explain she didn't want to make a habit
of going places with him, that she didn't want to see
him socially and that she didn't plan on kissing him—
or doing anything else with him—again. She told him
everything that she had rehearsed in great detail during the wee hours of the morning.

He just smiled and said, ''Okay, darlin', if you just
want us to be friends, we'll be friends. Come on. I'm
starving.''

''But I can't go like this.'' She gestured to her
stain-smeared shorts and faded T-shirt. Good heavens,
she'd barely run a brush through her hair before she'd
gathered it into a rubber band—and she hadn't even
considered makeup.

''You look fine to me—and trust me, sugar, you'll
fit right in with the Austin crowd. Nobody dresses up
much around here.''

''I've noticed that.'' She tried to think of another
legitimate excuse, but she couldn't come up with one.
And to cap things off, her stomach picked that exact
time to rumble.

Jackson chuckled. ''I'll take that for a yes.''

Before she could argue, his hand was under her
arm, guiding her down the driveway.

Jackson couldn't help but grin as Olivia polished
off the last of her pancakes. God, he was crazy about
her. Just being close to her, watching her, made him
feel ten sizes bigger. Funniest damn thing—he wanted
to laugh and whoop and climb up on the table and
crow like a rooster. He'd never felt this way in his

life—and been sober. Now he was beginning to understand why Kyle and Matt acted so goofy over Irish and Eve.

Woman-like, she'd been worried about the way she looked, but he thought she looked gorgeous. He liked her dark hair kind of rumpled, and, Lord knows, lipstick and rouge couldn't have made her any more beautiful. Olivia had natural beauty—good bones, lush lips and mysterious eyes that a man could get lost in. Even in her painting clothes, she carried herself with the confidence and grace of a dancer. She oozed sex appeal. Hadn't he noticed a half dozen men watching her as they walked in the café?

Olivia could talk about just being friends all she wanted to, but friendship wasn't what he had in mind for her. He wanted her by his side and in his bed. But he wasn't anybody's fool. He knew not to rush her, sensing that whatever made her skittish was some heavy baggage she carried. Irish had hinted at it but wouldn't tell him the details. Things were going to take some time, and he was determined to be patient—and persistent. He wasn't going anywhere, nor was he going to let her get away again. He would follow her to hell and back. Just call him glue.

He itched to touch her, to stroke her cheek with the back of his hand, to run his thumb along her bottom lip, then lick it to taste the syrup lingering there. But if he did, she'd probably give him another one of those "platonic relationship" lectures. Unable to keep his hands off her another second, he reached across the table and touched her cheek.

She startled.

"Eyelash," he said quickly, smiling.

"Oh. Thank you." She put down her fork and sighed. "I can't believe I ate so much. But you were right. The pancakes were delicious." Glancing around the room, she added, "And you were right. I'm not any more grungy than anyone else."

"Austin is pretty laid-back, and they have some of the best food in the state. We could eat at a different place every meal and not run out of restaurants for a couple of years. Have you ever tried rattlesnake?"

She laughed with that low, throaty sound that rippled his backbone. "No, and I'm not interested in trying it." She laughed again, and her eyes crinkled and sparkled the way he loved—the way he thought of her at night when he couldn't sleep.

"Actually, it's not bad. There's a really great restaurant just outside of town that has excellent exotic game dishes, everything from wild boar to alligator. I'd like to take you one night. We have some fine chili parlors and an Irish pub with food, drinks and music on Sunday nights. We can go there tonight if you want."

She laid her hand across his. "Jackson, didn't you hear a word I said to you earlier?"

He put his other hand over hers. "What was that, darlin'?"

"This…this thing between you and me. It can't go anywhere. I've told you that over and over."

"And what thing is that, darlin'?"

His eyes were riveted on her lips as she licked them. "This…this thing, this feeling…this feeling…"

He leaned forward and said softly, "You mean this feeling that comes over me and makes me want to lay you on the table naked and pour that jug of syrup over your body and lick up every drop?''

Her eyes widened suddenly, and she swallowed. ''Jackson!''

''Sorry, darlin'.''

She jerked her hand away. ''Please stop calling me that. I'm not your *darlin'*. Let's go. We need to discuss this. In private.'' She stood and strode toward the door.

Oh, hell, he thought as he fished for his wallet. He'd torn it now. Why couldn't he have kept his damned mouth shut? Just because he was thinking it, didn't mean he had to say it out loud. He heaved an exasperated sigh, threw a bill on the table and followed her out. Why couldn't she just admit that the chemistry between them was explosive? Anybody with half a brain could tell they were perfect together, and she was smart.

She was also sod-pawing mad. She tore up his pea patch all the way home. He tried to sweet talk her out of her peeve, but his best efforts didn't work. He finally figured that he was better off just to keep his mouth shut and hope that her anger would blow over. For the life of him he couldn't understand why she'd gotten so angry.

Olivia didn't understand why she'd gotten so angry. She had totally overreacted. If she had berated Thomas the way she had torn into Jackson, he would have beaten her senseless. Jackson hadn't even lost his temper. He'd simply said, ''Now, darlin', you're breakin' my heart,'' every time she took a breath.

Oh, come on, Olivia. You've had enough psychol-

ogy to know why you overreacted. It was an ego defense mechanism, pure and simple. The erotic syrup image was more appealing than she was comfortable admitting. He was coming too close, and it was scary. There was no denying that she was very drawn to Jackson, that she enjoyed his company, that she found him incredibly attractive and enormously sexy. That was the problem.

It would be so easy—

No. She wasn't ready to trust a man with her heart again. It had taken a lot of work to get to where she was now; she wasn't going to blow it for another man.

After a quick shower Olivia dressed and grabbed her backpack. She planned to spend several hours in the library doing research.

As she backed out of her driveway, a little red car pulled into the driveway across the street. A very cute blonde, who was at least ten years younger than Olivia and wearing teeny-tiny shorts and a sassy little cropped top went bouncing up to the gate of Jackson's courtyard. She opened the gate and went inside and out of Olivia's sight.

Olivia hesitated for a few moments, fastening her seat belt and adjusting the mirrors, but the blonde didn't make a quick exit.

So much for Jackson's broken heart, she thought as she threw the car into Drive and peeled away.

She muttered all the way to the university library, mostly about male mentality and her stupidity for caring one iota about what Jackson Crow did with his spare time. She *didn't* care, she reminded herself. And, as a matter of fact, if he spent time with Miss

Short Shorts, then he wouldn't be bothering her. Which was just fine.

Just fine.

Finally she settled down and got some research done, reading, making photocopies of articles and checking out a tall stack of books. By the time she lugged her material to her car and drove home, the sun was hanging low over the tree-covered limestone hills.

The little red car was still in Jackson's driveway.

Damn!

No, scratch that. She didn't care. Not one single bit.

Chin high, she wheeled into her parking space, gathered her stuff and slammed the car door behind her. She stomped up the steps to her apartment, dumped her belongings on the couch and went directly to the kitchen sink. She didn't go there because the window afforded a perfect view of the tile-roofed hacienda; she went there because she was thirsty. She drank two glasses of water, very slowly, then dusted the sink with scouring powder and began to scrub the shiny porcelain.

Her fingers were beginning to pucker when Miss Hot Pants bounced through the gate. Jackson sauntered along after her, and the two of them were laughing. When they reached the little red car, the blonde turned, tiptoed and kissed Jackson on the cheek.

Olivia slammed the sponge in the sink and stalked off. With her tiny apartment, she didn't have much stalking room, so she opted for a shower.

As he always did after one of those marathon sessions, Jackson had a splitting headache. He took a couple of aspirin and rocked back in his recliner to let them take effect. He dozed for a few minutes, and when he woke after about half an hour, he felt better. He washed his face and hightailed it across the street to Olivia's apartment.

On his way he checked the desk in the garage and found that the varnish was dry. He carried it upstairs and set it on the landing.

When he knocked on her door, she didn't open it. Instead, he heard a muffled acknowledgment from the other side.

"Hey, darlin', it's Jackson. Want to grab a hotdog and go to a movie?"

She opened the door a crack, and he tried to go inside, but the screen door was latched. He couldn't see much of her, but it looked as if she had a towel or something wrapped around her head.

"I'm sorry, but no. I'm conditioning my hair, and I have to make preparations for my classes tomorrow."

"How about I go pick up some barbecue or get some Chinese takeout? You've got to have dinner."

"No, thank you." And damned if she didn't slam the door in his face.

He knocked on the door again.

She didn't answer.

"I brought your desk up," he yelled.

After a long pause, the door opened again. "That wasn't necessary."

"I know that it wasn't necessary, but it's too heavy for you to be struggling with. Unlatch the screen, and I'll bring it in."

She didn't look too happy about it, but she did as he asked and stood back as he carried the writing desk inside.

"Where do you want this?"

"There by the window."

He positioned the desk and stepped back. "You know, it looks great. You did a fine job with that old green castoff we bought. I never would have thought something so pretty could be under all that ugly paint."

"Thank you."

"Glad to oblige."

He hadn't missed that she was wearing a robe, and she clutched the front of it primly to her throat. She smelled like bubble gum and wildflowers.

"Sure I can't talk you into some barbecue? Some ribs would really be good. Or maybe some brisket. I really hate to eat by myself."

"Perhaps Miss Hot Pants will go with you."

He frowned. "Miss Hot Pants?"

"The bouncy little blonde in the cropped top that you spent the afternoon with."

"Bouncy—you mean Tami?"

"Yes, I suppose her name would be Tami. Or Tiffany."

He laughed. By damn, if he didn't know better, he'd think Olivia was jealous. Well, well, well. He considered stringing her along for a while, but he decided not to chance it. The truth always worked best. "Sugar, Tami is one of my assistants."

"Assistants? She doesn't look much older than Bill Jurney—not that I had more than a glance at her. I mean, I just happened to see her arrive as I was leaving. She's very...cute.''

"Yes, she is cute. And smart as a whip. So's Paulie.''

"Who's Paulie?''

"Tami's little boy. Hers and Jimmy's. He's almost three.''

"Jimmy?''

"No, Paulie. I think Jimmy is about twenty-four.''

"Wait a minute,'' Olivia said. "Who is Jimmy?''

"Jimmy is Tami's husband. They've both worked for me at Crow's Nest for years. Tami's daddy and I go way back. They were real tickled when I took the appointment here. Jimmy graduated from the local junior college last May, and now he's going to take classes at UT. He plans on being a vet.''

"I see.''

Was he imagining it, or did her face soften after he explained who Tami was? No, there was a definite softening. "Can I convince you to change your mind about the barbecue?''

"No, I'm having soup. I was preparing it when you banged on the door.''

"What kind?''

"Chicken noodle.''

He grinned. "Great. That's my favorite. I'll eat with you.''

"But...but it's only canned soup.''

"I love canned soup. Long noodles or round?''

"Long.''

"Perfect. Where are the crackers?''

Six

Olivia tried every excuse she could think of to get out of going tubing with Jackson and the kids, but between Jackson, Jenny and, of all people, Cherokee Pete, she finally conceded defeat. Buddy, a young man who worked at Crow's Nest, had brought a mini-bus from the East Texas lodge on Friday evening, and Jackson's grandfather had come along for the ride.

"Wanted to see your new house," Pete had told his grandson. "Besides, I couldn't miss a chance at tubing." He'd even talked Tessa into joining them.

On Saturday morning, after Jen's early soccer game, the five adults and five kids piled into the mini-bus with their gear and drove to New Braunfels. The route through the hill country was breathtaking with its craggy limestone hills, still lush with cedar and small oak trees that covered the rises like mounds of green tufted pillows.

Olivia sat next to a window with Jackson beside her, his arm casually draped across the back of her seat. He commented on various points of interest as they rode, but for the life of her, she couldn't concentrate. He was very close.

She could smell his aftershave and feel the warmth of his body as he leaned across her to gesture toward some site or the other. He was so close that she could almost count his eyelashes, and she noted the laugh lines that radiated from the corner of his eyes.

He caught her watching him and winked. She quickly turned her attention back to the scenery. He didn't say anything, and neither did she, but the air between them vibrated with awareness. She was relieved when Jen and the twins got everyone involved in a game of twenty questions.

In an hour they arrived at the river where they rented inner tubes. Buddy took care of the rental details, and soon they were in the river, all wearing bathing suits and T-shirts and sneakers to protect their feet from the rocky shallows. Even Jackson traded his boots for well-worn sneakers.

Olivia had never had so much fun in her life. They drifted down the shallow stretch, sometimes slowly, sometimes at a faster clip, paddling around rocks and shouting to one another. They sang silly songs and laughed and splashed until they landed on a sand bar, then they hoisted the tubes and walked upriver to begin the trip again.

Cherokee Pete, at eighty-plus, stayed in the thick of things, and when they stopped for a picnic lunch, the kids gathered around the old man like bees to a honey pot.

Olivia stretched out on a quilt to allow her lunch to settle and listened to Pete's endless supply of tales—which captivated her as much as it did the young people. Jackson dropped down beside her, casually eased her head onto his thigh, then sat sipping the last of his soft drink and twirling a wildflower between his fingers.

"Having fun?" he asked.

"Umm," she managed to answer, her eyes closing. Feeling totally relaxed for the first time since she couldn't remember when, a delicious languor stole over her, and she wanted to drift in that peace forever.

Distant laughter, the river's rush, a balmy day and the smells of water and grass and mustard lulled her deeper. The company of Jackson and his grandfather and the others brought a comforting sense of security that wrapped her like a down bunting.

The kids left first, Buddy going with them to supervise. His grandfather glanced at the sleeping Olivia, smiled, then rose and headed for the river. Tessa winked at Jackson, then she, too, stood and left.

Jackson didn't have the heart to wake her, wouldn't have for the world. She looked as peaceful and trusting as a child, sleeping with her head on his lap. He hadn't realized how strained her face always looked until he saw it relaxed. He wondered for the umpteenth time exactly what it was that dogged her so.

Deep feelings for her began to stir inside him, catching at his chest and his throat. She sighed, shifted slightly and slipped her hand under her cheek and atop his fly—or where his fly would have been if he'd been wearing jeans instead of a flimsy bathing

suit. His feelings weren't the only thing that was beginning to stir.

He silently muttered a colorful curse and tried to
get his mind on something else, but his mind went
back like an oiled gate hinge. Things got progres-
sively harder.

Caught somewhere between heaven and hell, Jackson endured. He sat there and endured, sat there with
his sword and held off the dragon while she slept.

The following afternoon Cherokee Pete knocked on
Olivia's door while she was engrossed in lecture notes
for her classes.

"Come in," Olivia said, holding open the screen
door. "I was just about to stop for a glass of tea. I
hope you'll join me."

"Don't mind if I do, Miss Olivia," he said, stepping inside and looking around. "Right pretty place
you have here. Yessiree, right pretty. I like that rocking chair. Puts me in mind of one my wife used to
have."

"Thanks. I found it in a junk shop and refinished
it."

His gnarled fingers stroked the carving on the high
back, then set the chair to rocking. "Did a good job.
My wife was handy at that kind of thing, too."

"Has she been gone long?"

He sighed. "More years than I like to remember.
Say, I was hoping you wouldn't mind an old codger
interrupting your afternoon for a little bit. Jackson and
Tami were working on commission business, and
Buddy went to visit with Tami's husband, Jimmy.
I've already finished the murder mystery I brought

with me, and Jackson doesn't have a blamed thing in the house to read except cases coming before the Railroad Commission tomorrow.''

"If you're looking for something to read, you're welcome to look through my bookshelves. I like mysteries, too, and I've picked up several at garage sales lately. Seems like anywhere I land I start collecting books.''

"Me, too,'' Pete said, "and I'm much obliged for the offer. I could go to the bookstore, but Buddy took Jackson's pickup, and I wasn't too keen on trying to drive the bus or that fancy foreign job of Jackson's, especially since I'm not too familiar with the town.''

"Would you like for me to drive you to the bookstore?''

"Oh, no,'' Pete said, squatting to look at the titles on the lower shelf. "I see two or three here that I haven't read—if you don't mind me borrowing them.'' He selected two books by Mary Willis Walker, an Austin mystery writer Olivia had recently discovered.

"Those are excellent. I think you'll enjoy them.''

He also picked up a title by psychologist Carl Jung and thumbed through it. "I'm right fond of Jung. I haven't read any of his stuff in a while. I'm gonna do that when I get back home.''

Olivia tried to hide her shock, but it must have shown, for Pete chuckled. "Surprised that an old coot like me reads books by psychologists?''

She smiled. "A little bit, I suppose. Sorry.''

"No need to be sorry. Most people are shocked out of their gourds when they see my library at home. My wife—she was a schoolteacher, you know—well, she taught me to read and taught me a love of books that has endured for over sixty years. I read purt-near everything.''

''I'm impressed. I love books, too.''

''Speaks well for your character. I didn't have much in the way of formal education, but I put a high price on it. That's why I dangled a carrot for my grandkids to go to college. They were all good students, too. Well,'' he said, chuckling, '''cept for Jackson. He never cared much for books and schooling— had his mind on other things—but he kept on until he got that college degree.

''Always seemed peculiar to me. Of all my grandchildren, Jackson's the smartest of the lot, smarter even than Smith, and he's a whiz, let me tell you. You haven't met Smith, have you? He's into making computers. Lives down in the Valley and grows cotton and citrus fruit, too.''

''You're very proud of your grandchildren, aren't you?'' Olivia asked, smiling at the old man's preening comments.

''That I am. Shows, does it?'' He laughed and slapped his thigh. ''I've been real blessed. I have two fine daughters, five outstanding grandchildren, and two super-duper great-grandchildren—with another on the way.''

''Let's have that tea, and you can tell me about those super-duper great-grandchildren.''

He smiled broadly. ''I don't take much prodding to run off at the mouth. And, say, before I forget it, I've got a big pot of chili simmering on the stove, and you're invited to supper. I won't take no for an answer.''

"Then I suppose that I'll just have to say yes."

"While you're in such an agreeable mood, young lady, how about taking me up on that other offer I made?"

Olivia frowned. "Which offer?"

A mischievous sparkle lit his eyes. "The one where I give you five million to marry Jackson."

"Forget it, Pete. Not even for you would I get married again. Do you like lemon in your tea?"

Olivia couldn't believe how quickly the weeks passed. Perhaps it was because her life was full and she was content, but before she knew it, September was gone and October was almost over. The last Saturday in the month dawned with a bit of crispness in the air—still warm, but with a definite hint of fall. Olivia threw open the windows of her apartment and was about to make a bowl of cereal when she heard a scratching at her door.

She opened it, expecting to see Jackson with another invitation to breakfast or to the movies or to some other event. No one was there.

Then she looked down. A puppy sat on the landing, an envelope in its mouth. "Well, hello there, little fella," she said, scooping up the ball of brown and white fluff into her arms. "What have you here?"

She tried to take the envelope from his mouth, but he wouldn't let go. He growled a little puppy growl and shook his head from side to side in a tugging game.

"Hey, Sport," Jackson said from a spot halfway down the stairs, "you're supposed to deliver it to the lady, not mangle it." He grinned up at Olivia. "Sorry.

We practiced and practiced, but he's young yet. The only thing he has down pat is eating and piddling on the carpet.''

"He's adorable. What kind is he, and where did you get him?"

"What kind? Who knows? I believe that his mama was a golden retriever and his papa was a champion fence jumper. I got him at the SPCA. Jimmy works there part-time, and he and Tami talked me into it. Tami is a one-woman adoption agency for the commission. Everybody in the building will have a new pet before she's finished. Want a kitten? Or maybe a goat?''

"No, thanks. I don't think Tessa would appreciate it.''

"I don't think Mrs. Lopez is too thrilled about Rowdy here, either.'' Mrs. Lopez was the house-keeper Jackson had hired a few weeks before. "He hasn't quite gotten the hang of indoor living, and she banished both of us while the kitchen floor dries. Want to go to Zilker Park with us?''

"I was just about to have some cereal.''

"Poured the milk yet?''

"No.''

"Good. Dump it back in the box, and we'll stop for a sausage biscuit and orange juice. I want to try out my new kite.''

"Your *kite?*''

"Yep. It's a fine one.''

He wore his customary boots and sunglasses along with well-worn jeans, straw hat and a T-shirt extolling the virtues of a popular beer. He looked better outfit-ted for horseback riding or bar hopping than a romp in the park. "Somehow I can't picture you flying a kite."

"Oh, sure. Matt and my cousins and I used to spend most of the summer making and flying kites. We got pretty good at it. My new one is professionally made—a black bat wing with dual controls. Matt sent it to me for my birthday."

"Is *today* your birthday?" she asked, feeling terrible that she hadn't even bought him a card.

"Nope. Tomorrow. Come on. Let's go to the park."

She hesitated. It seemed that they were spending more and more time together—most weekends and several times during the week they went out to dinner or to a movie or to a play that Jackson had tickets for. She always enjoyed herself, but she planned to pass the current weekend alone for a change.

"Sorry, but I want to go to the bookstore and do some browsing this morning."

"Tell you what. Let's go to the park for a while, then we'll drop Roscoe here off, have some lunch and spend the afternoon browsing in the bookstore."

"I thought the puppy's name was Rowdy."

"I haven't decided on a name yet. I'm trying out different ones to see which one fits best."

"That may be part of your problem in training him. The poor thing is confused."

"Ach, an identity crisis you sink, Frau Freud?" Jackson asked in a terrible German accent.

"I sink," she said, laughing, "that you'd better stick to English."

"I'll have you know, darlin', that I had four years of Spanish and four years of French in college." He grinned. "'Course I only got credit for two of each. Come on, *cheri,* we're burning daylight."

As usual, Olivia ended up going with him. After all, she thought, making another in her endless list of excuses to herself, tomorrow was his birthday. And nobody could make her laugh and feel quite as carefree as Jackson Crow.

And nobody could make her feel quite as safe—or quite as vulnerable—as Jackson Crow.

At the park, before Jackson could slip the new leash on, the puppy barked and took off after a butterfly. Yelling didn't stop the determined little fellow, so Jackson went one way and Olivia the other, trying to corral him. Every time they were about to pounce, the puppy, thinking it was a grand game, slipped through their legs and shot off in the opposite direction.

"That little dickens is like a streak of greased lightning," Jackson said as he ran after the scamp. "Try to cut him off at the tree."

They chased him for a quarter hour until Jackson finally caught him by the scruff of the neck and fell laughing into the tall grass of the field. "Lord, I'm worn out," he said, rolling onto his back and holding the wiggling dog on his chest. "How about you, Streak?" he asked the puppy.

The puppy yapped and wagged his tail.

Olivia laughed as she dropped down cross-legged beside them. "I think you may have named him. How about it, Streak?"

The puppy yapped again and licked Jackson's nose.

"Streak it is," Jackson said, slipping the leash on. "I think I'm too tuckered to fly my kite."

"Absolutely not!" Olivia said, hopping to her feet "I want to see it."

They went back to the truck, retrieved the kite and Olivia held Streak's leash while Jackson got the big black bat wing into the air.

It was a glorious thing looping and diving and swirling high in the air. Jackson was very adept, and she enjoyed watching him put the kite through various tricky maneuvers. She also enjoyed watching the man—watching how his arms and back and shoulders moved with the strength and grace of a big cat. How familiar those arms had become.

How often, like now, she ached to have them around her. No matter how many times she told herself to keep her distance, she discovered that all those warnings were futile. The plain fact was she was attracted to Jackson Crow. She enjoyed his company. Why shouldn't she let him hold her or kiss her? She was a mature woman with needs. He was a mature man with needs. Perhaps they could have a relationship of sorts. Such an arrangement didn't have to mean a lifetime commitment. It wasn't as if she planned to marry him, for heaven sakes.

Hmm. She was going to have to give this some thought.

"Want to try it?" Jackson asked.

She almost blushed, then realized that he was talking about flying the kite. "Sure. Why not? What do I do?"

She tied the puppy to a signpost, then, standing between Jackson's outspread feet, took the controls. With her back against his chest and his arms pressed against the outsides of hers, he guided her. In tandem, almost as one, they stood while the kite tugged at the strings, strained at the controls as if it wanted to break free and soar to the clouds and beyond. It danced on the currents and dove with a pull of the cord, yet its goal seemed to be to snap the restraints and fly untethered to the top of the world.

For some strange reason, tears clogged her throat for a heartbeat. Silly, she told herself, that a kite could move her to such sentimentality, but at that moment she felt an overwhelming kinship with it.

And with Jackson.

As if they were one. Their arms and bodies continued to move in perfect synchronization.

Perfect.

They were perfect together.

Perfect.

From nowhere, panic rushed in and flooded her body. She struggled in his arms, stepping on his foot in her haste to get away from him, from the power of the moment.

"Ouch! Whoa, sugar," Jackson said, grabbing for the controls. "What's wrong?"

"Let me go. I can't breathe." She struggled wildly.

"Hang on a second." He nosedived the kite and dropped the strings. He grabbed her upper arms and faced her to him. "What's happening? What can I do?"

"Nothing," she said, splaying one hand across her heaving chest and pushing him back with the other. "Give me a minute." She turned, walked away and sucked in several deep breaths.

As she began to calm herself with a familiar ritual,

she felt like a damned fool. She hadn't had a panic attack in ages.

"Honey?" Jackson's voice sounded worried.

She made a big show of coughing and patting her chest before she turned around. She took another big breath, then pasted on a smile. "Sorry. Allergies. Must be something blooming around here that disagrees with me. For a moment there something took my breath away—literally."

"Do you need to go to a doctor—or to the emergency room?"

"Heavens, no. I have some pills in my apartment." That part was true. She had some antihistamines that the doctor had given her for problems caused by the terrible cedar pollen.

"Let's go get you one." He grabbed her elbow and started propelling her to the pickup.

"Hold on," she said. "It's not critical. We can't leave Streak and the kite. I'll get the puppy while you wind up the kite."

On the way home, Olivia had to caution Jackson twice to slow down. Realizing the extent of his concern, she felt terrible for fibbing to him. But she would have felt worse having to admit her anxiety. As a soon-to-be psychologist, she felt absolutely stupid for being prey to her emotions. In her head she knew that Jackson was a very different kind of man than Thomas or her father. She didn't feel threatened by him—especially after having gotten to know him over the past several weeks. But emotions didn't have brains, they weren't ruled by reason or logic. Propelled by the past, they sped directly from the unconscious to the nerve endings.

She was sure that she'd gotten over most of her anxiety, but obviously a lot of old baggage remained inside her, hanging around to give her grief if she strayed too far from safety. Therapy had been helpful but time often was the best healer.

Obviously, she wasn't ready to trust Jackson yet. A relationship with him was still too threatening.

Back at her apartment, Jackson insisted on coming inside while she took her medication. There was nothing to do but continue her charade.

Oh, what a tangled web we weave… she thought as she unlocked her door.

Jackson picked up the envelope that Streak had mangled earlier. "I forgot to tell you," he said, "that we're invited to the governor's mansion for a reception. This is the invitation. It's in three weeks."

"What's the occasion?" she asked over her shoulder as she headed for the kitchen alcove.

"Meeting the president and the first lady."

"You're kidding, right?"

"Nope. It's for real. Wanna go rub elbows with the movers and shakers?"

Her first inclination was to say no, but who refused an invitation like that? "I'd love to meet the president and the first lady." She picked up the medicine bottle on the counter and turned to Jackson. "I don't think I need this after all, I'm feeling much better now."

"Then we need to stay inside. No pill, no bookstore."

She took the blasted pill.

Seven

"**I** love this place," Olivia said as they walked into the large bookstore. She took a deep breath and savored the distinctive scent of pristine pages and new bindings. "Don't you love the way it smells?"

"Sure do," Jackson said. "Want a cup?"

She glanced at him and frowned. "Pardon?"

"Want a cup of coffee?"

When she caught the subtle aroma of coffee from the bar to the side of the huge area, she understood his question. "Not now. I was talking about the way the bookstore smells, better even than libraries. Libraries smell like history and tradition, and bookstores like this one smell like new beginnings. I love the scent of books, new or old."

"I guess I never paid much attention. Are you looking for anything special?"

She shook her head. "I thought I would check out the new arrivals, then browse the bargain tables. How about you? Interested in anything particular? We've never talked much about our favorite authors. Who's yours?"

"Oh, uh, I have several," he said. "What about you?"

She smiled. "Me, too. My list is endless. For fun I like to read mysteries or romantic comedies. What about you? What are some of your favorite books?"

"Well, let's see. Uh…uh, I like mysteries, too. And Westerns. I like Westerns a lot."

"Don't tell me. I'll bet you like Louis L'Amour." She grinned.

"He's not bad. Let's see, uh, I liked *Lonesome Dove*."

"McMurtry's great, isn't he? You know, I think he has a new book out. Want to check? You need to start filling up all those bookshelves in your den. Why don't we split up, and I'll meet you at the coffee bar in half an hour or so."

"Sounds good to me."

Jackson waited until Olivia disappeared behind the stacks before he hurried to the information desk in the center of the store. What on earth had possessed him to come to this place with her? He must have been nuts. He'd sooner walk barefoot through a field of grass burrs than to set foot in a bookstore—or a library. Being around all these books made him edgy. He shook his head. Of all people, he *would* have to fall head over heels with a book lover. Go figure.

At the information table, he eased over to a kid

with a badge on his chest and said quietly, "Say, I need some help."

"Yes, sir. What can I do for you?" His words seemed to reverberate through the store.

"Shhhh. Keep it down." Jackson glanced around to see if he could spot Olivia. He couldn't. "I want to buy some books, and I need help," he said softly. "I want a lot of books—in a hurry."

"What kind do you want?" the young guy whispered.

Jackson glanced over his should again, then said, "I want everything you've got by L'Amour and McMurtry, all the latest bestsellers, ten or twelve of your best new mysteries, and, oh, some romantic comedies."

Jackson had to hand it to the kid. His eyebrows barely moved. "Yes, sir. The bestsellers, do you want fiction or nonfiction?"

"Both."

"Hardback or paperback?"

"Hardback. And there's an extra fifty in it for you if you can help me gather them up in twenty minutes and keep quiet about helping me."

"Let's take a buggy."

The kid grabbed a cart and took off toward the back of the store like a prairie fire with a tailwind. Jackson took off after him. They stopped at a large display.

"These are the latest bestsellers," the kid said out of the side of his mouth. "Want one of each?"

"Yeah."

The kid grabbed one from each pile, dumped them in the cart, then took a hard right and went up two aisles. "McMurtry," he whispered. He pulled several books and added them to the rest. "Let's get L'Amour, then we'll tackle the mysteries."

They hurried down the center aisle, the kid steering the buggy like a speed demon. They stopped at another shelf, and his helper frowned.

"Something wrong?" Jackson asked.

"Well, most of our L'Amour are paperbacks. That and tapes."

"Tapes?"

"Yeah, you know, like cassette tapes for when you're driving your car. We have a couple of his big collections on tape."

"Tapes?" Jackson grinned. "Well, what do you know. Tell you what, I'll take whatever you've got, hardbacks, paperbacks and all the tapes. Have you got McMurtry on tape too?"

"Oh, yeah. Grisham, too."

"Who's Grisham?"

The kid picked up a book from the buggy and flipped it over to the author picture. "Him."

"Oh, *that* Grisham," he said, not recognizing the man from a walleyed calf. "I want tapes of every book here."

"Not all of them are available on tape."

"I want the ones that are," Jackson said.

"We're gonna have to hurry if we want to beat the deadline and get tapes, too."

"I'll give you an extra five minutes and an extra fifty bucks."

"You're on." The kid burned rubber on the buggy.

They had a close call once—almost ran smack into Olivia—but Jackson managed to grab the kid and duck behind a display of calendars before she saw them.

Jackson had to hand it to the clerk, he was as fast as a dust devil. In half an hour the cart was jam-packed with merchandise. He slipped the boy a hundred and wheeled his stuff to the checkout stand.

The cashier eyed the loaded buggy, then smiled. "You must really like to read," she said.

"If you only knew," Jackson said, stacking the volumes on the counter.

After he paid for his purchases, he took the three shopping bags full of books and tapes and went to the coffee bar. He was on his second cup when Olivia appeared.

"Sorry," she said. "I lost track of the time. I do that when I get around books."

"No problem. Want a cup of coffee?"

"I think I'll have an iced cappuccino instead."

"You got it, sugar." He rose and went to the counter.

When he returned with her cappuccino, she was peering into one of his shopping bags that was sitting on the floor.

"You bought *all* these?"

"Yep. You said my shelves needed filling. I figured this was a start."

She picked up a book on top and frowned. "Why on earth did you buy a book on menopause?"

Jackson damned near dropped the cup. "It's, uh, for Mrs. Lopez."

She looked at him strangely. "Do you think she reads English well enough to comprehend this?"

"Oh, sure. You'd be surprised at how she reads."

Olivia shrugged and picked up another book. Her eyes lit up. "Oh, wonderful! One of my favorite authors. Now I know where I can borrow the new Grafton book."

"Take it now, if you want."

"Oh, no. I'll borrow it when you've finished. Have you read all the other books in the series?"

He squirmed and took a sip from his cup. Damned if he didn't feel sweat pop out. "One or two. It's been a while. He's pretty good. Want another cappuccino?"

She looked at him funny. "I've barely touched this one. Tell me, which of Grafton's is your favorite?"

"I don't recall the title. Like I said, it's been a while. Given any thought to where we might have dinner tonight?"

"Not a bit. But I have given some thought to tomorrow night. You're invited to dinner at my place. I'll even bake a cake for the occasion."

"The occasion?"

She chuckled. "Your birthday. That is, unless you have something else planned."

"Not a thing." He grinned. "Are you really going to bake me a cake?"

"I am. What's your favorite?"

"Coconut."

Olivia must have had rocks in her head. She couldn't believe that she actually promised to make a coconut cake for Jackson. She'd never baked one in her life.

It showed.

One hunk of the top layer started to slide. She

grabbed it and stuck in another half dozen toothpicks to hold it steady. Thank heavens the frosting filled in most of the cracks. She patted it where the cake showed through, then licked the gooey white from her fingers and stepped back.

That wasn't *too* bad. She opened the package of coconut flakes and began to sprinkle them over the sides and top. The top went fine, but there was a logistical problem in getting the coconut to stick to the sides. When she tried tipping the cake, another crevice opened across the top, and she feared for a moment that the whole thing would slide onto the floor. She considered every means that she could think of, including using her blow-dryer to blow it on. In the end, she just slapped on wads of flakes as best she could.

She stepped back and surveyed her work again. It looked worse than a New York street two days after a snowfall.

She sighed. Well, it would have to do. Thank heavens the rest of the meal was simple. She'd shot her budget on pork tenderloin, which was baking in the oven with its plum glaze, as well as Greek salad and roasted new potatoes. She'd bought the Greek salad and new potatoes at the deli. Tessa had given her the recipe for the tenderloin.

The table was set, the candles in place, the gift wrapped and waiting beside his place. She just had time for a quick shower before the birthday boy arrived.

Jackson's head was pounding. He'd taken more aspirin than he thought was sensible, and still his temples throbbed and his eyes ached. He'd tried his damnedest to read that Grafton book last night—and didn't he feel like a fool when he discovered that Grafton was a woman? He'd tried hard, but he just couldn't. He'd finally given up in frustration and stayed up a good part of the night listening to the tape. Thank God the kid at the bookstore had put him on to those tapes. He would have been lost without them.

To top it off, Sunday afternoon was the time that he spent a marathon session with Tami going over all the cases for hearings on Monday morning. He had a legal assistant and another reader at the office, but the worst of it he did with Tami at home. This job, at least all the reading required, was a bitch.

Lord, he hated books. He hated newspapers and magazines and case reports and the backs of cereal boxes. He hated every damned thing in the world that was printed or written or carved in stone—hated it with a passion formed by thirty-odd years of frustration and humiliation and self-disgust. How could he go on pretending to Olivia that what was so wasn't so?

He held his face up to the shower head and turned on the cold water full force, trying to chase away his usual Sunday headache.

Why in the world was he putting himself through such torture? He was a damned fool, that's why.

Then Olivia's face flashed through his mind—her sweet, beautiful, laughing face. No, it was all for Olivia. He'd endure anything for her, do anything to make her happy and see her smile. He didn't know if he could keep up this charade, but he was blamed well going to try.

She was worth it.

She was worth anything he had to do. Thank God for Tami. He wouldn't have a prayer without her. Stephanie was a big help, too. And Jennifer. Maybe he could pay the girls to put in a couple of extra evenings during the week. That might work.

As he sat with Olivia at her little table, Jackson knew for sure that he was the luckiest man alive. She'd served him a fine meal—though he wouldn't have minded a bologna sandwich if they could have shared it. A little bouquet of flowers was in the middle of the table, flanked by candles that she lit before they sat down to eat.

Olivia looked beautiful. Her hair was pinned up, and she wore a kind of loose silky top and pants in fire-engine red that shifted with every move she made, teasing over her curves just enough to drive a man crazy. He had a devil of a time eating that good food. He just wanted to watch her. And touch her. And make love to her until next April. The lady was dynamite.

"That was great," he said, putting down his napkin. "You're a fantastic cook. I'm pleasantly surprised. A beautiful woman who can cook."

She laughed that throaty little laugh that he loved. "Actually I'm not much of a cook, and you'd better withhold judgment until after the cake."

"You really baked me a cake?"

"I really did. It won't win a bake off, but I hope it's edible."

She rose and disappeared into the alcove for a few moments. She returned carrying a white cake with a single tall candle lit in the middle. As she set the plate on the table she smiled and began to sing "Happy Birthday" in a slow, breathless style that reminded him of clips he'd seen of Marilyn Monroe singing to President Kennedy. Damned near drove him wild.

"Happy birthday, Mr....Commissioner, happy—"

Unable to keep his hands off her another minute, he pulled her down into his lap and kissed away the last words of the song.

She tasted of wine and plum sauce and wildfire. He groaned and probed deeper with his tongue, stroked her breast through the silk and groaned again.

"Lord, I want you," he whispered as he nuzzled her ear.

"But...the cake."

"The cake can wait. Let me make love to you, darlin'."

She tried to say something else, but he kissed away her protests, holding her tight, thrusting his tongue deep. He was about to explode.

"Jackson, no." She pushed him away and struggled to her feet. "I...I don't want this. I'm not ready."

Her cheeks glowed with high color; her chest rose and fell with ragged breaths. She licked her lips.

"Darlin', I'm not much a one to call a lady a liar, but it seems to me that you're about as ready as I am. And let me tell you, I'm *ready*."

Lacing her fingers together tightly, she took a shuddering breath. "I'm sorry. I don't mean to be a tease, but I...it's...it's, uh, a bad time for me."

"Bad—" Then he realized what she was talking about. He nodded. "I see." He unlaced her clamped fingers, which had gone ice-cold, and kissed each hand. "Don't worry about it, sugar. How about that cake?"

She turned and looked at her creation. "It's a mess, isn't it?"

"Darlin', it's the prettiest birthday cake I've ever had—because you made it for me. Let's cut it."

"You have to make a wish and blow out the candle first."

He laughed. "That's a no-brainer." He took a deep breath and blew.

She cut big slabs and handed him a plate. "Careful of the toothpicks. I used nearly a whole box keeping that sucker together. Want some coffee?"

"That would be great. I'll get it." He started to rise, but she motioned him down.

"Stay seated. It's your birthday." She handed him a blue-striped package tied with a bandana bow. "Happy Birthday."

"Oh, honey, you didn't have to get me a present."

"Of course I did. I hope you like it. Open it while I get the coffee."

It looked so pretty that he hated to tear off the paper, but, kid-like, he ripped into it.

A book.

He was holding it in his hands staring at the picture of the kite on the front when she returned with the cups.

Her eyes lit up. "It's a book on the history of kites. Do you like it?"

He swallowed, then smiled. "I love it. What a great present."

She beamed. "I'm glad you like it. How's the cake?"

He carved a bite with his fork, pulled out a couple of toothpicks, then tasted it. "It's damned good."

Looking skeptical, she said, "Are you sure?"

"Positive." And to prove it, he ate two pieces and took the rest of it home with him.

Actually, despite its looks, the cake *was* damned good. He ate another piece before he went to bed. Sitting at the kitchen bar, alone in his big house, he decided that the evening with Olivia had been one of the best birthdays he'd had in recent years. Only one thing could have made it better—to have spent the rest of the night with her.

He wanted her here with him now. He wanted to lay the world at her feet, give her everything her heart desired, make love to her until she moaned with pleasure and said the words he wanted to hear. He wanted—

Patience, he told himself.

Olivia lay in bed thinking. On her back in the darkened room, she stared at shadows made by a sliver of moonlight coming through the blinds.

Why had she chickened out?

She had fully intended for Jackson's birthday party to end here, in this bed. Hadn't she changed the sheets and put sachet under the pillows? Hadn't she worn the most seductive of her lingerie?

The stage was set. He was turned on; she darned sure was. Then, at the last moment—or very near it—

she'd panicked again. The anxiety wasn't as severe as it had been in the park when they'd gone kite flying, but it was there. She thought that she'd reasoned the whole thing through.

Obviously, she hadn't. Why?

She hadn't detected any cruelty or extreme possessiveness in Jackson. He wasn't like Thomas...or her father. He wasn't.

But then Thomas had been wonderful and thoughtful when he was courting her. It was only later that she learned it was all a front, a facade for the controlling, cruel man that he really was. Thomas was a liar of the worst kind. Olivia abhorred lies and deceit. Yet she was finding herself drawn in to doing the very thing she detested.

She hadn't been truthful with Jackson.

But had he been truthful with her?

It was such a small thing, she knew, but why had he claimed to have read Grafton's books when he obviously hadn't? He didn't even know that the famous mystery writer was a woman. She hadn't missed that. And she'd caught him in a couple of other fibs as well.

That's what made her nervous. She was terrified of deception.

No, she couldn't get any more involved with him until she trusted him totally—for Olivia was beginning to realize that she couldn't simply have a no-strings affair with Jackson.

Her heart was at stake.

Jackson had lied about the book. Why?

And what else was he lying about?

Eight

Olivia stood at the sink and watched another of Jackson's "assistants" leave. Heavy caseload, he'd told her. He was having to do a lot of extra work at home. This one was a redhead, tall, gorgeous. Young. Very young. She'd been at Jackson's twice this week. Monday night and Wednesday night.

Not that it was any of her business how many nubile blondes and redheads trooped in and out of his house.

Not that she was jealous.

Liar, liar, pants on fire.

Well, maybe just a tiny bit.

And she realized she was being silly.

She knew that Jackson held a very responsible position in the government and that he took his job seriously. He wasn't messing around with the redhead.

He'd been working. He told her that he planned to work, and she believed him.

But it was odd that none his "assistants" were plump and gray-haired. Or male.

Not her business, she told herself again. She and Jackson weren't a couple; they didn't have any sort of understanding. She had no claim on him.

None.

She quickly turned from the sink, and her gaze fell on the Grafton book that he'd loaned her. She'd just run over and drop it off.

Before she had time to change her mind or scrutinize her motives, Olivia snatched up the book and hurried toward Jackson's house.

It took forever for him to answer the door.

When he finally yanked it open, a green bath sheet draped around his middle and dripping water, he said, "Jennifer, did you for—" Stopping as soon as he spotted Olivia, he grinned and leaned against the jamb. "Well, hello, darlin'. What a pleasant surprise. Come on in."

Mortified, she could only mumble, "Sorry. I...I— Here's your book." She shoved it at him, turned and walked away quickly.

Jackson called after her several times, but she was too embarrassed to stop.

Served her right, she thought. What further evidence did she need? Rumpled sheets? Jackson was a normal, attractive, red-blooded male. Did she think he was celibate? Certainly not. And she had no right to expect it of him.

But if she didn't, why did it hurt so much?

Fighting back tears, she clattered up the stairs to her apartment and hurried inside.

Cursing his fumbling fingers, Jackson zipped his jeans, stomped on his boots and grabbed a T-shirt. He pulled the shirt over his wet head as he strode out of his front door and across the street. What had upset Olivia so? Something sure as hell had, but for the life of him he couldn't figure out what. But then he had a dickens of a headache, and he couldn't think straight. Sticking his head under the cold water usually helped to chase the pain away.

Had he shocked her by coming to the door with a towel around him? Nothing showed. She'd seen him in less when he wore a bathing suit.

Combing his hair with his fingers, he clomped up her stairs. "Olivia!" he shouted, knocking on the glass pane of her door. "Olivia!"

He saw her peek through the curtain as though she didn't know who was banging and caterwauling outside.

The door opened a crack. "Shhhh, you'll wake the dead with all that noise."

He pushed his way inside. "Why did you take off in such an all-fired rush?"

"I...I came at an inopportune time."

"Inopportune how? Because I was in the shower?"

"That and..."

"Spit it out, sugar."

"Well, obviously you and Jennifer—" She glanced away.

"Me and Jennifer...what?"

Olivia stared at the floor.

Then it dawned on him. "You think Jennifer and I—" He laughed. "By damn! You're jealous."

"I am not!"

"You *are!*" He laughed and hugged her to him. "As I live and breathe. You're jealous."

She poked him in the belly with her fist. "I am *not* jealous. I have absolutely no reason to be jealous. What you and Jennifer, or anyone else, do is none of my business."

"Yes, it is, darlin'. I'm not interested in having anyone in my bed but you. And until you're ready, I'll wait. I'm a one-woman man. For the record, Jennifer has a live-in lover who's a wide receiver for the Texas Longhorns. Heck of a nice kid. By the way, want to go to the game Saturday? We can grab some dinner and go boot-scootin' afterward. Ever been boot-scootin'?"

"Nope. I'm not much of a country and western dancer."

"Sugar, you've just never had the right partner. I'm a demon on the dance floor." He grabbed her and did a few fast shuffles and turns.

She laughed. "You're a demon everywhere, Jackson Crow."

He wiggled his eyebrows and winked. "You betcha!"

She pushed away. "How about a cup of coffee?"

"I'd love a cup. Got any aspirins?"

"I think so. Have a headache?"

He rubbed the back of his neck. "Yeah. Too much paperwork."

"Sit down, and I'll get the aspirins."

He didn't have to be told twice. His head was throbbing like a sonofagun.

It must have showed because when she came back, she frowned as she handed him a glass of water and the tablets.

"Do you have these headaches often?"

He shrugged. "Once or twice a week."

"Maybe you need glasses."

He shook his head. "Eyesight's twenty-twenty. It's just a tension headache."

She nodded and stepped behind him. When she started to knead the tight muscles of his neck and shoulders, he couldn't help but moan. "Man, that feels good."

"I used to do this for my father. He had tension headaches."

"You never talk about your family."

"No."

He waited a long time for her to say more. She didn't.

Her magical fingers massaged his scalp, his temples, his forehead, then went back to his neck and shoulders. He felt like he'd died and gone to heaven. The muscles relaxed, the pounding in his head slowly left.

He pulled her down into his lap and touched his forehead to hers, then kissed her gently. "Darlin', I may have to marry you and chain you to my bedpost."

She went stiff as a poker, then sprang to her feet. "In your dreams, Commissioner."

Damn! He'd set her off again. When was he ever going to learn not to crowd Olivia? He'd finally wormed enough out of Irish to know that her ex had been a serious control freak, and her daddy was, too. At the first sight of a rein, Olivia would bolt and run. Patience was the key. Patience to let her set the pace.

That ex-husband of hers must have been a real scumbag. Somebody ought to do him some serious damage for screwing up Olivia's life so badly.

Olivia hadn't been to a football game in…well, she couldn't even remember the last one. Certainly not since she'd been in college, she thought as she'd dressed in slacks, two-piece blue sweater set and loafers. She hoped she looked okay.

She needn't have worried. They'd sat with a gang of Jackson's old buddies and their ladies in the special club section of the stadium reserved for those who were big contributors to the school. Part of the group wore yuppie casual chic and part wore Western garb similar to Jackson's, though she had to admit that his jeans, plaid shirt and black felt hat looked twice as good on him. Everybody had yelled for the Texas Longhorns, laughed and eaten peanuts and popcorn and hot dogs.

Jennifer's boyfriend made two touchdowns, and they won twenty-seven to ten. Olivia had a terrific time.

"Are you a University of Texas alum?" she asked Jackson as they exited through the clubroom.

He grinned. "Sort of. I flunked out my first year. But I made a lot of friends. It's the best party school in the state. I always make a hefty donation so I can have good seats and decent parking at the football games."

"Jackson! That's terrible."

"It's the truth. Want me to lie about it?"

She shook her head and smiled. "No, of course not." That was Jackson. He was a straight shooter. That was one of the things she found endearing about him.

They went to their favorite Mexican restaurant, though Olivia was hard-pressed to find room for food after the junk she'd consumed at the game. She settled on a salad, and they ate on the patio. Although Olivia had experienced only a few cool nights since her move to Austin, she was amazed that the weather was still balmy enough in November to sit outside. Any chill was chased away with fragrant mesquite wood burning in a clay firepot.

After their leisurely meal, they went to a big barn-looking building and parked. Jackson's pickup truck fitted right in with the sea of others parked out front. She could already feel and hear the twang and rumble of the bass inside.

As she stepped down from the cab, a dozen "yee-haws" split the air, and the sound of a fiddle plucked strings of excitement inside her. By the time they went inside she was quivering on the inside and laughing on the outside, wiggling her shoulders and bobbling her head to the infectious beat.

Jackson slipped a bill to the waiter, and he led them to a table near the dance floor, where couples in a wild mixture of hats and jeans and designer capris whirled and stomped around the floor. Neon sizzled in reds, blues, yellows and greens, and beer flowed from endless pitchers and long-necked bottles. The music's potent throb vibrated the floor beneath their feet and challenged all comers to join in the revelry.

Jackson didn't even let her sit down. "Yee-hawww! Sugar, let's boogie."

He pulled her onto the floor with him, and, with a loose-hipped rhythm, swung her around and strutted with the counter-clockwise flow of the dancers. How she followed him, she didn't know—maybe it was a result of Miss Melear's dance classes—but follow him she did.

"Darlin', you're a natural," he said, grinning as he pushed and twirled and two-stepped to the loud country band.

They danced for a half hour solid until the band took a break. Decidedly damp from the exertion, Olivia fanned her face with her fingers, then mopped it with the handkerchief Jackson offered.

She plunked down in her chair and took a big swig of the bottled water she'd ordered earlier. "I'm not sure my heart can take this," she said. "I'm exhausted."

He laughed. "You're doing great. I thought you said you'd never done any country and western dancing."

"I haven't, but it's not too hard—especially if you've had twelve years of dance lessons and watched country music programs on TV. Plus, you're darned good and have a strong lead."

"Thank you, ma'am. What kind of dance lessons did you have in…?"

"California," she supplied, being vague about her origins as usual. "Tap, ballet, jazz, ballroom. My mother insisted—I think because she always wanted to take dancing when she was a child. Then after my mother…died, my father insisted that I keep it up. He contended that it encouraged discipline.''

"Did it?"

"I suppose. Mostly it kept me busy and out of his hair.''

Jackson took a swallow from his long-neck, then asked, "How old were you when your mother died?"

"Ten. She…she took an overdose of sleeping pills. I found her when I came home from school.''

"Oh, darlin'," he said laying his hand over hers. "I'm sorry.''

"It was a long time ago. And I don't want to think about it tonight. I'm having too much fun. Want to play some pool?" She nodded in the direction of the tables filling an anteroom.

He cocked one dark eyebrow. "*You* play pool?"

"What's so strange about that? Bet I can beat you.''

"Bite your tongue, sugar. I have a degree in pool.''

She grinned. "I thought it was poker.''

"Double major. Put your money where your mouth is.''

"Five dollars," she said.

"You're on.''

She, to borrow one of Jackson's colorful phrases, cleaned his plow. Cleared the table her first time up.

One hand on his hip, Jackson leaned on his cue and watched her. When the last ball dropped, he shook his head. "I think I've just been hustled.''

Olivia laughed. "I told you I was good.''

"Where'd you learn?"

"From my brother. When he got in trouble, my

father would ground him, and he would head for the third-floor billiard room. I felt sorry for Jason, so I'd tag along to keep him company. He was in trouble a lot.''

''I've never heard you mention your brother before.''

''No.''

''You see much of him?''

She shook her head. ''I don't even know where he is. Jason left home the day he turned eighteen. I haven't seen him since. Say,'' she said, changing the subject before she got maudlin—or revealed more than she wanted to, ''the band's back. I want to learn to line dance.''

''Let's do it.''

Olivia soon caught on to the steps and was keeping up with the most experienced of the crowd. Afterward Jackson taught her several other dances, but it was the slow ones that he liked best.

''I get to hold you close,'' he said, shooting her a wicked grin, then pulling her into his arms.

She had to admit that she liked the slow dances, too. With her forehead on his cheek, the top of her head fitted perfectly under his hat brim. Instead of taking the usual hand and arm position, he put both arms around her waist—after tucking hers around him.

After a couple of turns around the floor, slipping her fingers into the back pockets of his jeans seemed a very good idea.

Excellent, in fact. And rather cheeky. She almost laughed allowed at her Freudian slip. In fact, Freud

would have had a field day with her stream of con-
sciousness at that moment.

She'd never realized how erotic a man's posterior
could be. Well...not just any man's. Jackson's.

His butt turned her on like crazy.

Taut, sinewy, sexy. His muscles moved and rippled
slowly under her fingers.

He pulled her closer against him, and she realized
that he was turned on as well. She tried to pull away,
but he held her tight.

"But, you're getting, uh, er..."

"Hard as a rock," he supplied. "Yes, ma'am. But
I'll survive. The man who made a cowboy's jeans
tight was one smart hombre."

It was after midnight when they finally decided to
call it a night. The honky-tonk was still rocking, but
Olivia was pooped.

Outside, Jackson put his arm around her as they
walked to the truck. "Have a good time?" he asked.

"Wonderful." She snuggled into the crook of his
arm. The wind had kicked up, and the temperature
had dropped considerably. "It's cold." She shivered
against him.

"Front moving in."

The sky flashed with a streak of lightning, and a
couple of seconds later thunder rolled through the
hills. A few fat drops of rain pelted them.

Jackson plunked his black cowboy hat on her head.
"Let's make a run for it before the bottom falls out."

They almost made it.

Yards before they reached the truck, the sky
opened and a torrent of cold rain drenched them.

Jackson tried to shield her, but it was no use, they were both soaked and shivering by the time they made it inside the cab. He started the truck and pulled away, the wipers sluicing on high.

"It'll take a minute for the heater to get warm," he told her.

"How did it get so cold so quickly?" she asked, her teeth chattering.

"Texas weather."

She tried to dry off with a handful of paper napkins Jackson found under his seat. It was a futile effort. The only place on her that was dry was under the hat she still wore.

He turned the heater on. After an initial blast of cold air, blessed warmth began to push away some of the chill. Jackson leaned forward, concentrating on seeing the road through the deluge, and she watched him concentrate.

Never in her life had just looking at a man thrilled her so, set her blood to boiling and robbed her of sanity. All she could think about was taking off that wet shirt he wore and licking the raindrops from his chest and his face. She ached to feel his hands on her bare skin.

She squirmed in the leather seat, and he glanced at her. His thoughts must have been following the same line as hers. Raw desire etched his face, and he reached over and stroked her thigh.

His touch sent a shiver of electricity zinging through her; she sucked in a startled breath. Only the restraint of her seat belt kept her from doing something foolish. Sexual awareness bombarded the cab, ricocheted off the walls in frenzied currents, scorched the air.

He moved his hand from her leg, seized the wheel in a two-handed grip, and said, "I gotta pay attention to what I'm doing. I sure as hell don't want to wreck us now."

"No. Not now." Was that her voice? It sounded raspy, breathless.

Jackson drove safely, but quickly, to their neighborhood. He didn't pull into her drive; he headed straight for his own, poking the remote to lift the garage door as he made the turn.

She made a sound of protest and looked toward her apartment.

"We'd get soaked again going to your place," he said as he pulled into the garage. "Besides, my bed is bigger." He grinned. "And I'm gonna need a *lot* of room."

Nine

"Come on in," Jackson said, "and let's get you dry and warmed up. You're soaked to the skin."

"You're just as wet as I am."

"Yeah, but I'm tough."

She poked his arm as he guided her through the mudroom door. "I'm tough, too."

He kissed her nose. "No, you're like spun sugar, and I can't have you melting on me."

Streak, who had been left in the room with his basket and newspapers, started barking and jumping on Jackson.

"Hey, there, fella," he said, bending to scratch the puppy's head. "How's the food and water holding out? Looks good. You stay here and guard the house, and I'm going to take care of the lady."

As if he'd understood every word, Streak barked

and wiggled his tail. Jackson could charm anybody—
woman or beast.

He led her through the kitchen, where they pulled
off shoes and boots, to the den. "Let me get a fire
going. You go to the guest bath and get out of those
wet clothes. Down the hall, second door on the right.
There should be an extra robe in the linen closet."

Olivia didn't argue. She was soaking and chilled to
the bone.

The guest bath, beautifully decorated in dusky
green and terra-cotta, still smelled of newness. As she
unbuttoned her sweater, she caught her reflection in
the mirror and realized that not only did she look
totally bedraggled, but she still wore Jackson's black
cowboy hat. She took it off and set it on the tile
counter, then stripped off her wet clothes and draped
them over the shower rod.

After toweling off, she found a stack of white terry
robes in the closet and took one. Crow's Nest was
embroidered in black on the breast pocket. It was too
big, but she belted it snugly, then searched the drawers hoping to find a hair-dryer and a brush. She did.
Clever decorator, she supposed. Everything for the
guest's comfort. She even found an unopened box of
condoms in one of the drawers.

She opened them. Feeling a bit wicked, she put one
packet in the pocket of her robe and gave it a pat.

Using the dryer she'd found, she fluffed the damp
ends of her hair and restored a bit of order, then
leaned forward toward the large mirror and checked
for mascara smudges. Her reflection told her that she
looked decidedly mussed. The shivery rasp of terry
cloth across her nipples told her that she felt decidedly

sensual. The gleam in her eyes told her that she was decidedly ready for Jackson Crow.

This was it. This was the night.

Feeling even more wicked, she put two more packets in her robe pocket and smiled as she picked up his hat and left the bathroom.

Barefoot, she walked back to the den. She stopped at the doorway. Jackson was squatted in front of the fireplace, adding another log to the new fire. He was barefoot, too.

And bare-chested.

Olivia's breath caught as she watched him poke the log. A shower of sparks shot upward, the cozy scent of burning oak pervaded the room and the glow of the flames brushed his skin with copper. He wore only an oft-washed pair of jeans, and a towel lay draped around his neck. His dark hair was rumpled and waving as if he'd merely scrubbed the towel over his head a couple of times.

He must have sensed her presence, or perhaps she'd made some small sound, for he glanced at her over his shoulder and smiled. He stood and held out his hand. "Fire's going pretty good. Come warm yourself. I've got coffee brewing—or would you rather have wine?"

"Coffee first."

She joined him. "Nice fire."

"Naturally. I was a Boy Scout."

"I'll bet you were cute in your uniform."

"Absolutely."

"Here's your hat."

"It looks better on you." He plunked it on her head, then pulled her into his arms and kissed her.

His lips were still cool from the outside chill, but his tongue was warm. Hot.

And reckless.

He pulled her closer, and the hat tumbled from her head as she arched her body against him.

He kissed her thoroughly, then left her mouth to nuzzle his way down to her shoulder, pushing aside the robe as he went. She clung to his bare back as his lips traced her collarbone, sighed as he rubbed his cheek against the cap of her shoulder, groaned as his hands slipped inside her robe to cup her bottom.

"Oh, darlin'," he moaned against her ear as he stroked her breast, and she turned into pudding.

She ached for him, ached with a need so potent that she could hardly stand it. She'd wanted him for a long time, and to wait any longer was excruciating. Grinding herself against him, she grabbed handfuls of his hair and pulled his mouth to hers. Her breath was ragged; her heart pounded furiously.

"Oh, Jackson, I want—I want—"

"What do you want, darlin'?"

"I want you."

"You've got me."

He kissed her again, rubbing his chest across her breasts, pushing the robe farther and farther apart until it was skin against skin. His hand stole between them to thumb her nipple, then it dipped lower, and her knees went weak.

"Jackson," she whimpered.

"What, darlin'?"

"I want—I want—"

"Tell me what you want, sugar."

His fingers were doing marvelous things to her. She

could barely find words. "I want you. Inside me. Now."

He eased her down to the couch, and her robe fell open.

He knelt beside her, his eyes seeming to devour her. "In a minute, darlin'. I've got some more looking to do. And some more touching." He dipped his tongue into her navel. "I want to make sure you're ready."

His hand stroked up her thigh, over her belly, and up to make a figure eight across her breasts, then down again to probe more intimate places.

"Jackson, I'm ready!"

He chuckled. "I believe you are. I'll be right back."

He stood.

"Where are you *going*?"

"To get some protection."

She fished in the robe pocket. "Here."

He cocked one wicked dark brow and grinned. "Prepared were we?"

"I told you I was ready."

"So you did, sugar. I was beginning to think it wasn't going to happen." He stripped off his jeans, then kissed her while he put on the protection. "I've lain awake many a night imagining this moment."

He continued to stroke her and kiss her as he moved to a place between her thighs. She sucked in a long gasp as he slid into her, filling her deeply, completely.

They savored the moment of their joining, lying still for several seconds. A rush of wonderment swept over her, and she drank in the power of their coupling.

Then they began to move as one in a slow sensual dance that stoked sparks of desire in every cell of her body.

He stroked her as they moved, whispered praise for her body, her beauty as he thrust deeper and deeper. She rose to meet each thrust, and the power and tempo increased until the flames glowed white-hot.

Their lovemaking grew frenzied, and she bucked and groaned, and they rolled off the couch onto the rug.

Hotter and hotter, faster and faster—

Then spasms broke over her. They arched her back and stole her breath.

His climax came almost immediately.

She could feel the throb of his fulfillment. His back bowed and his arms taut, holding his weight off her, and with firelight glistening off his damp skin, he looked like a great primitive warrior. Strong, muscled, virile, supremely handsome.

Her heart ached at the sight.

Dear Lord, how she loved him.

Loved?

No, she told herself. She'd loved the lovemaking. He was a skilled lover. He'd made her feel like the only woman in the world for him.

She would bask in the feelings for now, enjoy the temporary intimacy.

Olivia crossed her arms behind his neck, pulled him down to her and snuggled close.

"Sugar, I do believe you're purring."

She chuckled and, imitating his drawl, said, "Sugar, I do believe you're right. That was delicious."

"The night is young yet, tiger. Want some coffee? Some wine? Some cheese? My heart on a pine plank?"

"You're crazy."

"Yes, ma'am. Crazy about you."

The storm continued throughout the night, and their tempestuous coupling continued, as well. They moved to Jackson's big bed, snuggling and napping, then rousing to make love again, both insatiable, wild. Was it the thunder and lightning, vibrating through the house and splitting the sky with its power, that roused her to such wildness, such abandon? Or was it simply Jackson? Never had a man stirred her the way Jackson did. Never had a man satisfied her the way Jackson did.

She slept, content and secure, in his arms.

Shortly before dawn Olivia woke. The storm had moved on, and the rain had stopped. She slipped from his bed and went to the guest bathroom. Her clothes were still damp. She hesitated to put on the clammy garments, but she didn't want to be seen skittering across the street in a robe, either.

Deciding to put her things through the dryer, she slipped on a robe and gathered up her belongings, then moved quietly to the laundry area off the mud-room.

As soon as she opened the door, Streak met her with excited barks and wiggles and jumps.

"Shhhh," she said, closing the door behind her. "We don't want to wake up your master. He had a very tiring night."

Streak wasn't very concerned about being quiet. He

barked and wiggled and jumped until she dumped her clothes in the dryer and picked him up.

"You rascal."

He licked her nose. She laughed.

"Hey, buddy," Jackson said from the doorway. "Are you trying to smooch my gal?"

Startled by his presence, Olivia turned. "Did we wake you? I'm sorry. I told Streak to be quiet, but he doesn't mind very well."

"You got that right. But the noise didn't wake me. The quiet did. I missed the sound of your breathing. What are you doing up so early?"

"Drying my clothes. I didn't want to sneak home wearing your robe and be the talk of the neighborhood."

"Don't worry about it. Come on back to bed and get some sleep."

She gave him a teasing smile. "I'm afraid that if I go back to bed with you, I won't get any sleep."

A wicked grin broke over his face. "You're safe for a while, darlin'. I'm plumb tuckered out. Come on." He held out his hand.

She took it and followed him back to his big bed.

He lied. Or else he got his second wind.

It was midmorning before she awoke. Alone.

Just as she sat up and stretched, Jackson stuck his head in the room. "Mornin', sugar. How do you like your eggs?"

"Poached."

"Will scrambled do?"

She smiled. "Sure."

"Good. I'll be right back."

In two minutes he came back, carrying a tray. He wore only his jeans.

"Breakfast in bed?" she asked.

"Yep. Eggs, bacon, biscuits, butter, jelly, orange juice and coffee. The jelly is homemade. Grandpa Pete puts up several pints every year when the dewberries come in." He put the bed tray over her lap, then slathered butter and jelly on a piece of biscuit and held it to her mouth.

She took the bit he offered. "Mmm. Very good. Where's your breakfast?"

"I already ate mine. And yours. Twice. Streak helped some."

Frowning, she tried to figure out what he'd just said.

He laughed. "I fixed breakfast earlier, but you went back to sleep. So I went ahead and ate. I thought you might be rousing about an hour ago, so I fixed you another breakfast. You were sawing logs when I brought it." He grinned. "I figured that the third time was a charm. Need anything else?"

Touched by his thoughtfulness, she swallowed back the lump in her throat and shook her head. "Thank you very much. Nobody ever brought me breakfast in bed before."

"Not even when you were sick or on your birthday?"

She shook her head again. "Not that I recall. Thank you, Jackson. Thank you very much."

"No problem." He gave her a peck and crawled in beside her. "Want to watch the news?" He picked up the TV remote control and clicked it on.

"Fine with me. Have you read the Sunday paper already?" She sipped her coffee.

"I don't take a newspaper."

"Good heavens, why not? I can't start the day without coffee and the morning paper. Sundays are a special treat. On Sundays, I take both the *Statesman* and the *New York Times*."

"Never liked to take the time for newspapers. Guess I'm a TV kind of guy. Want me to go get the papers from your driveway?"

"No, I'll read them later. I can't believe that you don't subscribe to a newspaper, especially now that you're in politics," she said in a teasing way. "I mean, how can you keep up with Doonesbury?"

"Is that such a loss? Look, I've got instant news around the world with CNN—and I can shave at the same time."

Olivia rolled her eyes and buttered another bite of biscuit. "Jackson, that's ludicrous. You can't get the depth of information from a TV show that you can get from a newspaper. TV is just a series of sound bytes. Newspapers give details."

"I listen to the radio for the details."

She sighed. "Deliver me."

He chuckled and took a bite of the biscuit she held. "To any place in particular?" He dabbed a bit of jelly on her chin and licked it off.

He tugged down the sheet that was tucked under her arms and put another dab on her nipple. "Have I told you how much I love your breasts?" He bent and licked the jelly smear away, lingering to lick long after the sweetness had disappeared.

"Mmmmmm. Several times. Careful, you're jostling the coffee."

He moved the tray from her lap to the floor.

"What about my breakfast?"

"I'll fix you another later." He ripped the sheet away.

Jackson wondered later why he hadn't told her. He'd had the perfect opening while she was eating breakfast and they were talking about newspapers. Why hadn't he told her the truth? Why hadn't he just told her that he hated the sight of newspapers along with everything else that was printed?

Why hadn't he just spilled his guts and told her what a damned moron he was? He felt like a dirty dog by not telling her the truth. He wanted things to be open and aboveboard between them. But he wanted her respect more. If she knew, how could somebody like her respect somebody like him?

He broke out in a cold sweat when he thought of her knowing his secret. She was so sharp, a damned brilliant woman. A scholar. He couldn't abide the notion of Olivia pitying him or being embarrassed by his ignorance.

Sooner or later, she was bound to find out.

Maybe not. Maybe he could keep faking it. After all, he was an expert at faking it. He'd faked it all the way through school and through all his adult life.

Hell, even his own family didn't suspect that he could barely read.

Ten

Late the following Sunday afternoon, Olivia hummed as she iced a coconut cake. She couldn't believe that she was feeling so domestic. After the disastrous birthday production, she'd sworn off cake making. Yet, she and Jackson had only been lovers a week and already she was baking again. She must be fond of the guy.

She smiled and stepped back and surveyed her latest effort. Not bad.

In fact, it looked darned good.

She picked it up and took it downstairs, calling to Tessa and Ed as she spotted them in the backyard. She and Jackson were joining Tessa and Ed for barbecue. Jackson was providing the beer; Olivia, the dessert.

Ed, a tall, silver-haired man, waved his mop brush

at her. "Do you smell those ribs? My mouth's already watering."

"They smell great. Are they almost done?" Olivia asked as she set the cake on a picnic table near Tessa.

"Another half hour ought to do it."

"Nice cake," Tessa said.

Olivia beamed proudly at the compliment. "There's something to be said for practice."

"I'll take it inside," Tessa said. "It's getting a bit cool to eat outdoors, don't you think?"

"Aw, you gals are sissies," Ed said. "It's pleasant out here. Say, where's Jackson with the beer?"

"He should be here," Olivia said. "I told him five-thirty."

Glancing across the street, she saw that Tami's car was gone. In fact, she recalled that Tami had left the usual Sunday-afternoon session quite a bit earlier than she ordinarily did.

Odd that Jackson hadn't arrived. He was always punctual.

"I'll run over and see what's keeping him," she told the Jurneys.

She hurried across the street and through the courtyard. After ringing the bell twice and receiving no answer, she grew concerned and tried the door. It was unlocked. She went inside, stopped and called out.

Nothing.

She searched the den and the kitchen. Then, thinking that he might have gone out for a quick errand, she checked the garage. Both his pickup and his Jaguar were in their places. Retracing her steps, she had started down the hallway to his bedroom when she heard a loud crash and muffled cursing coming from Jackson's study.

She hurried to the door and knocked. "Jackson!"

She knocked again, then opened the door. Only a dim desk lamp illuminated the room.

"Dammit!" Jackson shouted, hurling a sheaf of pages against a wall and letting out a string of vitriolic oaths.

Papers flew everywhere, and Olivia gasped at his behavior. "Jackson! What on earth is wrong?"

He turned to her, anguish, soul-deep and terrible, etching his face, despair burning from his eyes. He raked his fingers through his hair, then clamped them against his skull as if holding his head on. "I can't do it, Olivia. I can't. Dammit, I'm such a loser. You deserve better than me."

He slumped to his chair, put his elbows on his desk and dropped his forehead into his hands.

Alarmed by a Jackson she'd never seen before, a thousand thoughts went through her mind. Was he drunk? On drugs? Psychotic? She'd never seen him in a fit of temper, and it frightened her. Witnessing his behavior brought a torrent of old memories rushing into her head, memories that carried heavy emotions with them.

Her impulse was to hasten to Jackson's side and comfort his obvious pain.

She hesitated, shuddering as tapes of her father and of Thomas flashed through her mind, the countless times she'd suffered through their vehement outbursts, been left battered and demoralized. The sequence was always the same. First came their rage and violence, then contrition, often sorrowful self-abasement and empty promises. She'd endured enough of such behavior to last a dozen lifetimes.

Was Jackson the same sort of man?

No, she prayed. *Please, God, no. Not Jackson.*

She couldn't believe that she'd ended up repeating her mistakes, falling into the same pattern. Women did it all the time, ended up choosing a clone of fathers or former partners.

No. She wouldn't believe it. Jackson was a different cut of man, and she was a different woman from the one she'd been when she was younger. She was wiser, more experienced.

Wasn't she?

Dear Lord, she hoped so.

Her hesitation lasted only a moment more before she went to him, knelt beside his chair and laid her hand on his thigh.

"Jackson, what's wrong?"

Seconds seemed like hours.

Finally Jackson lifted his head. His expression was no less anguished. "I'm a stupid son-of-a-bitch. Damned stupid. And a fake. I'm a fake."

"Jackson, what are you talking about? I don't understand. Why are you so angry? What's going on?"

"Oh, hell, this is a mess." He swiped his hands over his face, then dropped his head back and stared at the ceiling. "Tami's little boy got sick, and she had to go home, and I can't locate Jennifer or any of the others that usually help. Hell, nobody's home on Sunday afternoon. I've got this whole blasted bunch of cases to go over before the hearings tomorrow, and I can't do it. I've been sitting here for two damned hours trying. Wanna know how far I've gotten? Two pages. Two measly, sorry-assed pages. A page an hour." He gave a hollow bark of laughter and rubbed his forehead. "I'm about as sharp as a rubber knife."

"One of those headaches?"

"It feels like somebody's hammering roofing nails into my skull."

"I'm sorry. Where are the aspirins?"

"Right here." He jerked out the drawer and dropped the bottle onto the desk top. "Aspirins won't help. I've already taken a handful."

She stood. "Then one of my massages ought to do the trick." Her fingers went to his shoulders, but he caught her hands and pulled her into his lap.

He cradled her close and laid his cheek on her head. "Darlin', I'd sooner fight the devil with a willow switch than admit this to you, but I've gotta do it. I've been wrestling with it for a while now, and if anything is to become of us, there's no way around it. I've got to tell you the truth about me."

He took a deep shuddering breath, and panic began to build inside Olivia. What was he trying to say? Her imagination raced from one wild notion to another. Did he have a secret wife? A terrible communicable disease? Some shocking sexual perversion?

"Is it…bad?" she asked.

"Bad enough."

One part of her wanted to clamp her hands over her ears or over his mouth to hold back this awful thing that he was about to reveal. The more sensible part of her said quietly, "What truth?"

She could hear his watch tick.

"I can't read."

The tension left her muscles, and Olivia laughed.

"Of course you can't read. You have a splitting headache." She pulled him to her and kissed his forehead. "Poor baby."

He captured her hands, kissed first one palm, then the other, then looked earnestly into her eyes. "Listen to me, love. I...can't...read. Headache or no. I...can't...read."

Puzzled, she stared at him. "Are you trying to tell me that you're *illiterate?*"

"All but."

She sat up straight. "That's ridiculous. You have a college degree. How can you be illiterate?"

"I didn't say I wasn't resourceful. I flunked out of four schools—some sooner than others—before I landed in the one where I got my degree. It's an...unusual college, small and unaccredited, kind of...experimental. I got my degree in dramatic arts."

"Dramatic arts? As in acting?"

"Well, yeah. I wasn't too bad at it. I'd always been a ham and the class clown."

"To hide the fact that you couldn't read."

He shrugged. "Maybe. I've never tried to analyze it."

"Your parents don't know?"

"Nope. I was always ashamed of how stupid I was compared to everybody else in the family."

"Jackson, I've known you for quite a while, and I'm very sure that you're not stupid. In fact, Pete told me that you're the smartest of his grandchildren."

"Me?"

"Yes, you. Didn't your elementary school teachers ever catch on that you were having problems?"

"Not really. Oh, I learned to read some, that is, I

could recognize words on flash cards, but developing a phenomenal memory got me by.'' He chuckled, but there was no mirth in the sound. ''I used the cookies from my lunch box to bribe a couple of kids in my class. They'd read the lesson to me, and I'd memorize it. If we had to read aloud, I'd always volunteer to be first so I'd know where to start, things like that. As I said, I learned to be resourceful. I was never much of a student, but I managed.''

''You compensated.'' She hugged him close, thinking of the little boy struggling with his awful secret.

''Yeah, I suppose. But this time I got in over my head. All the reading that goes along with being a railroad commissioner is a bitch.''

''That's what Tami and Jennifer and the other girls do,'' Olivia said. ''They read for you.''

''Yeah. They think I have an eye problem. Like I said, I'm resourceful when it comes to hiding my ignorance.''

''Have you actually had your vision tested?''

He nodded. ''It really is twenty-twenty. And through the years, I've hired tutors on the sly a time or two, trying to learn to read, but it's no use. The letters start running together, and they might as well be chicken tracks dancing around on the page. God, I hate telling you this. It's humiliating.'' He stared at the ceiling some more.

''Don't be silly. I'm a psychologist—or soon will be, anyway. I suspect that you have some specific learning difficulty—a form of dyslexia would be my first guess. We won't know exactly until we have you tested.''

''Tested? What's dyslexia?''

"Yes, tested. And I'm not an expert in the field, but, basically, the wiring in some people's brains is different, and signals get scrambled so that reading is difficult. Dyslexia is a wastebasket term that covers a range of perceptual problems."

"Great. Now I'm a freak with a miswired brain. I'm not sure that it wasn't better just to be dumb."

Olivia bit back a smile. "You aren't a freak. Or dumb. Lots of people are dyslexic—would you believe Albert Einstein, Thomas Edison and Pablo Picasso among others? And there are many kinds of dyslexia." She stood and walked to the wall switch. "Let me get some proper light in here, and I'll show you."

Jackson winced at the brightness. "Actually, I do better with dimmer light."

"Hmm," Olivia said as a thought suddenly struck her. Headaches, words moving on the page, now photosensitivity. "Does strong light bother you? Is that why you wear your sunglasses so much?"

"I suppose. But everybody wears sunglasses."

"That may be a clue, but I'll have to talk to JoAnna."

"Who's JoAnna?"

"She's a friend of mine from the university. She's doing her doctoral research on a special kind of reading difficulty and some new and unconventional techniques for ameliorating the problem. JoAnna's a whiz at this kind of stuff. We'll set up an appointment for her to test you."

He looked uncomfortable, and she chuckled. "It's painless. I promise. And speaking of pain, how's your headache?"

"Better. Almost gone. I guess confession is good for the head as well as the soul. But I still feel like a dope."

"Why? I told you that lots of very bright people have similar problems. And at least it's not catching. I was afraid that you were going to tell me that you had some dread disease."

He grinned. "Nope. I'm clean."

"Good. Tell you what. Let's go pig out on Ed's barbecued ribs, and then we'll come back here, and I'll read whatever you need to bone up on for tomorrow."

He stood and tucked in his shirt. "You're on. I could eat a dozen of those ribs right now."

"Then let's get the beer and go."

They walked to the kitchen where Jackson retrieved two six-packs from the fridge and set them on the counter. He took her into his arms and kissed her—a long, slow, sweet kiss.

"Have I told you what a very special lady you are?" he asked. "You never cease to amaze me."

"I never think of myself as amazing."

"You are. I sweated blood over telling you about— you know—and you didn't even bat an eyelash."

"Why would I? Your problem isn't shameful. We can handle it."

He smiled at her, and an expression of infinite tenderness came over his face. "You're something else."

He kissed her again, almost reverently. "We'd better get a move on."

"You're right. We don't want to miss out on the

ribs. And I baked a coconut cake. Without a single crack.''

He laughed and grabbed the beer.

''Where's Streak?''

''Oops. I forgot about the little dickens. He was banished to the patio for chewing up one of my favorite golfing boots.''

''Golfing boots? You play golf in *boots*?''

''Yep. I have a pair of boots for just about everything.'' He held up one foot and showed off a pair of well-worn black ones. ''Now, these are my eating ribs and drinking beer boots.'' He grinned.

''Oh, you!'' She laughed and swatted his bottom.

''Miss Olivia! Such liberties.'' He gave her a quick peck. ''Let me tend to the animal, and we'll go.''

After Streak was fed, watered and left in the mud room with newspapers, they went out the front door.

Outside, dark was falling, and as they crossed the street, they could see Tessa and Ed waiting on the porch. ''Darlin','' Jackson said quietly, ''if you don't mind, I'd just as soon you didn't mention my, uh, problem to the Jurneys.''

''My lips are sealed. I won't tell a soul but Jo-Anna.''

On Tuesday afternoon Jackson felt like a wiggletail in hot ashes as he paced the hall waiting for Olivia's class to be over. His boots were too tight and his tie choked him and he thought he might be coming down with a fever.

He jiggled the change in his pocket and paced some more.

Finally the door opened and a deluge of students

poured through the door. Was he getting old or were college kids getting younger? And he couldn't believe the garb they wore to class.

When the herd cleared, he stepped inside the room. Olivia was at the lectern talking to several lingering class members. As he approached, one of the girls elbowed another standing beside her. They stared at him, looked at each other, then giggled.

Yep, he must be getting old.

In a few minutes the stragglers left, and the two gigglers giggled again as they passed him.

Olivia grinned as he approached. "You really are a hottie."

"A *hottie?*"

"That's a compliment. Bridget and Emily think that you're very handsome."

"Who are Bridget and Emily?"

"The gigglers."

He grinned. "A hottie, huh?"

"Don't let it go to your head, Commissioner. If you were precocious, you could be their father."

"Don't rub it in. I feel 103 today. Is the meeting with JoAnna still on?"

Olivia nodded and glanced at her watch. "She should be in the lab by now. Nervous?"

"Naw. I always trim my fingernails with my teeth."

She laughed and tucked her arm through the crook of his elbow. "Come on. I'll introduce you to Jo-Anna. And, by the way, you really do look very handsome today."

He glanced down at his gray suit. "These are my

commissioner duds. I came straight from the office. Are you going to stay with me while I get tested?''

''Do you want me to?''

''I don't know. One part of me says yes, I want you glued to my side. Another part doesn't want you to witness my humiliation.''

''Why don't we ask JoAnna what she thinks?''

They went to a room on the next floor, and Olivia introduced him to a short woman with a bush of kinky red hair. She had a friendly smile and a handshake like a linebacker. They shot the breeze for a few minutes, then JoAnna Armbruster suggested that Olivia drop back by in a couple of hours.

''I hate for you to hang around so long waiting for me,'' he told Olivia. ''Why don't you go on home, and I'll stop by later.''

''Sure?''

''Positive.'' He winked. ''Thanks.''

''Take off your coat and relax,'' JoAnna told him after Olivia left. ''I promise this will be painless. Want a glass of water?''

''Please.'' He stripped off his coat and tie and rolled up his sleeves, then downed the glass of water in one gulp.

''Nervous?''

''Does it show?''

She gave a laugh that seemed twice her size and motioned him to a chair. First she asked a lot of questions and filled out a form, then she had him read a bunch of stuff and asked him some more questions. That went on for a while, and his head began to pound.

After more questions and some *hmm*s she opened

a folder and removed several colored plastic sheets. "I think that Olivia was right. I think that you may have Scotopic Sensitivity Syndrome, also known as Irlen Syndrome."

"Say what? Is it catching?"

She laughed. "Not the last I heard, but if I'm right, you'll make a dynamite subject for my study. Irlen Syndrome is a perceptual problem named after Helen Irlen, the woman who first diagnosed it. Read this for me." She pointed to one of the pages on the desk.

He labored with the words as the letters danced and converged.

"Okay, try this." She laid two sheets of colored plastic over the page.

It wasn't any better.

After trying several combinations, she laid a purple and a turquoise sheet over the page. "Now try."

Growing more disheartened by the moment, he sighed and looked at the page.

He glanced up at JoAnna, then looked at the page again. "Well, I'll be damned."

"What?"

"The letters. They're not moving. They're not dancing or blurring or sliding off the page. They're just sitting there—as clear as can be. Well, I'll be damned."

A grin broke over his face, and he let out a whoop.

The grin stayed on his face while they finished the session and JoAnna put the specific colored overlays into an envelope for him.

"Placing these over the pages will help you read books or other printed material," she told him, "but you should also be fitted for special filtered lenses at a clinic. The glasses are expensive, but I think you'll be amazed at how much they will help you." She handed him a sheet of paper. "This is a list of locations in the United States that do testing for filters."

"JoAnna, I can't tell you what this means to me." He cleared his throat. Twice. Damn! For a little of nothing, he would start bawling like a baby. "It's a miracle."

She smiled. "The difference is so dramatic with some people that I know it seems that way sometimes. You're one of the lucky ones."

"You don't have to tell me twice. Listen, do you need any help with your studies? A grant or something?"

"Are you kidding? Grad students always need grants."

He whipped out his checkbook, wrote a sizable check and handed it to her.

Her eyes widened when she saw the amount. "You've made a mistake. I—I can't take this. This is for—"

"It's for a drop in the bucket compared to what you've done for me. Take it." He pumped her hand again and strode from the room.

Olivia sat just outside the door.

His heart swelled up to twice its normal size to find her waiting there. "You stayed."

She smiled. "I did. What's the verdict?"

"Not guilty." He grabbed her and swung her around, laughing. "I'm not an ignoramus after all. I just needed a little more color in my life. Can you believe it? I swear it's a miracle." He held up the envelope JoAnna had given him. "All I have to do is put a purple sheet and a turquoise sheet of plastic over a page, and I can read it. Olivia, I can *read* it. The letters don't jiggle or dance or run together. The words just sit there and let me read them.'' He laughed and swung her around again. ''Let's go home. This calls for champagne!''

Eleven

Olivia was dressed and waiting when she heard boots hit the bottom stairs. She and Jackson had parted at UT just over an hour before with his admonition to go home and get her glad rags on. They were going out to celebrate. She smiled thinking of his exuberance. She'd never seen him so deliriously happy.

"Open up, woman!" Jackson shouted. "My arms are full."

She threw open the door to a beaming Jackson with armloads of flowers—red roses, yellow roses, magnificent lilies and a huge potted orchid.

"Good heavens! Did you buy out the florist?"

"Just about. I'd already gotten the roses when I remembered that you once said you liked this kind of lily—"

"They're stargazers," she supplied, laughing as

she caught his infectious mood. "And they're beautiful."

"Right. Stargazers. And you went on so over that pot of orchids at the Chinese restaurant last week that I got the same kind for you. I would have brought more stuff, but this is all I could carry." He kissed her, then said, "Grab the pot, will you, darlin'? I've got a thorn sticking my finger."

She took the orchid along with the bundle of lilies and started to the kitchen, wondering what in the world she was going to use for vases. After a bit of searching, she found containers that would do.

The huge bouquet of red roses went into the single large vase she owned, a cut glass one that she'd picked up on a junking spree. The two dozen yellow roses went into a tall pickle crock, and the lilies into a blue glass pitcher.

When she'd finished with the overwhelming mass, Jackson was still beaming. He seemed so excited that she didn't dare mention that he might have gone a tad overboard. "The flowers are lovely, and they smell heavenly. Thank you."

Wrapping his arms around her, he laid his forehead against hers. "I know I got a little carried away, sugar, but I owe you a lot more that an armload of flowers for what you've done for me. Do you have any idea what a difference you've made in my life? I couldn't repay you if I gave you every flower in Texas."

He reached into his pocket and pulled out a small box wrapped in gold paper. "I want you to have this, too."

She frowned. "Jackson—"

"Now, darlin', don't go getting on your high horse like you do every time I try to give you something. This is a red-letter day for me. You can't imagine how it feels to know that I'm not really stupid, that I can read a book now like a normal person, that I don't have to fake my way through every single day. Please, honey. I want you to have this. Okay?"

The expression on his face was so tender and so entreating that her heart simply melted. "Okay." She tore away the paper and opened the small box. A pair of exquisite diamond studs sparkled against the dark velvet interior.

"But, Jackson, I can't accept these. They're huge. They must have cost a fortune."

"Naw. I charged 'em."

A smile escaped her despite her best efforts. "I appreciate the thought, I really do, but I can't accept these."

"Too late. You already said okay. Here, let's put them on, and we're going to go out for a champagne dinner. There's that fancy place outside town that we haven't tried yet. I think I mentioned it to you. They serve wild game of all kinds and pour a whiskey sauce over ice cream that'll make you swear you've died and gone to heaven."

Olivia didn't argue any more. This was a special day for Jackson, and she didn't want to spoil it for him. She took off her plain gold loops and laid them in the kitchen window. Standing in front of a small wall mirror in the living room, she inserted the studs, then turned around for his reaction.

"Beautiful, absolutely beautiful. I knew you were made for diamonds." He pulled another gold-wrapped package from his coat pocket. This one was longer and narrow. "Here."

"No."

"But, darlin'—"

"No. Absolutely not. The earrings are too much."

He caught her around the waist and penned her in his arms. After a small kiss and a nuzzle, he asked, "Aren't you even curious?"

"Not in the least. I'm not going to take another expensive gift."

"What if I told you it was just a fountain pen?" He nuzzled the other ear and nipped at the lobe.

"I wouldn't believe you. I thought you were taking me to dinner. I'm starved."

"Oh, can't have that, sugar. Where's your coat? It's nippy outside."

Jackson was like a kid when he whipped out his colored overlays and placed them over the menu. "Looka there, I can read every word. You want rattlesnake or wild boar?"

She wrinkled her nose.

"Don't worry about it, darlin'. I promise that everything here is de-licious and like nothing you've ever tasted before. They floosy it up so that you don't even know what you're eating half the time. How about venison?"

"You want me to *eat* Bambi?"

"Sorry, sugar, bad choice. Ever tried alligator? How about duck? That's not too different from chicken."

"Why don't you order for me? Just whisper it to the waiter so I won't know."

He grinned, but he ended up doing just that. When the waiter left, he picked up his glass of champagne and touched it to hers. "To a remarkable lady, and to the future."

"To new horizons," she added, then sipped from her glass.

He drank also, then he sat holding his glass and simply watching her for the longest time.

"What?"

"I was just thinking how bright you are. And how beautiful. And how much I love you."

Her breath caught, and she looked quickly away. This wasn't supposed to happen. She hadn't wanted this to happen. She didn't want declarations and commitments. She wasn't ready.

"Honey, don't look at me like that."

"Like what?"

"Like you're about to panic and start circling the wagons. I just said what I felt. I'm not pushing."

She turned her glass round and round, then took another sip. "When are you going to get colored filters?"

He sighed, then said, "I'll call the closest place in the morning and go in as soon as they can take me. I'm mighty anxious to get those glasses."

Olivia was relieved that he didn't mention the *L* word any more, not even when he came to her bed later that night.

Her apartment smelled of roses and lilies and desire when he kissed her and caressed her and unzipped her dress slowly. She savored each moment, returned every caress and unbuttoned his shirt to touch his bare skin.

Their lovemaking was slow and sweet and sensuous. Her body sang to his whispers, swelled under his seduction and slipped over the edge of the world with wonderful racking spasms of fulfillment.

She snuggled close, content in his arms, taking comfort from his size and strength and slept.

"Darlin'," he whispered, waking her from a lovely dream, "it's morning. I've gotta go."

She roused only to smile and flutter her fingers.

He chuckled and kissed the back of her neck. "I'll set your alarm."

She fluttered her fingers again and didn't move until the alarm jerked her awake. She smacked it off and rolled back onto her stomach, bunching and hugging the pillow under her head.

Her hand encountered something hard beneath the pillow, and she patted it, trying to figure out what it was. Pulling out the object, she raised up and squinted at it.

The other gold-wrapped box.

Pushing back her tumbled hair, she squinted at it some more.

Dare she?

No. Absolutely not.

She put the box on her bedside table and went to the bathroom to brush her teeth.

Curiosity itched inside her. She peered around the door and saw the box still sitting there. Tearing her gaze away, she scrubbed her teeth harder.

She dressed and made her bed and tried not to think about that box. She carried it to the kitchen with her when she fixed coffee.

The coffee seemed to take forever to drip. She leaned over, put her elbows on the counter and her chin in her hands. Her eyes went from the slow drip-drip of brewing coffee to the box. The package seemed to beckon her.

"Oh, go for it!" She snatched up the package and tore off the wrapping paper.

She gasped when she opened the box. It was a diamond tennis bracelet—five carats at least. A small gold tag was attached near the clasp. Something was engraved on it. Holding it close to the light, she read the three words.

I love you.

She sank to the floor and wept.

Dear Lord, she loved him, too.

Olivia was about to leave for the university when the phone rang.

"Hey, sugar, I'm glad I caught you," Jackson said. "I'm on my way to the airport. The soonest I could get an appointment at an Irlen Clinic is this afternoon at one o'clock in Houston, so I'm going to fly down. I have some other business to tend to, so I'll be gone until Friday afternoon."

"You certainly move fast."

"You betcha. I wanted to go to the head honcho's place in California, except they can't see me for two weeks. With this deal, I'll come home with the glasses."

"I hope this solves your problem. You know that this might only be part of your difficulty."

"I know, I know. JoAnna briefed me on all that,

and she gave me a book. I'm going to read it on the plane."

Olivia smiled at the pride in his voice. "That's great."

"Listen, sugar, I'm almost at the airport. Would you do a couple of things for me?"

"Sure. What?"

"Would you check on Streak at night? Let him out for a run and give him food and water. Mrs. Lopez will tend to him while she's there."

"No problem. What's the second thing?"

"Call Irish and tell her that their suites are confirmed at the Driskill for this weekend and that I have a tee time at eight on Saturday morning for Kyle and Matt and me to play golf with Mitch. She can pass on the word to Eve and Matt."

"Will do."

"I've gotta go, darlin'. Call you tonight. Love you."

He hung up before she could reply.

She'd almost forgotten about the special weekend coming up. The president's reception at the governor's mansion. What in the world was she going to wear? she wondered as she punched in Irish's Dallas number. Her choices were severely limited. Maybe Irish had some ideas.

She did.

"Oh, heavens, Olivia, you can't wear that old bridesmaid dress," Irish said. "I have a closet full of gowns, some of them with the tags still on, and I'm already too poochy to wear them. In fact, I have one in mind that would be perfect for you, but I'll bring along two or three to try. Would you believe that I even convinced Eve to buy a new dress for the occasion? I can hardly wait to get there. We're flying in Friday afternoon after Kyle gets through at the hospital.''

"Wonderful," Olivia said. "We can get together Saturday morning while the guys play golf."

"Count on it. And Friday night for dinner, too."

"If Jackson gets in from Houston in time."

"What's Jackson doing in Houston?"

"Business," Olivia said quickly. She didn't dare reveal his secret, even now.

"Are things heating up between you two?"

"It depends on how you define heat," Olivia said, trying not to giggle.

"Oh, I think we define it pretty much the same way, m'dear. Is there a serious romance blooming?"

"Oh, I wouldn't call it…too serious. You know Jackson. He's not the serious type. And neither am I. We enjoy each other's company. Say, how's the morning sickness these days?" she asked, steering the conversation in a different direction. They chatted for another minute or two, then Olivia said, "I could yak all day, but I have to run. I have a seminar."

The days crawled by slowly. Even though she was busy, Olivia discovered just how much Jackson had insinuated himself into her life. Without him around, there was a big, empty space.

The second evening that he was gone, she went across the street to play with Streak and feed him. The puppy seemed lonely, too. He looked at her with such pitiful eyes that she stayed longer to keep him company. They watched a movie on TV, she on the couch and Streak on her lap. She hadn't meant to fall asleep, but she did. She awoke at two o'clock in the morning, Streak still curled against her and an infomercial on the TV.

Darn it! She'd missed Jackson's phone call. He'd called the night before to tell her that his exam had gone well, and his glasses should be ready on Friday afternoon. He'd be flying in as soon as he picked them up.

Olivia dialed her own number to see if he'd left a message.

He'd left four.

The last one was at one-thirty. "Where are you, darlin'? I'm worried about you. Call me when you get in."

Should she or shouldn't she?

She should. She tucked a warm throw around her and called his hotel. He answered on the first ring.

"I'm sorry to call so late, but I fell asleep on your couch."

"You gave me a scare. I was afraid something had happened to you."

"Nope. Streak and I watched a movie."

"John Wayne?"

She chuckled. "Not on your life. It was a very urbane romantic comedy. I only wish I knew how it ended."

"They lived happily ever after," he said. "Isn't that the way they always end?"

"In movies." A sudden melancholy swept over her, clogging her throat and bringing a sting of tears to her eyes. "Real life doesn't always work that way."

"It does if the two people involved want to make it work. I want us to live happily ever after. Don't you?"

A glib answer died on her lips. What did she want? Was there a future for Jackson and her? She tried to picture it and couldn't. At least she didn't panic thinking about it, but she wasn't ready to promise any lasting commitments, either.

"I won't crowd you, sugar," Jackson said after the long silence. "But I can't help but wonder sometimes just how you feel about me."

"I care very deeply about you, Jackson."

"Do I hear a *but* in there?"

She let out a slow breath and stroked the puppy's soft fur while she thought about her answer.

"Darlin'?"

"I think you deserve to know about my past, and perhaps someday I'll tell you the whole story, but not tonight. It's late and we both need to get some sleep. The short version is that I've been abused by the men in my life, and it makes me very cautious."

"Olivia, I would cut off my right arm before I would ever harm a hair on your head. I swear by all that's holy. Trust me, darlin'. I love you."

Deep down, she knew what Jackson said was true. Even so, she could feel tiny fingers of panic starting to unfurl as he pursued the issue. She loved him, too, but she wasn't ready to say the words, nor was she ready make the commitment that went with them. Not yet. Not yet.

Maybe not ever.

"Are you going to be home in time to have dinner with Irish and Kyle and Eve and Matt?" she asked.

She heard only the barest of sighs from the phone. "Yes. I talked to Matt this evening. Everybody's coming over to my house, and we're going to keep things casual. Six-thirty okay with you?"

"Fine," she said, yawning. "Do you need me to do anything?"

"No, but thanks for offering. Tami arranged for a caterer to handle stuff. Darlin', would you do a favor for me?"

"Sure. What?"

"I don't want you out alone this time of night. Why don't you stay there and go to bed."

"Jackson, my place is just across the street."

"Humor me."

She smiled. "Okay. I'll stay."

"Dream of me," he whispered.

Twelve

Olivia felt like Cinderella as their group rode in a long and imposing black limousine to the governor's mansion in downtown Austin. The six of them had enjoyed their casual get-together the evening before at Jackson's, and on Saturday, while the men played golf, the women had primped for the occasion. She could hardly believe that the same bunch that had eaten fried chicken in their jeans one night could be turned out like fashion plates to share paté with the president and the first lady the next. Well, everybody except Eve, of course. Irish's younger sister was a vegetarian.

The sapphire panne velvet dress that Irish had insisted was perfect for Olivia, was. Its lines, from the bateau neckline to the hem that just touched the floor, were simple but elegant and the long sleeves were comfortable for the cool November evening. Irish had even insisted on loaning her a spectacular diamond and sapphire pin that set off the dress perfectly. And she wore the diamond studs that Jackson had given her.

But not the bracelet. As beautiful as it was, she was going to return it to him. She simply hadn't had a chance. The only moment they'd had alone was when he picked her up at her apartment—and the others were waiting downstairs in the limo.

"You look scrumptious, sweetheart," he'd said when she'd opened the door. "Fantastic! That dress matches your eyes exactly."

She beamed and her hand automatically went to her upswept hairdo. Borrowing the gown and spending most of the afternoon with Irish and Eve in Austin's finest beauty salon had paid off. They had gotten the works: fabulous hair styling, manicures and facials. Even her toenails were painted siren red. Eve had groused the whole time, but Olivia had enjoyed it. She'd felt positively decadent.

As Jackson put the matching wrap around her shoulders, he'd kissed her nape and whispered, "How about you and me skip this shindig and stay home in bed?"

"Not on your life, buster. I didn't go to this much trouble to spend the evening in the dark."

He'd grinned. "We can leave the lights on."

"I don't think so," she'd said, picking up her evening bag. "Let's go see the president and the first lady. By the way, how are the new glasses working out?"

"Great. They're even better than the overlays. And,

uh, sugar, I haven't told Matt and Kyle about…you know.''

''Then I won't tell them, either.'' She'd given him a quick kiss on the cheek before they went downstairs to join the others.

Now the limo was pulling up to the front of the stately governor's mansion with its huge white columns and view of the state capitol and grounds. The place was ablaze with lights and thick with security.

Irish and Kyle were the first out of the limo, then Eve and Matt. Jackson climbed out and offered her his hand, smiling as she exited the car.

Cherokee Pete would have been proud of his grandsons, three handsome men in their tuxedos going to meet the president of the United States. Irish was gorgeous in an emerald-green suit with a floor-length skirt and a boxy beaded jacket to accommodate the first signs of her pregnancy, and Eve was equally beautiful in a dusky-rose silk gown.

Jackson tucked Olivia's arm in his, and, after they passed through a security check at the gate, they started up the walkway with the others. She felt like a movie star, smiling and girlishly giddy as cameras flashed around them.

Inside, she actually met the president and the first lady, though later she couldn't for the life of her remember what she'd said to them. She hoped it was something sensible.

Mitch had hugged her, and Jackson had glared at him. They nibbled from the bountifully filled buffet tables and chatted with the movers and shakers in attendance. Jackson seemed to know everyone—and those he didn't know, he quickly befriended.

He was a charmer, no doubt about it. Men liked him, and women grew more animated when he was around. And she thought his new glasses made him look more distinguished.

Matt had noticed the glasses first thing. "Had to break down and get some cheaters, huh, big brother?"

"We're all getting older, fly boy," was all Jackson had said.

The evening passed in a whirl of introductions and conversations, and before Olivia knew it, it was time to leave.

At Irish's insistence they all stopped by the hotel to have a nightcap. Olivia had fallen in love with the historic old Driskill with its Romanesque exterior and sumptuous Victorian interiors. The bar was a huge room done in a Western motif with overstuffed leather sofas, ranch paintings and a stuffed longhorn head over the fireplace.

"Gruesome, isn't it," Eve said, shuddering and sitting with her back to the steer head.

"Sweetheart, not everybody is the animal lover that you are," Matt said. To Olivia he said, "Would you believe that not only do we have two cats, four dogs and an aria-singing parrot, we have a *pig* as a house pet?"

She laughed. "I understand that pigs are very bright."

"Minerva is extremely bright," Eve said. "And neater than Matt." She winked at her husband.

After everyone ordered drinks, Irish said, "I almost forgot to mention it, Olivia, but Kyle and I are having Thanksgiving at our house this year. I hope you'll come with Jackson. We'd really love to have you.

Everybody is pitching in, and it will be so much fun. We're doing the turkey, Grandpa Pete is making cornbread dressing and gravy, Mother is making pumpkin pies, Kyle's mother is providing vegetables—''

"And we're bringing homemade bread and butter," Eve added.

"Mom and Dad are springing for the wine," Matt said.

"Mom doesn't cook anymore," Jackson added, "not since they live in the hotel."

"I didn't realize that your parents lived in a hotel," Olivia said.

"Mmm-hmm. In San Antonio. They own it and live in the penthouse when they're in town. They travel a lot. Where are they now, Matt? I forget."

"I think the last postcard we got was from Japan. They should be on their way home about now."

"Well, anyhow, Olivia," Irish said. "I hope you'll come."

"Sure she will," Jackson said.

"What can I bring?"

Jackson grinned. "She makes a mean coconut cake."

"Great!" Kyle said. "Coconut is my favorite."

Irish rolled her eyes. "Any kind of cake is your favorite."

"Can I help it if I have a sweet tooth?" He leaned over and playfully gnawed on Irish's shoulder.

Olivia laughed at the bantering of the two couples who were obviously so much in love. She wondered if it was wise to spend the holiday with the families. She had a premonition that there would be a lot of matchmaking going on.

After they finished their drinks, Olivia and Jackson said their farewells and rode home in the limousine. Jackson had the driver drop them off at his house.

''My bed *is* roomier,'' he said as he unlocked the door, ''and I've been itching to unzip that dress all night.''

They were barely inside when he tossed her wrap aside, pulled her into his arms and kissed her. She felt his fingers at her back and the slow slide of the zipper as he drew it down. She shivered and melted against him.

Their tongues met and their moans mingled and her dress fell into a puddle around her feet.

His jacket joined it. Then his tie and cummerbund.

His studs and her shoes were scattered along the path to his bedroom.

''New undies, I see,'' Jackson said as he kissed her shoulder and unclasped her bra.

''Mmm. Irish and Eve talked me into buying them at Victoria's Secret. They matched the dress. Like them?''

''Love them.'' He tossed the bra across the room. Her panties landed on top of the lamp. ''I think garter belts are sexy. Remind me to buy stock in Victoria's Secret.''

She slipped off his shirt and ran her tongue along his collarbone.

His boots landed with a *thud, thud,* and he shucked his pants and hung them on the bedpost. The last of his clothes landed in a heap near the chair.

''I've never made love to a woman wearing only stockings and a garter belt, but I always thought it would be a turn-on. Saw a picture in a magazine when I was a kid, and I've fantasized about it ever since.''

''You told me, and I remembered.''

''Did you now?'' He circled her nipple with his tongue, then sucked gently.

She gasped at the sensation. ''I did. Nobody wears garter belts with stockings much anymore.''

He laid her on the bed and stroked up the length of her leg. ''They should. It feels sensational.''

He kissed her and stroked her and touched her until she was begging him to enter. At last he slipped into place and plunged deeply. He moved slowly at first, but she urged him on, and the pace quickened.

Their rhythm was wild and sensuous, and their climaxes powerful.

When the last shudder had stilled, Jackson ran his hand up one of her stockinged legs and over the garter belt.

''Darlin', I may have these bronzed.''

On Sunday morning they lay in bed, sipping coffee and reading the papers.

''I still can't believe this,'' Jackson said. ''I'm actually *reading* a newspaper. It's amazing. Oh, I'm going to have to have some extra tutoring for a while to improve my skills, but, dammit, I'm actually *reading*. And looka here, sugar, our pictures are in the Austin paper.''

''Where?'' She craned her neck to peer at the section he held.

''Right here in living color. There's a write-up about the president's reception.'' Very slowly and deliberately he read: '''From left to right—Dr. Kyle

Rutledge and his wife Irish, the former New York model. Matthew Crow of Crow Airlines and his wife Eve, Dallas ad executive. Olivia Moore, university professor, and Jackson Crow, railroad commissioner.'''

"Let me see that. I'm not a professor! I'm merely an instructor."

He grinned. "Wanna sue?"

"I'll pass. That's an excellent picture. I wish I had a copy."

"I'll check with the newspaper office. Maybe I can wangle one out of them." He touched the picture, then ran his finger over the caption. "You know, it's a miracle, Olivia. With these colored filters I can actually see your name. It's so beautiful."

Tenderness filled her, and she rubbed her cheek against his. Things were just about perfect.

Olivia was in her living room grading term projects and half listening to the evening news on TV, when "president" and "Austin" caught her attention. She looked up and saw the last of a story about the president's vacation in Texas and the Saturday reception at the governor's mansion. There was a film clip of Mitch and the president and the first lady receiving guests, and—ohmygod! There she was! And there was Jackson and the others.

Panic rushed over her. What if Thomas saw that? She'd been so careful to lie low and cover her trail, and now here she was on television. Slapping her hand on her chest, she forced herself to breathe deeply and relax. But panic clawed at her insides. Her picture in the local paper had made her uneasy; seeing herself on television was horrifying.

When she realized that she'd been watching a local newscast, she sighed with relief. It was highly unlikely that Thomas Fairchild, in California, had access to Austin newspapers or TV broadcasts.

Keep calm, Olivia, she told herself. Thomas wasn't going to find her. In all probability he had given up on her by now and moved on with his life.

She hoped.

No matter how much positive self-talk she used, a niggling doubt lingered and worried a corner of her mind.

She slept poorly that night and awoke early to sit in her rocking chair, her gown tucked around her toes, and stare into space. And she prayed.

When the phone rang, she almost jumped out of her skin.

It was Irish.

"Have you been watching CNN?" Irish asked.

"No. Why?"

"We're on. They have a film clip of the president's visit to Austin and all of us shaking hands with him at the reception. Isn't that neat?"

Olivia's mouth went dry. "No, Irish. It's not neat."

There was dead silence for a moment.

"Thomas," Irish said.

"Thomas."

"Oh, Lord, Olivia, I'm sorry. But I'm sure you don't need to worry. Even if he sees the film, he might not realize that it was you. I mean, you were only on for a fraction of a second. I recognized the dress first. And you aren't identified in any way. You've changed your name, and your phone is unlisted. It's unlikely that he'll find you.''

"Unlikely. That's what I've told myself.''

"Olivia, have you told Jackson about Thomas?''

"No, not really.''

"Tell him, sweetie. Tell him and let him protect you.''

"I'll think about it.''

"We'll talk more when you come to Dallas. When are you arriving?''

"We'll be driving up Wednesday afternoon and staying in a hotel. We'll see you Thursday morning.''

"Oh, I wanted you to stay with us. We have scads of room in this big house.''

Olivia smiled when she recalled Jackson's reaction to the suggestion. Not no, but "Hell, no,'' he'd said. "That place will be like fleas on a farm dog with all the relatives coming in. Let's stay where we can have some privacy.''

"But I suppose you two would rather have a place with more privacy,'' Irish said.

"Those were almost Jackson's exact words.''

Time dragged by, and Olivia was exhausted by the time she returned home Tuesday afternoon. It seemed that everyone she'd met for the past two days had seen her picture in the paper or on television. Apprehension and lack of sleep had her nerves on edge.

The phone rang.

She started and cried out at the sudden sound. Her hand hovered over the receiver, and it rang again.

It was probably Jackson. Or Tessa. Or Irish.

It rang again.

She snatched it up.

"Hello?"

Nothing.

"Hello?" she repeated, louder. After the third hello, she slammed the phone down and rubbed her arms to ward off a prickly chill.

Thomas, the frightened part of her said. *Wrong number,* her stoic self said.

The phone rang again. She reached for it but couldn't make herself pick up the receiver. Instead she let the answering machine click on. Ed Jurney's deep voice said, "This is 555-6304. Leave a message and we'll call you back."

Thank heavens that Ed, for security's sake, had made the recording for her when she'd first moved in.

"Hey, darlin', it's me," Jackson said. "I'm going to have to work late—"

She snatched up the phone. "I'm here."

"Good. I was afraid that I'd missed you."

"Did you call before?"

"Before now? No. I have another hour or two's work to do here, and I didn't want you to wait on me for dinner. Mrs. Lopez said there was one of those casserole things that you like in the refrigerator. She said all we have to do is heat it up and toss a salad to go with it. Go ahead and eat, and I'll eat when I get home. And, babe, would you mind taking care of Streak?"

"Not at all. And I'll wait for you. I'm sorry you have to work late."

"Everybody wants to get off early for the holiday,

so we're trying to finish up some things. Gotta go, sugar. Love you.''

He was gone before she could say anything else— not that she would have confided her fears. This was something that she would deal with. Thomas was her problem, her nemesis, her nightmare.

Familiar anxiety began to build inside her.

If he hadn't seen the TV clip, she was sure some mutual acquaintance would have seen it and told him about it. Pretending that she was safe was a fantasy. Hadn't he told her that last time? Hadn't he shouted, as she hid behind a neighbor's shrubbery, that she could never escape him? Hadn't he tracked her and almost caught her three times?

She grabbed the stack of student papers from her desk and fled her apartment. She ran across the street, unlocked Jackson's front door, then reset the alarm and dead-bolted the heavy door behind her.

But she couldn't lock out the memories or outrun the fears. They followed her inside. She could never forget that night.

Thomas had beaten her before, once so badly that she had to be hospitalized. She'd told the doctor that she'd been attacked when she surprised a burglar. She'd had to lie. Thomas was standing at the foot of the gurney—acting like a loving, overwrought husband—and had threatened to kill her if she didn't lie. Anyhow, who would have believed that Thomas Fairchild would have done such a thing? He was a federal judge, highly respected in the town. He played golf with the mayor and the chief of police...and her own father. Besides, everyone knew that he adored his wife, doted on her.

In his own sick way, he had loved her. And in the beginning she'd loved him, too, but as their marriage deteriorated, as his abuse escalated, her love had quickly died.

She'd tried many times to leave him, but he always found her and brought her back. Twice, when she'd fled to her childhood home, her father, the bastard, had called Thomas and told him where she was. Thomas was always contrite after one of his outbursts, begging her to forgive him, showering her with gifts, proclaiming his deep love for her. Things would be fine for a while. He would be the perfect husband—loving, tender, considerate. Then something would set him off again.

She was sensible enough to realize that his abuse wasn't going to end, but she was terrified of the man. And with good reason. Controlling her in every way, he'd made her an emotional cripple. The mere mention of her getting a job would send him into a tirade. She never had more than a few dollars in cash, nor did she have access to their bank accounts. Oh, he'd been generous with her, but everything had to be charged, and she knew that he could cut off her credit with a phone call. He kept the most costly of her jewelry in a safe in his study, not trusting her with the combination, but taking out pieces as she needed to wear them—even the things that had been her mother's.

But she'd learned to be devious. She searched until she found the combination to the safe. She began stockpiling cash, charging lunch with friends and taking their money, returning purchases and getting cash. A little here and a little there began to add up. She hid it in an old purse in the back of her closet, waiting for her chance.

That last night, she'd finally screwed up enough courage to tell Thomas that she was divorcing him. He'd grown wild with rage, slapped her to the floor, then dragged her back up and shaken her, shouted obscenities and struck her again. He threw her against a wall mirror and her head shattered the heavy glass.

"You'll never leave me, Olivia. You're *mine!* No other man will ever touch you. I'll see you dead first."

When he reached for the fireplace poker, Olivia knew that he meant to kill her. Somehow she'd found the strength to run from the house. Keeping to the shadows, she'd hidden behind the oleanders at the Almont's house, a block away.

She'd waited there for hours, bruised and bleeding and terrified, until she saw Thomas leave in his car. She'd hurried back to the house and grabbed money, jewelry and what she could fit into her car and fled.

She hadn't stopped running.

A coldness rippled over her and set her to shivering.

He was going to find her. She knew it.

Her instincts told her to run. Fast and far away.

Thirteen

Olivia didn't relax until they were on the freeway headed to Dallas. Even then, she kept looking behind them to see if anyone was following the car.

"Sugar, what's the matter with you? For the last few days, you've been jumpier than a cricket in a hot skillet."

"Just nervous about the prospect of being around all your relatives, I suppose."

He reached for her hand, squeezing it. "No need to worry about that. You've already met and charmed every one of them. Mama even said she brought you a present from Japan."

"Jackson, your parents don't think that we—"

"That we—what?"

"I mean, they're not expecting us to get engaged or anything like that, are they?"

He was quiet for a moment, then said, ''We haven't discussed it.''

She relaxed a bit more. For the next few days she was going to forget about her worries and enjoy herself. It was unlikely that Thomas would track her to Dallas, and she would be surrounded by powerful people. Even if he did find her, he wouldn't dare try to harm her.

No, he'd wait until he had her alone.

The bustle of preparing Thanksgiving dinner—which was served at noon rather than in the evening—kept Olivia's mind off her worries about Thomas. Jackson's parents, Anna and Sam Crow, had brought everyone, including Olivia, lovely silk robes from their trip to Japan. The men's were emblazoned with embroidered dragons and the women's with exquisite flowers and birds.

She really liked Jackson's parents, who, despite over forty years of marriage, still appeared to be very much in love. They were a striking couple, both tall with dark eyes and dark hair going gray, his more than hers. Anna looked very much like her sister, Sarah Rutledge, Kyle's mother, though Sarah's hair was lighter. Both had an ageless sort of beauty with their wonderful high cheekbones and sculpted features that were part of their native American ancestry.

Kyle shared his blond coloring with his father, who had blue eyes and light hair that was now almost white. Dr. T. J. Rutledge was a cardiologist, newly retired. Since they were both heart specialists, Olivia would have bet that T.J. had met her father at one medical convention or another through the years, but she didn't dare ask.

Irish and Eve's parents, Beverly and Al Ellison, both as tall and fair as their daughters, were as warm and welcoming as they'd always been. They loved being new Texans, and Al especially bragged on the mild climate of their adopted state and his skills as a fisherman on the lake where they'd retired.

When the food was ready, everyone gathered around Irish and Kyle's massive dining table. By popular request Cherokee Pete sat at the head. After leading the Thanksgiving prayer, he and Kyle carved two huge turkeys.

Since Irish had given her housekeeper the day off, the meal was served family style, and food was plentiful. It seemed that everybody had brought extra things, and bowls and platters were passed around amid laughter and joking.

"Oops," Irish said, rising. "I forgot the cranberry sauce. It's in the fridge."

"I'll get it," Kyle said. "Stay off your feet."

When the turkey was served and the plates were heaped with dressing and green beans and sweet potatoes and salads and a half dozen other dishes, Jackson said, "Maybe I'd better use one of those platters. I'm running out of room."

His father laughed and agreed, as did Al Ellison.

"I'm planning on seconds," Matt said.

"Save plenty of room for dessert," Sam Crow said. "I've had my eye on that coconut cake Olivia brought."

"Me, too," Kyle said, "but I plan to have cake and pie both."

Irish laughed. "You would."

Gaiety and the drone of congenial conversation filled the large room and sparked warm fuzzies inside Olivia.

She looked around at all those gathered—the whole clan except for Jackson's sister and her family and Kyle's brother. They were such likable people, warm, funny, down-to-earth despite their wealth. They had opened their arms and made her feel welcome. Strange. She felt more a part of this group than she'd ever felt at home.

Family meals had usually been an ordeal when she was growing up. More often than not, her father would go into one of his tirades about some infraction or another. After her mother had died, Jason had been his whipping boy, but Olivia had endured many of her father's tongue-lashings as well. And after Jason left, there had been no buffer between Olivia and her father's vitriolic eruptions. She had become his only target. Yet, as controlling and emotionally abusive as her father had been, he hadn't hit her as often as he had hit Jason, in all likelihood because she had tiptoed around her home like a mouse. On the other hand, Thomas—

No, she told herself, no thinking about Thomas. Not now. She focused her attention back on those gathered in the dining room. It was then that she realized thirteen people were at the table. Bad luck if you believed such things.

A shiver went over her.

"Olivia, what's wrong?" Jackson asked.

"Nothing," she said with a nervous laugh. "I just realized that I'm the thirteenth person."

"Nope," Irish piped up. She patted her tummy. "He makes fourteen."

"Do you know that it's a *he?*" her mother asked.

Irish nodded and caught Kyle's hand. "We were going to wait until dessert to make the announcement, but—"

"But we're having a son," Kyle finished, beaming.

Cherokee Pete rose and lifted his wineglass. "I'd like to propose a toast to our family's new additions. To my new great-grandson and to our most welcome friend, Olivia."

"Hear, hear!"

Olivia felt herself blush, but she also felt her heart expand. She'd never realized just how much she'd missed in not being part of a large and loving family.

That awareness grew when, after the meal, the men rushed to the den to watch the Dallas Cowboys football game, leaving the women to clean up the mess.

"Male chauvinist pigs," Eve shouted after them, laughing after she said it.

Anna Crow laughed as well. "They're all like little boys. Never," she told Olivia, "get between one of these men and a Cowboys game. They're all die-hard fans, always have been."

"That's the truth," Irish said. "They have season tickets to all the games. Only on threat of death did they forgo being there in person today."

Olivia smiled and pitched in to clear the table, but she realized that this was probably the first Cowboys game Jackson had watched this season. He'd spent all his Sunday afternoons with Tami, preparing for the commission's Monday hearings and suffering blinding headaches. Jackson was truly dedicated to doing his job well. Her admiration for him rose another notch.

The weekend in Dallas seemed to fly by, and Olivia thoroughly enjoyed herself. The day after Thanksgiving, they went out to see the new farmhouse that Matt and Eve were building, and she got to meet Minerva, the wonder pig, as well as all Eve's other animals.

She and Jackson spent time with his family and managed to squeeze in some time on their own as well. On Saturday night they went to a performance of a Broadway musical on tour, drank wine and made love.

On Sunday morning they started home.

Fears that had been suspended for the holiday suddenly recurred with a wallop. The closer they came to Austin, the more her anxiety grew.

By the time Jackson carried her bags upstairs to her apartment, dread filled her stomach like a hot stone.

"Darlin', are you okay?"

"I'm fine," she said, forcing a smile. "Just tired. But I had a lovely time. I really like your family."

"And they like you." He dropped her bags in her living room and took her in his arms. "I do, too."

He brushed noses with her, then kissed her. She wanted to hold on to him forever, but she knew he had work to do.

"Get some rest this afternoon," he told her, "and I'll call you later."

When he had gone, she hurried to her answering machine and checked messages. Four hang ups and a call from Tessa playfully asking for a report on the weekend.

Four hang ups.

Probably wrong numbers or randomly dialed computer calls trying to sell her something.

Probably. After all, her number was unlisted.

But Thomas was a judge, friends with police officials and others who could easily secure unlisted numbers.

She locked the door carefully, using both dead bolt and chain as a backup, and took three slow deep breaths. Then she unpacked and called Tessa.

Tessa wasn't home. After leaving a message on her machine, she went to fix a cup of hot tea. She couldn't seem to get warm.

The phone rang.

She hesitated a moment, then picked it up. "Hello."

Silence.

"Hello! Hello! Dammit, who's there?"

"Ah, so it is you."

Olivia's heart almost stopped, and she ceased to breathe. Her blood ran ice-cold.

Thomas.

Her worst nightmare had just become real.

"What do you want?" she asked, trying to remain calm.

"I want what I've always wanted. You, at home with me where you belong."

"I don't belong with you, Thomas. We're divorced."

"You do belong with me, Olivia. You're *mine!* You'll always be *mine.* I'm coming to pick you up."

Trembling with panic, she ran to the kitchen window, terrified that he might be outside. "I'm not going anywhere with you, Thomas. We're divorced. Leave me alone."

"I saw you on television, and I saw the newspaper picture of you with that bastard's hands on you. He can't have you, Olivia. You belong to *me*. I'll be coming for you. You'll leave with me, or I'll see you dead."

She broke the connection and flung the phone aside. Grabbing the edge of the sink, she held on tightly and clenched her teeth as her body shook. *No,* she prayed. *No, please no.*

Run! Run! She had to pack her bags and get out of there before he came. He said he'd kill her, and she knew that he would.

She glanced up and saw Jackson's house across the street. If she called him, he'd be there in an instant. Thomas would be no match for Jackson Crow.

Or would he? Thomas might have a gun, and as furious as he was, he would shoot Jackson with the slightest provocation. Thomas had always been violently jealous, even when there was no reason, and he was an excellent shot. Jackson might be killed if she called him.

A sudden calm moved over her, and she stood straight and tall. No, she wasn't calling Jackson, nor was she going to run away. She was done with running. She was making her stand here. Now.

A car stopped in the driveway, a big luxury car. Thomas Fairchild got out.

Her stomach tightened, but for the most part, Olivia remained calm. She picked up the phone and dialed

911. Her voice was shaky, but she managed. After giving her name and address, she said, "My ex-husband has just threatened to murder me, and he's walking up to the door now. Hurry. For God's sake, hurry!"

"We've dispatched a car," the woman said. "Stay on the line and don't open the door."

"You couldn't pay me to open it. I hear him walking up the steps to my apartment. Oh, God, he's coming!"

"A car is less than a minute away. Hold on."

Thomas knocked on the door. "Olivia!"

When she didn't answer, he banged on it. "Olivia! Open the door!" After a moment he banged again, harder. "You're *mine,* dammit, and you're coming with me!"

"Don't open the door," the dispatcher warned.

"I'm not crazy," she whispered.

"You're coming with me, or I'll kill you! I swear I will. No other man is having what's mine!" The door shuddered as he threw his weight against it.

"He's trying to break down the door," she whispered. "Go away, Thomas!" she shouted. "I've called the police."

"You're lying. Open up! Now!" He hit the door like a battering ram.

The power of his fury shook her to the core, but she clenched her teeth and strengthened her resolve. She'd never reported him to the police before, and he thought she was the same cowed woman she used to be. She wasn't. If she went down, this time she'd go down fighting.

Wood splintered, the glass in the door shattered.

Olivia picked up a pewter candlestick, preparing to defend herself. "He's coming in!" she shouted, running to the door and smashing her candlestick against the hand that reached through the broken pane and tried to unlock the dead bolt.

A siren came screaming down the street. Two sirens.

"The police are here, Thomas!" she shouted, but he was too enraged to stop his battering.

"I'll kill you, you bitch! You're dead! You're dead!"

"Stop! Police! Stop right there!" she heard yelled from outside. Footsteps hammered up the stairs, and she heard scuffling and shouting on the landing.

"They're here," she whispered into the receiver.

"Stay where you are. Wait until an officer identifies himself to you," the voice on the phone said.

It seemed an eon before a voice said, "Ma'am, I'm Officer Rodriguez. It's okay now. He's cuffed and my partner is taking him to the car."

Still trembling, she put down the phone and unlocked the dead bolt and chain of the ruined door. "Thank you," she managed to whisper. "Thank you. I'll file charges. I'll do whatever is needed. He meant to murder me, you know."

"Yes, ma'am. We'll take him down to the station and book him. Don't you worry about him hurting you."

The policeman left, and she slumped against the jamb, still clutching the candlestick in her hand.

"Olivia! Olivia!"

She glanced up to see Jackson bolting down the driveway bellowing her name. He tore up the steps two at a time and, when he reached her, gathered her into his arms.

"My God, are you all right? What happened? Who was that?"

"Thomas Fairchild. My ex-husband. He found me. He saw me on television, and he found me. God, I was so scared. He was going to murder me."

Rage flashed over Jackson's face, and he clutched her to him. "That sorry son of a bitch! I'll kill him if he ever comes near you again. You're *mine!*" He hugged her tighter. "You're *mine,* and I won't let him touch you!"

Olivia's spine stiffened as fury shot over her. "Don't you dare say that! Don't you dare. I'm not *yours!* I'm not his, and I'm not yours. I belong to no man." She struggled from his grip. "Get your hands off me!"

He tried to gather her into his arms again. "Olivia, darlin', calm down."

Flailing her hands and slapping at him, she elbowed her way out of his hold. "Don't you *darlin'* me. And I'm perfectly calm. Go away. Just go away!"

"Sugar, I'm not leaving while you're in this state. Let me take care of you."

"Dammit, don't you hear me?" she screamed. "Go away! I don't want you here. I don't need any man to take care of me. I can take care of myself. Go away!"

Jackson looked hurt, but she was too raw and too distraught to worry about his feelings. She was in survival mode and teetering on the edge.

He turned and walked slowly down the stairs. A

crowd of neighbors had gathered and were watching the spectacle, but she didn't care.

She went inside and slammed what was left of her door, then threw herself on her bed and wept. She cried and cursed every man who had tried to control her and humiliate her, beating her fist on the mattress and venting her anger and her fear.

When the well of tears was empty and her anger and fear had dissipated, she rolled over onto her back and stared at the ceiling. Maybe she had overreacted with Jackson, but his words had shaken her. Twice now she'd witnessed his fury. Jackson Crow had a temper.

And his proclamation that she was *his* had pierced her heart and struck at her most vulnerable spot. What was it about her that made the men in her life so possessive? What made them think that they could declare ownership of her as if she were no more than a pet dog?

Never again would she allow this. Never again. Not with Jackson, not with anyone. Good thing that she saw this side of him now rather than sometime in the future. She knew the pattern.

Her first impulse was to pack and leave, move far away from Jackson, abandon her quarters now that Thomas knew where to find her. But, then again, that had always been her custom. Flee.

Not this time. This time she was staying. She loved her job; she loved Austin. She was almost finished with her dissertation. She refused to let any man ruin her life again. She was going to live life on her own terms.

Rising, Olivia washed her face and called JoAnna.

She would spend a few days with her friend until her door was repaired and until she could be sure that Thomas wouldn't bother her again.

She wasn't leaving Austin.

Fourteen

Jackson hadn't wanted to leave Olivia, but she had been so upset, he hadn't known what else to do. He'd tried to call Tessa, but the Jurneys weren't home. He would have called JoAnna, but he didn't know her phone number, and he couldn't find it in the directory. He didn't want to phone Irish, in her condition, and get her all upset. He did the only thing he knew to do. He called his mother.

Wise woman, his mother.

She told him to make sure Olivia was safe from her ex-husband and to give her some time. "Let her know that you care and that you're there for her, but don't push. And for goodness sakes, don't start beating your chest and making all those he-man noises. It won't help."

"Yes, ma'am."

"Jackson, your father and I really like Olivia. We think you've hit another jackpot with her."

He grinned. "Yes, ma'am. My luck seems to be holding. I love you, Mama."

"I love you, too, son. And I have a feeling that things will work out between you and Olivia. You seem perfect together."

After he hung up, he considered what he could do to make sure that Olivia was safe. The number-one thing was to make sure her ex-husband stayed locked up and far away from Olivia.

He picked up the phone again and called the person he knew with the most political clout—Mitch. He briefly explained the situation and asked if he could help.

"As governor, I can't do much directly," Mitch said, "but the chief of police owes me a couple of favors. Let me call George and find out what's going on. I'll get back to you."

For an hour Jackson tried to read the material for the upcoming commission hearings, but his heart wasn't in it. Mostly he paced, waiting for Mitch's call.

When the phone rang, he eagerly snatched it up. Instead of Mitch, Tessa was on the line, asking what had happened. "I had a cryptic message from Olivia, telling me about the break-in and that she was going to stay with a friend. Is she there?"

"No, I believe that she's with a girlfriend, Tessa, and I'm glad to know that she's safe." He filled her in with the details, as much as he knew. He even told her about Olivia's reaction to his trying to help.

Tessa's advice was almost the same as his mother's.

"I have the governor looking into things—but for gosh sakes don't let Olivia know that. And I'll call a carpenter to fix the door."

"Forget the door," Tessa said. "Ed and Bill will take care of it. See that she's safe, Jackson. She's been terrified by that man for so long it's almost ruined her life. Be patient with her."

"I will."

Half an hour later Mitch called. "Did you know that Thomas Fairchild is a federal judge in California?"

"A *judge?* My God."

"Yep. Would you believe Olivia called me for help not fifteen minutes after we talked?"

"I hope you didn't tell her that I'd called you."

"Sorry. I did. I didn't realize it was a secret."

Jackson groaned. Now she was really going to be hacked at him. "What's going on?"

"I found out that Fairchild was about to worm his way out of jail in a few hours when George got involved. The most he can do is hold him for twenty-four hours, then the bastard can post bail and be out. Olivia can get a restraining order, but they don't always do much good. I have a better idea."

"Which is?"

"Harlon Swain and I are going to go visit Fairchild in jail." Harlon Swain was also a federal judge, one with many years of service, who had the ear of the powers that be in Washington as well as a supremely commanding voice and presence. He was a male version of the late Barbara Jordan.

"We're going to see if we can put the fear of God and Texas in this fellow," Mitch said. "Ride him out of town on a rail, so to speak."

"Think it will work?"

Mitch laughed. "You've got me, but Harlon seems to think it will. He's asked around, and from what he's found out about Fairchild, and from what Olivia told me, appearances are important to him. So is his judgeship. We can escort him to the airport and send him back to California with the charges dropped, or we can pursue the matter and get him thrown off the bench. If we let him off, he has to swear that he'll get some psychological help and never set foot in Texas again."

"Do it."

"Say, buddy, what's going on with you and Olivia? She was colder than a marble gravestone when I mentioned your name. Are things off with y'all?"

"Don't go getting any ideas, Mitch. She's still— spoken for." Damn, he'd almost said "mine." He was going to have to erase that word from his vocabulary. "Keep me posted, will you? And don't mention to Olivia that we talked. She gets pissed if she thinks somebody is interfering in her business."

Now, Jackson thought, if he could just manage to be patient.

He tried his dead-level best for the next few days. From what Mitch told him, he and Harlon had put on quite a show, and Fairchild had taken the first plane back to California. The bastard jumped on the chance to keep his job and his good name. Olivia was rid of him for good.

And she was back at her apartment. The door was

fixed, and he saw her coming and going, but she wouldn't take his calls or return his messages.

He sent her flowers and cards every day. Hell, he even had dinner delivered to her door every night with a note to call if she needed someone to share it with.

Nothing. *Nada.* Zip.

Not even a polite thank-you note.

Patience, his mother warned.

He muttered—and waited.

Olivia could ignore the prime rib, the lobster, the fillet of sole and chicken Florentine, each with a bottle of the finest wine, but when she opened the latest dinner box, she almost wept. Inside were four hotdogs with mustard, chili and cheese, and a big bag of potato chips. Instead of wine, there was a six-pack of Jackson's favorite beer. The note said: "Call me, darlin'. I'm starving to death."

She had tried to cut Jackson from her life, told herself that she was crazy to make herself vulnerable to a man again. Trouble was, she loved Jackson Crow, plain and simple.

She freely admitted that she'd overreacted to him the day of the break-in, but she'd been so keyed up that she couldn't help it. Now that her life belonged to her again and she had time to think rationally, she realized that Jackson was nothing like Thomas or her father. Protective? Absolutely. Hadn't he called Mitch to help her even before she thought of it? But manipulative and domineering? No.

And, darn it, she missed him something awful.

Picking up her phone, she punched in the familiar number.

Jackson answered on the first ring.

"Want to come over for a hotdog?" she asked.

"Damned right. I'm on my way."

He didn't even say goodbye, just hung up. From her kitchen window, she saw him charging out the courtyard gate, dragging a shirt over his head. She laughed. He was barefoot, and it was cold outside.

She heard his feet hit the stairs and in three seconds he was knocking on her door. When she opened it, he was leaning casually against the jamb, grinning in that delightfully endearing way of his.

"Come in," she said, resisting the urge to throw her arms around him and kiss him senseless. "Want a beer?"

"Don't mind if I do." Thumbs hooked in the belt of his jeans, he sauntered in.

"Aren't your feet cold?"

He looked down and, as if noticing for the first time that he was barefoot, wiggled his toes. "Damn! And I was trying to be so cool."

She laughed. "You are cool, Jackson Crow. Supercool. Or is it hot?" Unable to resist any longer, she put her arms around his neck and pulled him to her.

He didn't need any urging. His lips met hers in a kiss that made her knees sag.

He kissed her eyes and her cheeks and nuzzled his way under her chin. "Oh, darlin', I've been out of my mind. I love you so much."

"I love you, Jackson."

"Do you mean it? Honest to God?"

She smiled. "I do. I've missed you, too."

"Promise that you'll marry me, darlin', and put me out of my misery."

He reached for her lips again, but she pushed him away and took his face in her hands. "Jackson, I can't promise you that. I'm not ready to make that kind of commitment again. I may never be. There's so much that you don't know about me, about the kind of life I've had."

Leading her to the sofa, he sat down and pulled her into his lap. "Tell me. Tell me everything."

She did. She told him everything about her father's abuse of her mother, then of her brother and her, about her college fiancé's abuse, about her ex-husband's abuse. She related every ugly bit of the story.

Jackson closed his eyes during parts of the account, and she could see the muscles in his jaw moving as he controlled his anger, but he didn't say a word until she was finished. He only held her close and stroked her.

"So now do you see why I'm anxious about relationships?" she asked quietly. "It's not that I don't love you, Jackson. It's just that I'm...very wary."

"I'll wait."

"Jackson, I may never be ready to get married again. You should know that."

"Olivia, I love you with all my heart and soul. I'll wait. And in the meantime I'll settle for what I can get. You've brought joy into my life beyond measure." He smiled and traced her lips. "And you've brought colors that opened up a new world to me and changed the way I perceive everything, but the only color that's worth a damn is the color of your name.'' He kissed her deeply. ''I'll wait.''

Epilogue

The roadsides were a blanket of blue as Texas blue-bonnets bloomed in profusion. Here and there along the highway to Dallas were patches of orange Indian paintbrush, pink evening primrose and other breath-taking spring wildflowers.

Olivia and Jackson were on their way to see Irish and Kyle's new son. Joshua had been born three days before, and mother and son were doing fine.

"Kyle sounded like he was about to pass out," Jackson had told Olivia after the call came, "but Irish and the baby are doing great. Seven pounds, nine ounces and gorgeous."

Olivia was anxious to see her friend. They talked weekly and had visited again at Christmas, but she could hardly wait to see that adorable baby.

She settled back, content to be with Jackson as he

drove. In the months they had been together, she'd learned a great deal about him. He was totally different from her father and Thomas. He had a temper, yes, but his anger was never directed against her. Jackson was a strong man with strong opinions, and he was very protective of her, sometimes overly so, but she knew for certain that he would never hurt her. Hadn't she deliberately provoked him several times to prove it to herself?

Every day she grew more and more sure that she was ready to commit to a permanent relationship. Instead of making her shudder, the notion filled her with warmth. She did adore the man. She smiled. And he was such a hottie.

After what seemed forever, they arrived in Dallas and went directly to Irish and Kyle's home. All the clan had gathered, even Jackson's sister, Congresswoman Ellen Crow O'Hara and her husband were there. Only Kyle's brother Smith was missing. He hadn't shown up at Christmas, either.

"I don't know what's the matter with that boy," Cherokee Pete said. "I miss him like the dickens."

"So do I," Sarah Rutledge said. "I wish he was here to see his new nephew and my new grandson. Isn't he beautiful?" she asked, folding back the blanket for Olivia and Jackson to get a better view of the bundle she held.

"He's precious," Olivia said. "May I hold him?"

Sarah transferred the baby to her, and as Olivia held him in her arms, a flow of maternal tenderness stole over her. "How wonderful to create this little soul." She smiled up at Jackson. "Why don't we have a little one like this?"

"I'm willing. But only if you'll marry me." He brushed her cheek with his knuckle, love shining from his eyes.

"I will."

"Do you really mean it, darlin'?"

She nodded. "Yes."

Folks could hear his whoop all the way to Austin.

* * * * *

Look out for more from Jan Hudson in April when she brings us Her Texan Tycoon.

▼ SILHOUETTE®
DESIRE™ 2 IN 1
AVAILABLE FROM 21ST MARCH 2003

THE SHEIKH TAKES A BRIDE Caroline Cross

Dynasties: The Connellys

Sheikh Kaj al bin Russard was determined to lure Princess Catherine to the altar. His fiery power and potent masculinity made him a formidable foe, but the 'Ice Princess' was ready for battle…

THE SEAL'S SURRENDER Maureen Child

Dynasties: The Connellys

Chance Barnett Connelly always got what he wanted, but single mum Jennifer Anderson had vowed not to let him into her heart. The navy SEAL secretly longed for a family—but was his wish impossible?

ROYAL DAD Leanne Banks

The Royal Dumonts

Prince Michel Phillipe was used to women who agreed with his every breath, but feisty tutor Maggie Gillian was different. The sexy royal dad was a man, with a man's needs—and what he needed was Maggie…

HER TEXAN TYCOON Jan Hudson

The man gazing at Jessica looked just like her dead husband, but how? Millionaire Smith Rutledge was mystified. Would his quest for answers bring him to her bed?

FALLING FOR THE ENEMY Shawna Delacorte

Paige Bradford intended to expose corporate hunk Bryce Lexington for the ruthless shark he was, but her intentions were foiled by the sparks they shared. Could she be losing her heart…to the enemy?

THE SECRET MILLIONAIRE Ryanne Corey

Anna Smith needed a boyfriend-of-convenience, and wealthy policeman Zack Daniels was eager to help. But she knew it was a dangerous game—for there was nothing make-believe about Zack's hold on her heart…

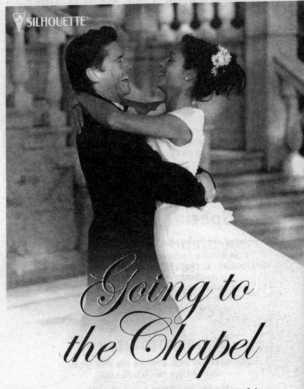

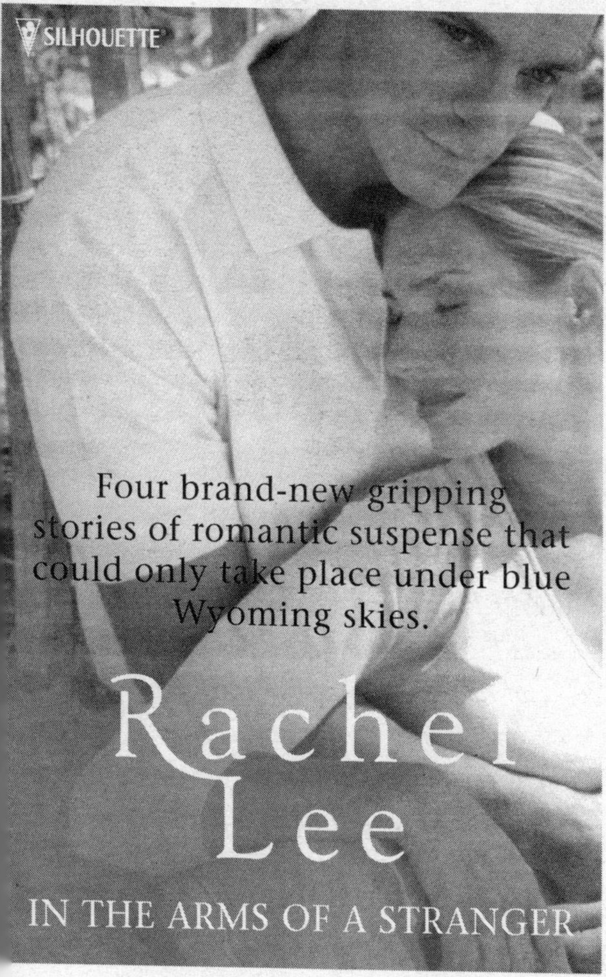
SILHOUETTE
Four brand-new gripping stories of romantic suspense that could only take place under blue Wyoming skies.
Rachel Lee
IN THE ARMS OF A STRANGER

THE COLTONS

FAMILY   PRIVILEGE   POWER

BOOK FOURTEEN
SWEET CHILD
OF MINE
JEAN BRASHEAR

Whilst Prosperino mayor Michael Longstreet was facing a town crisis, he also faced one of his own—his powerful family was demanding he produce a bride! Only Suzanne Jorgenson was desperate enough to agree—needing to find a husband to solve her own problem of losing custody of her child. After they seal their pact with a kiss, sparks fly, changing everything between them!

Available from 21st March 2003

THE COLTONS

FAMILY PRIVILEGE POWER

BOOK FIFTEEN
CLOSE PROXIMITY
DONNA CLAYTON

*Even before the death threats, Rafe James
knew high-powered attorney Libby Corbett
wasn't safe. Whisking her away to safety,
Rafe offered her round-the-clock protection.
Libby was only interested in Rafe as her
bodyguard and that suited him just fine —
until Libby was kidnapped.
The only place Libby could truly be
safe now... was in his arms.*

Available from 21st March 2003

THE
COLTONS

FAMILY   PRIVILEGE   POWER

BOOK SIXTEEN
A HASTY WEDDING
CARA COLTER

*Holly Lamb was hopelessly in love with
her sexy boss, but Blake Fallon seemed
content to keep their relationship strictly
business. A crisis draws them together,
and suddenly Blake's plain-Jane secretary is
transformed into a stunning Cinderella.
But will the Colton investigation shatter
Holly's fairytale fantasies...or result
in a fairytale wedding?*

Available from 18th April 2003

▼ SILHOUETTE®
DESIRE™

is proud to introduce

DYNASTIES:
THE CONNELLYS

*Meet the royal Connellys—wealthy,
powerful and rocked by scandal,
betrayal...and passion!*

TWELVE GLAMOROUS STORIES IN SIX 2-IN-1 VOLUMES:

SILHOUETTE® SENSATION™

presents

ROMANCING THE CROWN

The Royal family of Montebello is determined to find their missing heir. But the search for the prince is not without danger—or passion!

SILHOUETTE®
SPECIAL EDITION™

proudly presents

a brand-new trilogy from

SUSAN MALLERY

DESERT ROGUES

Hidden in the desert is a place where
passions flare, seduction rules and
romantic fantasies come alive…

March 2003
THE SHEIKH AND THE RUNAWAY PRINCESS

April 2003
THE SHEIKH & THE VIRGIN PRINCESS

May 2003
THE PRINCE & THE PREGNANT PRINCESS

0203/SH/LC55

FREE

1 BOOK
AND A SURPRISE GIFT!

We would like to take this opportunity to thank you for reading this Silhouette® book offering you the chance to take another specially selected title from the Desire™ ser absolutely FREE! We're also making this offer to introduce you to the benefits of Reader Service™—

- ★ FREE home delivery
- ★ FREE monthly Newsletter
- ★ FREE gifts and competitions
- ★ Exclusive Reader Service discount
- ★ Books available before they're in the shops

Accepting this FREE book and gift places you under no obligation to buy; you may cance any time, even after receiving your free shipment. Simply complete your details below return the entire page to the address below. ***You don't even need a stamp!***

YES! Please send me 1 free Desire book and a surprise gift. I understand that unless hear from me, I will receive 2 superb new titles every month for just £4.99 e postage and packing free. I am under no obligation to purchase any books and may cancel subscription at any time. The free book and gift will be mine to keep in any case.

D3

Ms/Mrs/Miss/Mr ....Initials..
BLOCK CAPITALS

Surname..

Address..

....

....Postcode ....

Send this whole page to:
UK: FREEPOST CN81, Croydon, CR9 3WZ
EIRE: PO Box 4546, Kilcock, County Kildare (stamp required)

Offer valid in UK and Eire only and not available to current Reader Service subscribers to this series. We reserve the ri refuse an application and applicants must be aged 18 years or over. Only one application per household. Terms and subject to change without notice. Offer expires 30th June 2003. As a result of this application, you may receive offers Harlequin Mills & Boon and other carefully selected companies. If you would prefer not to share in this opportunity please w The Data Manager at the address above.

Silhouette® is a registered trademark used under licence.
Desire™ is being used as a trademark.